"*Tandem* is gripping, p When economics profe~~ssor Mike Kovacs causes a deadly~~ accident, leading to an unconscionable crime, we're ushered into a morality tale of the highest order. Mozina shows expert control over a shocking range of moods and motivations. By turns sad, frightening, disturbing, haunting, and—most surprisingly—funny, this novel wrecked me in all the best ways. *Tandem* is at times difficult to read, yet even more difficult to stop reading."

— **Darrin Doyle, author of**
The Beast in Aisle 34

PRAISE FOR TANDEM

"A delicate web of intrigue. Fans of Kimberly Belle, Alex Kiester, and Greg Olear will appreciate Mozina's ability to blend the drama of a domestic thriller with the heartbreak of loss in many forms: death, divorce, and distance."

—***Booklist***

"Reading *Tandem* is an education in crime, punishment, and the dark side of human compassion—and somehow it also manages to be hilarious. Mozina's signature hapless characters, through their own foolish decisions, can only manage to make difficult circumstances worse as they move from guilt to grief to absurdity. A psychological tour de force!"

— **Bonnie Jo Campbell,**
author of *The Waters*

TANDEM

A NOVEL

Andy M--- *(signature)*

ANDY MOZINA

TANDEM

ANDY MOZINA

TORTOISE BOOKS
CHICAGO

For my mother, on her 97th birthday

1.

The sun was setting when Mike Kovacs pulled out of the parking lot of the Arcadia Brew Pub and entered what seemed like a reasonable gap in westbound traffic on Kalamazoo Avenue. A horn meeped. Was it in front of him or behind him or coming from inside his head? He'd had one Double IPA too many. There was something like 10% alcohol in those beers.

Dinner with Dave and Sarah had been great. The mid-May evening was warm enough to sit on the pub's patio overlooking the swift and glittering Kalamazoo River. Fluffy dandelion seeds blew overhead, passing in and out of bands of horizontal sunlight. A folk guitarist sang incomprehensible lyrics through portable speakers with just the right feeling. Mike had feasted on smoked beef brisket, baked beans, and jalapeño corn bread. Bearded Dave told stories with fingers splayed; angular Sarah made clipped, sardonic comments. They'd had some big laughs.

Cutting through the mid-rise edge of downtown, the street became one-way and picked up a third lane. Another horn sounded. Mike seemed to have drifted from his lane, or maybe he had not definitively chosen a lane. He would do so now.

"I accept that you had to meep your horn," he said aloud, darting his eyes into his rearview. A red Jeep veered out of the mirror, reappeared much larger on his left, and roared past him. "My bad."

He had become extremely happy during dinner, but when the patio filled like a swimming pool with shadow,

Tandem

Sarah had said, "Well, some of us have to work tomorrow," and grabbed her handbag from the weathered picnic table.

"Mike's still got his beer," Dave observed.

True: he had about half of a golden twenty-ouncer in front of him. Serving sizes were trending larger across multiple beverage types. What did that say about supply? What did that say about demand? Mike foresaw a not-too-distant future when a standard beer would be forty-eight ounces, cost $30, and come in a Freon-lined tankard. He wondered if there was a way to get that vision on the record somewhere.

"No, I totally respect that," Mike said to Sarah with an ingratiating smile. It was a Thursday night, after all, and though Dave and Mike didn't have to teach tomorrow, Sarah had to report for duty in her lab at Zoetis. Mike was tempted to leave his third beer, but he hated to waste resources, and it would be funny to chug the rest—just like one of his degenerate students.

"Mike, Mike, Mike!" Dave chanted while he guzzled, and even Sarah grinned when he'd slammed his empty glass down, eyes watering, and shook his head like a wet dog.

The whole evening had been so spontaneous. Mike had learned that his latest article—"Three's a Crowd?: Financial Stability and the Federal Reserve's Dual Mandate"—had finally been accepted at the *Journal of Economics and Business,* a very good venue. Promotion to full professor was at last within reach. He'd texted the news to Dave, who called for a celebratory dinner that very evening because he and Sarah would be at a wedding in Chicago over the weekend.

Hanging out with Sarah and Dave gave Mike hope that things were finally getting back to normal after his divorce. They were the first couple he and Anne had really bonded with when they'd moved to Kalamazoo. Mike and Dave met at the college and brought them all together. Anne sold real estate and could be loud and silly. Sarah developed animal vaccines and was more wry and reserved. Yet after taking Zumba classes together, Sarah and Anne had become friends on their own terms, and during the unraveling of his marriage, Mike had never been quite sure where Sarah's loyalties lay. He couldn't stand being the bad guy. Anne's hasty and unceremonious move to Tucson four months ago had shifted things with Sarah. When it had come up tonight, Mike had predicted producers of margarita mix would notice a steep sales drop in Michigan and a corresponding rise in Arizona, and Sarah had allowed herself a laugh. This sign of sympathy created an enormous sense of reprieve, as when a firing squad unexpectedly stands down.

Two sets of lights at intersections up ahead turned green at almost the same instant. They were so beautiful! All at once the license plate on the SUV in front of him grew large and clear like a line on an eye chart brought into sudden focus. He flopped his foot onto the brake, braced for impact—the SUV had just begun to accelerate, moving inches away as he came to a skidding stop. He had seen the light change from a distance and assumed the way was clear.

"Wow," he said to himself. "Wow. Wow. Wow."

Mike regripped the wheel at ten and two, established a safer following distance, and leaned forward slightly as if it would improve his vision.

The irony was that after years of holding back because Anne was sliding into alcoholism, Mike was very drunk. He had evidently forgotten how to manage more than one beer. Things had been so shitty for years, but now they were looking up. At this precise moment, they were fantastic. He was almost used to being alone in the old cedar-shingled house. His son Connor, a rising junior at the University of Michigan, wouldn't be coming home for the summer. This was consistent with Connor saying that Mike and Anne had "fucked up" and were "a shit example" for him. (Connor, like his mother, had a knack for saying blunt and devastating things when stressed.) But the real reason was Connor's excellent marketing internship with Google in Ann Arbor. Connor would be fine, and using his parents' catastrophic marriage as a negative example wouldn't be the worst thing.

In any case, Mike didn't want this glorious night to end. He was tired of Netflixing *Breaking Bad* back at the house. Maybe he could meet someone, or even get laid.

Anne's departure had thrown him badly, but why not get back on the horse this very night? He was a single man—fifty years old, yes, but a good fifty, a young fifty, an in-pretty-good-shape fifty.

Mike believed there was no reason to decline physically at his age. For god's sake, a fifty-seven-year-old ex-Marine had recently set the world record for continuous abdominal planking—five hours, fifteen minutes, and fifteen seconds. Mike could plank for four minutes. This meant he had the potential to increase his plank time approximately 7800 percent over the next seven years. He couldn't be over a hill he had only just begun to climb.

He approached the weird intersection where Kalamazoo Avenue split—two lanes curving left and up West Main Hill toward his house, and one lane curving right to merge with Douglas Avenue. At the last second, he made a no-look lane change and swooped onto Douglas.

The night wasn't ending. He had always wanted to see the sunset from the beach at Saugatuck Dunes State Park. With its ornate tree-limb driftwood and picturesque boulder twenty yards from shore, it seemed the only place within a fifty-mile radius that offered both soulful vistas and the possibility of a romantic encounter. He envisioned a bonfire ringed by single ladies and empty bottles of Pinot Grigio. Divorcées, tragic young widows, wisecracking loners at loose ends.

Mike felt fortunate to be living in a golden age of attractive middle-aged women. He saw them everywhere: in his neighborhood, on campus, at the farmer's market. One such bored woman on the edge of the bonfire would invite him over and let him ask questions about her life. He was dying to know what made people happy and how they dealt with reality. He wondered why he'd never broached such topics more directly with others, including Anne.

And if the beach was deserted, the shushing waves and the solitude would still foster spiritual reflection, or at least mindless enjoyment. He would pass out and sleep on the sand. He would wake up to seagulls landing on him, like morning birds perching on a Disney princess, nipping his pockets for signs of Cheetos.

As he headed north on 131, the sun fell below the horizon but the air was still lit somehow. In the span of a few miles, he passed a dead deer twisted in the breakdown lane, a tidy lump of inert raccoon, a licorice braid of shorn truck tire tread. Who moved these objects from the middle of the freeway? Why always carefully arranged? Why not remove altogether? The dashboard said it was 9:17 and 63 degrees outside. Dusk came late and took forever in this gently hilly and randomly forested edge of the Eastern time zone. The park would probably be closed when he got there, though running into the sort of people who would defy such rules seemed promising. The temp ticked down to 62, but he had a college hoodie on the backseat.

He exited 131 and took M-89 west through a dense commercial strip burning with superstores and fast-food franchises. Early streetlights passed over his car like a great bright hand stroking a cat. He turned off the AC and cracked his window. The night air was humid and indeed cooling. On the other side of Otsego, he got up to speed again, rolling past the Lynx golf course through a sudden bank of ground fog that barred the road. Then on a straightaway, he saw patches of fog that were strangely discrete and well-organized, hovering masses about one story tall, no taller, taking the shape of long corridors, or a whole warehouse-like building, floating over low-lying areas in the undulating earth. It was as if clouds had come in for a landing. Or maybe this was how clouds were born before they rose up and took their place in the sky. His dash said 60 degrees. But he still looked forward to the lake, which he now hoped would be eerie or surreal under the hazy moon.

By the time he was on M-40 heading toward Holland, the darkness had thickened and the ground fog was a problem. If it didn't sober him up, it at least focused him. Shoals of cloud dissipated just when he worried he couldn't see well enough to drive. Then he passed Bruce's Party Store, a friendly oasis, windows blinded with beer prices; the parking lot lights seemed to disperse the fog. He went due west on 140th Avenue, then came back south on 65th street, overshooting the road that led into the park. He had to stop and back up to make the turn.

It was full night now, just after 10:00 PM. He was in a maze of fog banks and clear ground. He wound down the road, broke through wisps into wider visibility, and saw the park ranger hut, dark inside but lit by an exterior lamp, and no chain across the entrance.

The road split and he bore right on a lane headed for the horseshoe parking lot. A mass of bushes loomed on his passenger side. In front of him, a wall of cottony fog, which he entered like an airplane entering a cloud. A tandem bicycle materialized in his path, two people on the bike lit for an eternal instant as if by a flashbulb: a young man on the front seat, polo shirt, board shorts, backwards ball cap; a woman on the backseat in an open, white button-up shirt, the tail of which lay on her bare thigh as it depressed the bike pedal. The man's face was panicked, eyes magically locking on Mike's through the windshield; the woman's eyes were closed, expectant, more dreamy than alarmed, as if she were only jumping into a lake.

Their paths crossed at an angle. A hard thunk sent the two bodies flying over his hood in a terribly convincing 3-D effect. The man's head glanced off the top left corner of the windshield; the woman's face smashed high into the right side of the glass. Spiderweb bloomed there. Sick twin pineapple clunk of heads, the clatter and scrape of the bicycle grinding against the front of his car. The bodies falling away from the windshield like soapy flaps in a car wash. He hit his brakes way too late. His airbag didn't deploy.

He threw the car into park and sprang out, hoping he was only the victim of a lucid dream, a hallucination, a prank. Only the left headlight was working, but the fog bounced its light around the front of the car. The vapor was moving and filled with tiny sparkles, which mesmerized him for a suspended moment. He could make out the shape of the man on the ground a few yards to his left and slightly behind him. He pulled his phone out of his pocket and switched on its light, as if this would simply rouse the stunned body and he wouldn't have to call an ambulance. The man was lying on his stomach, eyes half-closed, his head turned to the side but wrenched more, it seemed, than was normal. He was a young man, probably Connor's age.

He tried to slow everything down, because maybe if he could stop time, he could also reverse it.

"Hey!" he said to the man. The man was unresponsive.

The car idled. He gathered the strength to approach the body. He stepped over, reached for the hairy wrist flung toward him, felt for a pulse on the tender bare underside. He thought he detected something faint and widely spaced; he squeezed harder to be sure, but as he squeezed, whatever pulse might have been there seemed to recede. He let go, then started over. Detected nothing. He pressed still harder, hoping this would have the collateral effect of waking the man up. Nothing. He shone his phone at the quiet face and broad shoulders. Eyelid ajar. No sign of breathing. Blood seeped from a slashed contusion on the man's forehead, ball cap gone.

A wave of nausea swept over him. He switched off his phone light and was able to keep from throwing up.

He didn't think about turning off the car and the headlight, but he reached in and did this. He didn't want to see the woman at all. Somehow it was easier to face killing the man, though he kept waiting for the man to stand up and be okay. His headlight had been bringing out the surrounding blackness; now with the light off, the darkness was less absolute. A thick gray glow emanated from above the ground fog, maybe from the stars or town lights reflecting from high clouds. The faded asphalt road glowed faintly compared to the dark grass and the fog-shrouded outlines of trees. He heard peeping tree frogs and his own shallow breath.

He opened his phone, bracing himself to call 911, but from the direction of the woman on the other side of the car came a sudden shifting sound, like a sleeping person kicking out a leg in a dream. He turned on his phone light again and ran over to her.

The woman lay on her back, a geyser of long straight hair spouting from the top of her head. Blood ran over her closed left eye and down the side of her cheek. The left corner of her forehead seemed slightly pushed in. She was utterly still. His head sank forward and he fell on all fours, leaning on the wrist of the hand that held his phone. A spasm of something related to weeping overtook him; his head jerked back, as if he'd been garroted from behind. Neither of them had worn helmets. Had he really been going that fast? Had he hit them that hard? He could not take her pulse. He could not go any closer. He sat up on his knees and banged his free fist repeatedly against his forehead. He saw himself guzzling that beer. His intent had been ironic.

"Okay," he said, as if answering an imploring bystander. "Okay! Okay!"

He would dial 911, and when the cops arrived, he would explain what had happened.

He was just driving.

It was so foggy neither had seen the other until it was too late.

It was no one's fault.

But, like pedestrians, bikes always had the right of way. The car driver was always the cruel bastard picking off the defenseless cyclist. Plus, he was still drunk. Three twenty-ouncers. His BAC was no doubt still some egregious multiple of the legal limit. Did it make a difference? Would he have hit his brakes sooner or swerved to lessen the impact? The couple had seemed to come out of nowhere; maybe they had hidden their bike behind the bushes while they explored the park. He hadn't hit his brakes until they were flying toward his windshield. The physical evidence of his drunkenly slow response seemed easily discoverable—the location of his skid vis-à-vis the bodies, the speed of impact, etc. A bicycle built for two. They would throw the book at him. They would not believe his uncorroborated tale of cottony fog at the exact site of impact. Untold years of prison time were likely. His shoulders shivered and a tingle spread over the back of his head.

This was insane! He hadn't had more than one beer in a night in four years. Four years of modeling moderation for downward-spiraling Anne. She was the drunk!

He stood up. He put his phone in his pocket without calling. He dragged moisture off his cheeks with his fingers, knuckled his eyes as if he wanted to push them out the back of his head. Could these people have been the last in the park? Ahead to his right he could discern two small restroom huts, cream-colored, slightly luminous. But most of the parking lot was not visible; there were trees in the center of the horseshoe and pesky patches of fog. He had to leave immediately, before he was seen. Get to a calm place where he could think what to do.

He got in his car but couldn't turn the key in the ignition. He banged his forehead against the steering wheel. He popped back out of his car. He had to be sure the woman was not alive, even if it meant getting caught and losing his own life. He walked over to her, waded into her distress, his responsibility for it, a sensation crawling up his legs like ice-cold lake water. He shined his light. More blood. Her face, less face-like. Bare sternum between bikini top and open white shirt. Cuffs rolled up her forearms as if to facilitate the taking of her pulse. He held her slender wrist. There was no pulse. A breeze stirred the forest that framed the parking lot. He shivered so violently he dropped her arm.

Nothing could be done. They were completely and irrevocably dead.

He got back into his car and rested his head on the steering wheel. "I'm sorry," he whispered. He closed his eyes insanely hard, squeezing oily moisture onto his lower lashes. Why was no one driving by and catching him? Why wasn't some force smashing him? Why hadn't they worn fucking helmets? The only certainty was that if he called the cops now, he would go to prison. Prison was simply a way to bring together all the people let down by teachers. He would be beaten and raped on a schedule modeled on the periods of a school day.

Of course, he still needed to turn himself in. But they were dead, so, at this point, why? There was his own conscience, but was his own conscience important? Up until now, his random fits of conscience had only caused trouble at work and in his marriage. And if his conscience didn't feel

13

right, who would suffer other than himself? He'd really done nothing wrong. The accident seemed truly unrelated to the fact that he'd been drinking. The fog, the suddenness. But no one could be trusted to grasp that truth. He couldn't even get his colleagues on the Planning and Budget Committee to accept Xeroxed financial facts staring them in the face. Then again, he hadn't braked fast enough or swerved at all, and maybe that was because of the drinking, and maybe that was the difference between treatable serious injury and instant death. It was always wrong to drive drunk, but all over the world millions of other people had done so tonight, were doing so right now, without killing anyone.

In economic theory, Pareto-optimality is a state in which it is impossible to make someone better off without making someone else worse off. Would the bereaved be better off if he turned himself in? Their loved ones couldn't be brought back to life. On the other hand, the civil suits would wipe out his TIAA-CREF, his house, everything.

The tree frog chorus entered the car through the slightly open driver's side window, through the other closed windows, through the cracked windshield glass.

He had to be careful when thinking about the bereaved. Leave them alone for now. Disrupting Pareto-optimal solutions was, by definition, inefficient. The tree frogs said the marginal utility of turning himself in was minimal.

But he certainly deserved to be caught. If he was meant to be caught, someone would drive by right now. He wouldn't even try to escape. "My wrists want your handcuffs," he would tell the cops.

Then it seemed he had started the car and, without turning on the lights, put it in reverse, dragging the bike, which was caught somehow. He backed for twenty feet before he heard the tandem clatter loose. Only then did he turn on his one working headlight.

He was about to make a Y turn and head home when he realized that pieces of his car might have come off. Even just the few *CSI* episodes he'd watched with Anne convinced him a trace technician could easily turn a curve of plastic or a piece of metal into a life sentence. If he was going to leave, he couldn't leave any evidence behind.

He got out and opened his trunk. He pulled out a reusable grocery bag, and in the refracted shine of his headlight plus his phone's flashlight, he examined his car. The right front headlight was well-smashed. It contained slots for four lamps, two encased in clear plastic and two smaller lights in amber. He fingered out shards of loose plastic and put them in his bag. The hood was puckered slightly in the front but whole. There wasn't a bumper like he imagined bumpers—he hadn't really looked at the front of a car for decades. There was a shallow U-curve of molded plastic that went from wheel well to wheel well with an air grill down front and center he had never noticed before. The plastic was cracked in several places, and small pieces were missing. There was also damage to a silver grill positioned higher up at the front seam of the hood. More pieces were missing from this grill, including part of the Toyota emblem.

Blood jittering through his veins, he swung his phone in an arc like a metal detector to scan the pavement, working back to the spot of the accident. Along the way, he searched under the pretzeled bike without touching it, then came upon items that had spilled out of the bike's side baskets—a towel, a half-filled bottle of pink lemonade, a light blue scrunchie. He lifted the towel with a stick and waggled it to make sure no car part nestled in its folds. Most of the car pieces were near the point of impact. He frantically picked up every shard of plastic or bit of metal he could find—it was all plastic or fiberglass by the feel of it, though some pieces looked metallic. He half-listened for groans or movement from the dead couple but heard nothing.

As he worked, the wind accelerated in the trees and blew more steadily, making a rushing sound like ghostly cheering in a distant coliseum. There seemed to be less fog. Now the cops would be even less likely to believe his cotton excuse. But his focus on scrubbing the accident scene brought some calm. He checked and double checked, covering dozens of square yards of road, running his hands in smoothing motions, brushing over grit that could have

Tandem

been pieces of his headlamp or bits of sand that had been on this gray asphalt for twenty-five years. He finally told himself the grit didn't matter—*It didn't matter!* He had picked up every broken piece—there were not a lot of them; the biggest was only a few inches long.

On his way back to the car, he couldn't stop himself from making a second pass around the bike because it had been temporarily caught on the bumper. He saw a streak of dark blood on the frame. Impulsively, he reached out and dabbed it with his finger. But it was dry. It wasn't blood, it was maroon paint. From his car.

When he looked up, raising his hands in supplication, he glimpsed through trees two cars on the far side of the parking lot. The fog had cleared enough, or his night vision had sharpened. People were still in the park! Maybe a bonfire was burning on the beach after all.

Every heartbeat told him to get away—quick!—but he couldn't risk a single clue. Better to be caught here before he had run than to have his car paint start the cops on a trail that would lead to him a week from now. At the first sign of approaching headlights from the road or flashlights from the beach trail, he could scatter the contents of his bag and press the emergency call button on his phone. He ran and grabbed a jug of wiper fluid from the trunk and snatched the hoodie off the backseat. He doused the frame and rubbed with the hoodie. Still mostly there. He spilled fluid on the spot again, scraped the line of paint with his thumbnail. The paint came off. He saw another streak of paint. He gripped the surprisingly heavy bike with the hoodie and shifted it to get at the new streak. He erased that too. He needed to systematically check the entire bike for more paint. The contraption was old, faded green, a Schwinn. He darted his eyes toward the dark trailhead. A shudder moved through him, like the mechanical mixer vibrating at the paint store. He could not be systematic. He ran his eyes wildly over the bike, saw no more streaks. With the hoodie, he rubbed parts of the bike he might have touched. Then he gathered up hoodie, jug, and reusable bag, ran, and threw it all in the trunk.

He made his Y turn and drove off, back the way he had come. Leaving the scene of an accident was bad, but it didn't seem as bad as drunken vehicular homicide. Driving off was incidental, like neglecting a tip when he'd already refused to pay the bill.

He turned up tree-walled 65th Street. He saw mailboxes studded with reflectors, but few houses were visible through the trees. On 140th Avenue, an oncoming car cruised by him without incident. He realized that on an unlit two-lane road a car's headlights obscured everything else about the car. Windshields and bumpers just weren't visible. His single headlight was obvious, but only a cop would care about that. If a cop stopped him, he would tell them what had happened with impeccable honesty.

When he got back to M-40, he didn't turn right. He couldn't risk going through Allegan and the franchised glare of Otsego. He would take 140th Avenue over to 131 and then hope to get lucky.

140th Avenue proved a good choice. It was all farmland. The air stank of freshly manured fields. The smell seemed to enter his sinuses through his eyes. How could people stand to live with that 24/7? A few vehicles approached and went past him, tagging his car with their wind. One oncoming pickup flashed lights at him and he calmly flashed his single headlight back. "Thank you, I know," he said aloud.

The fog lessened the further east he went. As he slid down the 131 on-ramp to Kalamazoo, the clear air revealed so many attentive motorists on the freeway his heart accelerated like his car. The spiderweb of windshield cracks crinkled slightly and two thin whistles of air sounded at slightly different pitches, growing louder until his speed plateaued at 68. He would take the right lane the whole way home, keeping the smashed side of his windshield as far as possible from the curious eyes of fellow drivers.

His detour meant he'd be on 131 for a dozen miles more than if he'd gone back on M-40 and M-89. Between here and Kalamazoo, the odds of a trooper running a speed trap in the median were probably 50/50. The trooper would see the single headlight, and, if there was enough light, also the windshield and the grill as he passed. The trooper would pull him over, but that would be okay, because then this moment would end. He felt so horrible it didn't matter whether he got caught or made it home. If he got caught, he would gladly confess everything. He would accept full responsibility, if necessary.

This was just one of the bargains he made as he drove. Another was that he would be a much better person to everyone, from now on, all the time.

"I will be very good," he said aloud.

He would be more patient with his students, less argumentative with his colleagues. He would volunteer for things so other people wouldn't have to do them. He would never let his frustrations show, with anyone, as he sometimes had. He'd recently had a testy exchange with his young, aggressive dentist, who recommended a bite splint to keep him from grinding his teeth during sleep, which was apparently wearing his enamel and recessing his gums. Mike had suspected an upsell scam and implied as much to the cologne-wearing small businessman. What an ass he'd been! He would have no more of the petty thoughts that had led to so much correcting and sniping and score-settling with Anne, which had brought out similar behaviors from her, until a billion bird-pecks had caused the same destruction as twin jackhammers.

They had debated such issues as whether it was okay to turn on the heat right after starting a frozen car (he wanted it blasting right away; she wanted to let the engine warm up first); how meaningful were sell-by dates on processed food (he trusted his eyes and nose; she insisted many deadly bacteria gave no sign); and in which rooms of the house was it appropriate to clip one's toenails (she decreed bathrooms only; he felt their bedroom and his home office were viable alternatives). There might have been a constructive way to help her with her drinking—as opposed to saying nothing night after night and then finally blowing up about it, to which she had responded, more than once, by throwing her wine glass at him, shrieking at him, until Connor told them both to shut the fuck up—but it was now clear he had lacked the patience and empathy to figure that out. Then again, she had called him a workaholic cheapskate who sucked all the joy out of life, so maybe her empathy tank wasn't topped off either.

Now he would let pretty much everything go. He would be a force for goodness and kindness in the world. He would love everyone as hard as he could. He couldn't bring those two people back to life, but he could make over-stressed students want to live. (It was scary how many of them had severe mental health issues, were suicidal or close to it.) He would impose on himself a sort of moral house arrest that would be far more socially productive than prison. Wasn't closing prisons the cutting edge of social justice activism these days? There'd been a speaker on campus for MLK Day who'd advocated just that. Why throw himself into a dehumanizing system that King's disciples considered a racist tool of state violence? He would pursue his own style of restorative justice—the speaker's alternative to incarceration—with the world at large. Besides, morality trumped legality. Slavery had been legal, the Holocaust had been legal, the Great Leap Forward had been legal. He was living on the moral plane now. Legally, he was completely fucked, getting worse by the instant; morally, he had enormous potential.

When he was deep in this line of thought, he was no longer indifferent as to whether he got caught or reached his garage: he wanted to reach his garage.

Up ahead on the freeway, blue and red lights spun and flashed. An ice pick of adrenaline stabbed his heart, radiating nerve shock that nearly cracked his molars.

But some other poor lawbreaker had been stopped, and the cop, leaning hip-sprung over the driver's side window, wasn't in a spot where he would have seen Mike's cyclopean headlight and nabbed him. He just might make it.

He took the 131 spur toward downtown, the dark lanes empty as usual. He exited at Douglas and motored through a neighborhood that was disconcertingly well-lit but where people generally didn't call the police. Soon enough he was back at the intersection that had been his point of departure. This time he merged with Kalamazoo Avenue, which became West Main as he took the S curve up the hill. A block later he angled left onto his street well ahead of a stream of cars coming the other way down the hill. All that remained was three blocks where he knew many of the families behind the array of windows facing the world. But it was a leafy road, with infrequent streetlights, and despite being the dog-walking capital of America, no one seemed to be out. He turned into the ring of alleys behind his own and his neighbors' homes.

He pushed the opener for his detached garage, and as the big door rose, he exhaled a gust of sour air that tasted like chewed cardboard. He parked, lowered the door behind him, and sat in his car, disbelieving what had happened, disbelieving he had made it home. When the automatic garage light timed off, he felt he would burst out crying, but his eyes were dry and his chest subsided. Nothing would ever be right again.

He finally got out of the car. He left the garage and pulled the back door closed behind him. He locked this door, which he otherwise never locked. He traversed the twenty-five feet of walkway to his back patio and entered his house.

2.

Uneasy and alert, Claire Boland woke up at 5:41, just before first light. Colors slept. The bedroom was light grays and dark grays. Outside the open windows, birds on the feeders were cheeping and chirping intensely. It reminded her of that moment during book club when the text was left behind for good and the discussion became a free-for-all on some social or political issue. The birds could be discussing seed quality or predator sightings—cats, raccoons, red-tailed hawks. Whose song was good lately? Anything juicy happen last night?

She believed that creatures of all kinds shared news, worries, and fun things—in their way. All the science pointed in this direction. Any sign of playfulness, desire, pleasure, fear or pain in a living being conveyed an obvious message to her. Once she had fully grasped this message about ten years ago, she became a vegetarian, except for eggs and dairy (rennetless-cheese only, of course). She'd put up the feeders to begin the process of karma repair, and usually she loved to hear the sound of birds, emblems of all the lives she had saved by not eating meat. This morning, however, the birds were unusually numerous and excited, and she wished they would pipe down so she could get back to sleep.

Ryan snored softly, facing away from her. In the dim light, his bald spot gazed blankly at nothing. He called it his third eye, to tease her about her foray into Ayurveda, but she never teased him back. In her teens and college years, she'd found herself in the grip of "tall, dark and handsome" fantasies, which she eventually dubbed the TDH Syndrome, or just TDHS. "I want a man I can climb," she'd gushed to her roommate freshmen year. It took several difficult relationships for her to find a cure for TDHS. She had ultimately fallen for average, fair, and humorous. It had proved to be a durable choice.

She felt an impulse to kiss the bald spot, maybe as a way of affirming the span of their relationship, and to spoon Ryan from behind. But he might interpret the cuddle as a sexual overture, and she was too distracted and tetchy for sex right now. She just wanted to absorb through his warm skin a bit of Ryan's seemingly effortless good humor, his optimism, even his cluelessness. But it was not always easy to send her husband a nuanced physical message and, besides, he needed his sleep, too.

Their son Nathan was taking the ACT tomorrow, and despite a prep course and a phone book of practice exams he was supposedly working through, his only complete dry run had yielded a result a good deal lower than what she had hoped. She had caught him working a timed practice section *while watching the Tigers on his laptop.* Though she knew it reflected an unhealthy sense of boundaries, she experienced a simmering panic at the prospect of one of her children not excelling academically. Nathan was sweet and considerate, but he couldn't be persuaded to do his homework or study for his tests until it was far too late. He wanted to be a sports announcer. *That* he would practice rigorously, sitting for hours hunched over the orange foam windscreen of a microphone mounted on a tiny tripod, doing the play-by-play for various games with the TV sound off, going so far as to record himself with his laptop and DVR the games and then compare his commentary to the TV announcers. Claire was always encouraging, and they had gladly paid for his teen sports broadcaster camp last summer at Hofstra, but she thought professional sports were idiotic. The way athletes let go of thought, the delirious fawning hype for someone who could throw a ball through a metal ring or across a field of fake grass, the billions of dollars that could have been spent on something socially useful—it all depressed her.

She was also on edge because her daughter Emma had just come home from her first year of college and things felt off between them. She had hoped their battles were mostly over when, at the last minute, Emma had decided to go to Oberlin (Claire's stated preference) instead of the University of Michigan. But Claire feared Emma's choice was tainted by resentment over Claire's influence, and it turned out Oberlin wasn't far enough away to cause Emma to break up with her high school sweetheart, a serious Christian boy whose conservative upbringing made Claire deeply uncomfortable. Emma had spent yesterday with him in Holland, where he attended Hope College, and Claire had gone to bed before she had come home.

The two had met at the Math and Science Center, a prestigious public magnet program that drew students from all over Kalamazoo County. Part of the student's day was spent at their home high school and part at KAMSC. The workload was fiendish, and though she was good at it, Emma was not that into math and science. But Claire had worried that colleges would perceive Kalamazoo Central as a weak high school, and she didn't want to move to a high-performing district in white-flight Portage or Mattawan; persistent school segregation, she felt, was at the root of most of our nation's problems. Therefore, she would cast her lot against racism and income inequality by sending her daughter to a Kalamazoo public high school but maximize her college prospects by encouraging her to take the exam for KAMSC. Via a long campaign of sly manipulative comments and two overt soul-searing arguments, she had betrayed her motherly ideal of healthy boundaries and unconditional support and possibly permanently damaged their relationship by more or less bullying her daughter into what was best for her.

She tried to be more hands-off when it came to Emma's college decision, but that had proved difficult. While Claire insisted on public schools for K—12, she had a soft spot for small liberal arts colleges. As a graduate of a Kalamazoo public high school, Emma was entitled to a Promise Scholarship, made possible by the wild generosity of anonymous donors, for free tuition at any public college or university in Michigan, including the University of Michigan, but Claire believed Oberlin's individualized attention and activism-intensive environment would be worth it, and implied as much in her conversations with Emma. One must hold to one's values on certain issues, regardless of the cost.

Emma had resisted until, after a visit to Ann Arbor, she pronounced the pervasive Greek life "gross" and the student body "too white and too rich." She expressed a sudden fondness for rural Ohio and profusely thanked Claire and Ryan for the chance to follow her bliss at the more expensive option. Claire wondered if Emma ultimately chose Oberlin, and its higher cost, as a convoluted way of spiting Claire for exerting an overbearing influence on her school choices. That's how twisted things felt between them.

There was no hope of falling back asleep. She would make the most of this wakefulness and go for a run.

She rolled out of bed. The shift in the mattress made Ryan turn onto his back and open one eye.

"Are you getting up?" he asked groggily.

"No, I'm lying next to you."

"Mmm, feels good," he said with his eyes closed, running a hand under the covers where she had been. "Have you lost weight?"

"You're still dreaming," she said.

She quietly dressed in her running clothes, unplugged her phone from its charger, and headed into the hallway. Nathan's door was closed; Emma's door was open.

She smiled wickedly to herself: Had her daughter spent the night with Jeremy? Had Mr. Abstinence finally cracked? She turned on her phone to see if there was a text from Emma. While her phone booted up, she poked her head into Emma's room. No Emma on the unmade bed. About three days of clothes on the floor—the number of days she'd been home. A waxed Sweetwater's bag stood on the desk among empty glasses, crumb-sprinkled plates, and wrung teabags staining napkins. No posters or pictures of any kind on the walls. Not a single one. It had been this way even before she'd gone off to college. Claire wondered if the bareness was a rebuke or a deliberate withholding, as if her daughter didn't want to show her mother (an art museum curator who presented images and objects for a living) any outward sign of her interests, tastes, or affiliations. Instead she dated a holy roller with pecs the size of footballs who openly declared his desire to save himself for his wedding night.

"He's got good values," Emma had said. "He treats people well."

This was exactly the humanistic morality she and Ryan had worked so hard to teach their children, yet those words felt flung at her like the harshest accusation. Accusing her of what? She had spent many a night hoping—yes, *hoping*, she had to admit—for Emma to come home and announce that the mask had fallen off: he *was* a jerk hypocrite fundamentalist.

"He's studied the Gospels, Mom. He says Jesus would be totally for LGBTQ rights."

Their arguments often had the mystifying quality of a role reversal. Instead of acting like a jaded, teenage know-it-all or bombarding her with you-don't-understand's, Emma yelled things like, "I know you have everything figured out, but I don't!"

"That's okay," she'd responded. "I don't expect you to, and I don't either!"

"Oh, God, perfect answer," Emma had grumbled and stomped away.

"Let's talk about what you're figuring out, okay?"

Slam of bedroom door.

Her phone was all booted up. No text from Emma. Fear. Anger. Fear. Anger. She texted: *where are u?* No instant answer. Emma's phone went right to voice mail. After the beep, as calmly as she could, she said, "Just checking in. Expected you home last night. Give me a call."

Of course, Emma wasn't up yet. Claire herself normally wasn't up at this hour. *Let's not get ahead of ourselves*, she thought, a phrase she had frequently used with Emma when she had catastrophized about some debacle with her friends or worried about playing time on the volleyball team.

She went downstairs, used the bathroom, put some clips in her graying bobbed hair. (She wasn't coloring it on principle.) On her phone, she cued up the audiobook she'd been listening to—Amy Waldman's *The Submission,* a novel about a Muslim architect who wins the new World Trade Center's design competition; clipped her phone to the waistband of her shorts; and put in her ear buds. She hydrated with a glass of warm water, the benefits of which she had learned on her sojourn in February to an Ayurvedic resort at the southern tip of India.

Without knowing anything about Ayurveda, she had gone at the invitation of her friend Sandy, who wanted to open a yoga studio. Claire had gone with practical goals— painful stress knots periodically formed in her shoulders and neck, and she planned to leave with a potent treatment plan and some top-drawer meditation techniques. She had also dared to hope for something more, something spiritual, even transformative. They would be empty nesters soon, and she was already anxious about the next phase of her life.

In some ways, India had been an amazing experience—slathered with herb-infused oils, poulticed with smashed plants, yogaed to the point where she no longer felt individual joints but one connected, limber lifeforce. She got used to the rivers of oil and the disposable underwear they wore during treatments. She loved how Indians said "veg" and "non-veg," as if vegetarianism was the norm. But there had also been painful stretches suspended from ropes, an inordinate amount of time spent upside down, and too-warm oil dripped on her forehead to open a third eye she knew she didn't have; it had given her a terrible headache. When she'd told her practitioner, he seemed insufficiently concerned. Online, she discovered a limited amount of hard science behind Ayurvedic medicine, and a troubling use of arsenic, mercury, and lead in mineralizing treatments. On her way home, lifting off over smog-shrouded Delhi, she'd chided herself for the *Eat, Pray, Love* fantasy she should have seen through.

Still, some of Ayurveda made sense to her—the diet, the principle of balance, the holistic view of mind and body. She tucked away her disappointment and took from it what she could.

Ryan sometimes mocked her relentless drive for self-improvement in all its forms. It was true she assigned her children selected TED talks the family would discuss at dinner. It was true she forwarded them links to podcasts like *Another Round*, which afforded them insights into how African Americans saw and experienced the world. Yes, she occasionally put sticky notes on articles in the Sunday *New York Times* to draw the attention of different family members. Her need to do these things was profound and, to some extent, out of her control.

•

When she came in through the back door after her run, Ryan stood before open cupboards, in his smiley-face boxers and plain T-shirt, gut flab meeting uncertain resistance at his waistband, eyeing his cereal collection.

"Don't rush me," he said, one finger raised. "This is a critical decision."

He wiggled his fingers dramatically.

Claire knew that Seinfeld had been famous for having a lot of cereal in his apartment. Ryan was a movie- and TV-quoter, able to re-enact lengthy scenes with his friends (or on his own, if need be), and she suspected his "cereal collection" was an homage to the show. She was sometimes stunned by, and jealous of, the ways in which he found gratification.

"Emma didn't come home last night," she said.

"Really?" he replied, not sounding concerned, and drew out a box of Cinnamon Life.

She poured herself a glass of water from the filtered pitcher on the counter and drank, hoping to calm herself before she spoke again. But by the time she'd put her glass down, her anger paced inside her head like a large tiger in a small cage.

"You didn't see her door was open?"

"Now that you mention it, I do believe it was," he said, pouring his cereal into a bowl.

"So what do you think that means?"

"Counsel is badgering the witness."

Ryan was a lawyer in the County's Friend of the Court office. He specialized in wringing child support from deadbeat dads, witnessing some of the most dysfunctional broken families in Southwest Michigan. She wondered if being schooled in all of that nastiness gave him an unfair advantage in their arguments.

"You know," she said, "it'd be good if you helped me carry the emotional ball sometimes."

"The emotional ball?" He gave her a sideways look. *"The emotional ball?"*

She doubted he would let her live that down. He could work a pet phrase for months at a time. He had just finally given up sarcastically adding "God willing" to everything.

"You know what I mean. The burden of caring."

"Who says I don't care? I care by not caring. Let her fuck up horribly. Builds character."

There was something to this. But had she waited up for Emma? No. She had let go. *She had not helicoptered!* Yet it wasn't like Emma to not say where she was going to be, and any red-blooded parent *needed* to be alarmed right now.

"Great! Everything's fine!" She threw up her hands and slipped into a doltish imitation of Ryan: "'If she's screwing up, it's fine, and if she's fine, it's fine. Everything's fine.' Well, since you've got this, I'm just going to forget all about it and take a shower."

She headed out of the kitchen, trying not to feel ridiculous.

Ryan whistled. "And there she goes—the only person in America in touch with reality. I'm a lucky man."

"That's right!" she yelled back.

•

She made it to her office early. More shipments were expected later today for an upcoming exhibition by Rita Bowman, an African-American multi-media artist from Philadelphia. The theme was African religious ideas threading through Black urban communities. The artist was arriving Monday afternoon, and Claire would be working with her on the final layout, with an artist's reception Thursday evening and a formal opening on Saturday. Most of the pieces had already arrived, in copious bubble wrap and an absurd amount of tape that she had spent yesterday afternoon fighting through. She and Marta, the associate curator, had tentatively placed the art around the galleries on movers' pads covering the terrazzo floor or leaning against the walls resting on carpet squares, roughly dividing them between the first and second half of the exhibition catalog. There were paintings, photographs, sculptures, a video installation, a church pulpit installation. So far over phone and email, Rita had been gracious and responsive, understandably finicky about lighting and wall color, open and funny, and generally not crazy, and Claire forecast no cryptic silences, passive-aggressive battles, or bizarre meltdowns when she was in the building.

In the meantime, the morning's task was trying to decide between two exhibitions for late fall/early winter: abstract paintings that looked like eruptions of molten, spiraling matter in outer space, and a group show of representational artists. The usual Rubik's Cube of variables—cost; quality; audience appeal; organizational difficulty; timing; relationship to current, past and future exhibits; likely board opinions—felt unusually intractable today. Teresa, the executive director, wanted her proposal by Monday.

She usually had her phone on silent, so she wouldn't be disturbed or forget to turn it off before a meeting and then have an interruption, but this morning she'd put the sound on, because she needed to hear from Emma.

A little after nine, two police officers wearing contrasting uniforms approached her open office door. Her shoulders seized and she avoided looking at their faces, like a child caught doing something bad. The colors of their uniforms drew her focus, maybe because raw color had always been a comfort to her—one tan, the other such a dark blue it was almost black.

"Claire Boland?" the dark-blue officer said.

3.

It was after 1:00 AM, but Mike had no plans to sleep. His head throbbed to a diabolical beat. In his study upstairs, he sat at his desk with a legal pad and a tall glass of ice water, his right leg bouncing on the ball of his foot, scrawling a mix of plans, excuses, dictums, confessions, and resolutions.
He wrote:

> *Guiding thought: I can't bring them back. Living morally, loving everyone, is the only thing that can justify my existence outside of prison.*

> *Must make secret recompense to the families.*

> *Must confess if necessary to fend off madness.*

> *Must confess if necessary to keep someone in the victims' families from going insane or committing suicide.*

> *Focusing on the tasks to escape being caught could actually help fend off madness.*

> *It was very foggy right there. It was nobody's fault.*

> *Before whatever-God-is and all other humans, I acknowledge the following: I was drunk, I am bad, I am sorry, and I will make it up to you.*

Tandem

*The legal system is a crutch for those who can't feel
real guilt and make amends in their own way.*

This was a thrilling thought, and to counteract this
thrill he put three question marks in brackets immediately
after it: *[???]*.

He imagined in detail a trip to Saugatuck Dunes
during which the accident did not happen. He combed his
memory for small moments he hadn't noted along the way
that affected the instant at which he arrived at the particular
spot where he'd collided with the bike riders. He had scooted
through a yellow light in Otsego. He had passed a farting
pick-up on M-89. If Sarah had just let him finish his beer in
due time, the tandem riders would have been long gone. The
sun might have been so far sunk he wouldn't have even
contemplated a trip to see the sunset.

His imagination ran toward these alternatives like a
dog forgetting an electronic fence—only to be jolted back
into reality.

Then he remembered where he had hit them: the
right lane just before the parking lot. The traffic flowed
counterclockwise around the horseshoe. There was an
outbound lane on the other side. They were going out
through the in lane. It was their fault!

But maybe he had actually entered the parking lot by
then, at which point lane assignments dissolved into the
bumper-car free-for-all that every parking lot effectively
represented. He tried to remember, but of course he hadn't
been focused on that at the time. Something about their
nearly head-on angle suggested they were headed down the
wrong lane, he was pretty sure.

What a fool he'd been not to notice that! If it was
partly their fault, he might have stayed and called the cops,
who would have been in a fried-dough coma some distance
away, which would have given him precious minutes to
incrementally sober up, which would have—

He hadn't done that. He had run. He was here.

He tried to recenter himself with his guiding thought: I can't bring them back; living morally, loving everyone, is the only thing that can justify my existence outside of prison.

This was reasonably effective. He did not have the mental energy, or the desire, to interrogate his guiding thought. He did not want to think about the bereaved.

Because staying sane was required for doing the right thing, and because compartmentalizing was required for staying sane, he made a commitment to compartmentalize. This approach seemed magically validated when he realized the word "mental" was safely tucked inside "compartmentalize."

He began to focus on practicalities: 1) Disposal/fixing of the car 2) Need for an internet research tool he could easily hide or destroy.

He knew everything in his life could become evidence. Paper could be burned, so he was free to write whatever he wanted on his legal pad. His computers and his car were the main things he would have to scrub or keep clean. He had a laptop that was technically school property, and on which he did all his professional work as well as his personal email and web surfing. His desktop computer in his school office was also college property, of course. He remembered that he used to have an iPad mini that Anne and Connor had given him for his birthday several years ago, but he hadn't really needed it, so he'd let Anne and Connor use it. Now it seemed the perfect burner for doing incriminating Google searches. (*What are the penalties for drunken vehicular homicide in Michigan? How does one dismantle a car?*) Let the police seize and scrutinize his phone and two other computers—the documents and browsing history would only reveal his three obsessions: macroeconomics, U.S. History, and the Green Bay Packers.

But he had lost track of the mini—hadn't seen it for years—and he hadn't thought to account for it when he and Anne had split up their stuff. It occurred to him that Anne had gotten so accustomed to using it that she had simply taken it with her without telling him. A gusher of rage caught him off guard. He swung his palm hard against the side of the metal file cabinet which was a few feet from his desk. This made a very loud noise. Some bones in his palm felt fractured.

Maybe his emotions were not totally in his control. Being loving and kind at all times was going to be incredibly hard.

"Maybe she didn't take it," he said aloud. "Think before you act out."

His mother's face cruised across his consciousness, slowly, at a great height, like the Goodyear blimp. She could be extremely warm and indulgent, or extremely judgmental, depending on one's relationship at any given time to her moral code. He didn't have to focus too intently on her floating visage to imagine her Old Testament mood.

He had to snap out of it. Mentalize.

He threw himself into searching the house for the mini. Where Anne's desk had sat on the first floor was emptiness, so he headed for the basement. Anne herself had been known to compartmentalize on occasion. Or at least she liked to organize and store things in large stackable plastic tubs arrayed on shelving units he'd installed. He had to admit, it did make it easier for her to move out when the time came, though, obviously, she didn't take them all. One huge, coffin-shaped bin housed their plastic Christmas tree, in three segments; other tubs held Halloween and Christmas decorations, rolls of wrapping paper and bags of gift bows, aluminum chafing dishes and Sterno cans, etc. All kinds of crap, but no mini.

Frustration boiled quickly. Now, however, he observed it from a remove, like a general viewing a Bikini Atoll nuclear test with high-powered binoculars: great brightness on the horizon, yes; the terrible burgeoning cloud, yes; a forceful unnatural wind, yes—but no immediate devastation nearby. He had successfully mentalized it into a compartment.

"Be systematic," he told himself.

He spent forty-five minutes going through every tub. He found Connor's old sports equipment, superfluous kitchenware, framed and illustrated inspirational poems Anne had collected. So much crap! He found a tub of baby bath towels: each had an extra triangle of cloth sewn in one corner, making a little pocket that would fit perfectly over the baby's head. Around the perimeter of these towels were stitched tiny ducks. He remembered two-year-old Connor, fresh out of the tub, with the pocket over his head, the rest of the towel falling behind him like a caftan as he did his "bath dance" on the mat—a berserk cherub. He hadn't exactly been feeling close to his son before the accident, and the memory almost brought tears. He resolved to love Connor more carefully. Then he renewed his search for the mini.

When he came up empty in the basement, despair was waiting for him, ready to throw a gunnysack over his head and pummel his face, neck, and kidneys.

"I will systematically search the first floor," he said aloud, Jedi-mind-tricking his way past despair.

He started with the built-in bookcases, and within three shelves he saw the slender mini holder slipped between a pair of books of similar size. Why hadn't he looked there in the first place? His low-grade OCD made him start at the base of the house and work his way up, a time-wasting outrage. On the other hand, maybe he had just the right amount of OCD to survive committing this...crime, for lack of a better word.

Watching movies as a kid, he'd wanted Bonnie and Clyde to rob banks forever; he'd hoped John Dillinger and Al Capone and Pretty Boy Floyd would elude the Feds and enjoy the fruits of their depredations in sober peace. A sweaty part of him even hoped *In Cold Blood* didn't have to end with arrests—and those murderers were awful in so many ways! Was this a sign of his latent criminality, or was it just impossible not to identify at some level with the bad guy, or with *any* guy, once you knew what was going on inside them?

Mentalize it, for here inside the beige leather was the mini itself. He found a charger and power cord in a junk drawer in the kitchen.

On a low nearby shelf was a compact edition of the *Oxford English Dictionary*. Anne was a real estate agent, but she had fiddled with poetry writing for a year or so and belonged to an all-women writers group. By Mike's reckoning, approximately fifteen percent of the women in

Tandem

Kalamazoo were either poets or at least willing to take a poetry workshop. It was a strange town. A poet friend had given her the Compact OED and encouraged her to study it, saying it contained just about everything English-speaking people knew about themselves, and much that was generally forgotten. Mike had counted three nights on which Anne had sat at the kitchen table, wearing her glasses instead of her contacts, with both volumes open, a glass of white wine providing inspiration. In a fancy moleskin notebook, she drafted poems. It was a good memory, he had to admit. Anne had been happy. It seemed sad and significant that she had not taken the dictionary with her to Tucson.

The dictionary didn't seem compact at all: two heavy volumes that slid into twin sleeves in a cardboard display box that included a small drawer on top for a magnifying glass. The pages were tall and wide. He would cut out a hole in the center pages that would exactly hold the mini. When the cops were closing in, he would slip the mini into the P – Z volume.

He found a pencil and a box cutter. A musty smell wafted up from the binding. He tried to determine how many book pages equaled the thickness of his mini. Twice he thought he had removed enough pages, but realized he had to take out a few more. Finally the mini fit snugly. He took the volume out and let the book stand on its own outside of the case. It stood well. The covers parted only slightly and the pages all slumped slightly to the right, just enough to rest on his desk. The top of the pages held together, albeit with a slight ridge in the center from the mini making a second spine inside. This wasn't ideal, but maybe the cops would be getting lazy at this point in ransacking his house. He returned the book to its case with the mini inside.

Satisfied with this hiding place, he removed the mini and hooked it up to its charger. He put the cut pages and the leather case in the trash. The accomplishment of this task seemed to put him on the other side of something, though he wasn't sure what that was. It was almost 5:00 AM. He felt himself relax slightly, and blinding fatigue followed. He decided to accept it. He went into his bedroom and lay down.

Mozina

He told himself there was nothing more to be done for now, nothing more to be done. Mercifully, his mind let him sleep.

4.

The dark blue officer was a young man with alert brown eyes and a prominent chin. The tan officer was older, soft and ruddy in the face, big in the chest; she realized he was not a Kalamazoo cop.

"I'm sorry," the tan officer said. "Your daughter Emma was involved in a hit-and-run last night."

Claire stared back at him, meeting his clear blue eyes, which did not waver. Her mouth trembled open on its own. She could not seem to re-set it.

"She was hit riding a bicycle," the officer continued in an even, subdued voice. "She died before anyone got there."

Claire covered her face with her hands, a leaden, unwilled movement, as if her arms were moving through heavy water. She saw her daughter asleep in her bed, in unconscious abandonment, on her back, arms flung up toward the headboard, sky-blue comforter foaming around her, mouth half-open, totally vulnerable. When was the last time she had seen her like that?

"She was with a young man named Jeremy Vanden Berg?" the officer continued, inviting a reaction to the name. "In a parking lot at a state park in Saugatuck. He also died."

Jeremy's name crushed any remaining possibility of mistake, escape, resistance. A space opened in her torso, as if everything inside her were gone, leaving a bare wooden floor. She wanted to scream, but screaming in the museum would be like screaming in church, and for a flash she hated herself for not being abandoned enough to scream. Still, the urge to scream rose like an elevator up her throat.

She stood up and walked past the men and out of her office. She opened her mouth: "OAH!" came out. She wanted to continue downstairs to the Ahn light box exhibit. She wanted to hide there. But three steps into the hallway, she realized this was too much. These men had to do their job. She needed to get rid of them as quickly as possible so she could go somewhere to cry and scream as much as she wanted. She turned around and walked back into her office, as if to start over. The men turned as she re-entered, but they kept their eyes down. They turned again as she resumed her seat behind her desk. She put her elbows on her desk and her hands over the bridge of her nose. She had assumed she'd have all summer to reconnect with Emma. She felt her tears on her fingers. The molecules that made up the world swam and churned, but reality didn't come apart, though she wished it would. She closed her eyes, trying to stop everything from happening. She sobbed helplessly.

After some gap of time, the dark blue officer said, "Her body's been brought to the medical examiner's office here in Kalamazoo. Because of the criminal investigation. They're doing an autopsy this afternoon." A slight pause between each sentence, as one pauses when taking steps on a lake that may or may not be frozen.

"Does my husband know?" She pulled several tissues out of the box on her desk and held them to her face.

"Officers should be with him right now," the tan cop said.

"I know your husband," the dark blue cop said. "I'm very sorry."

"Can I see her?" Her voice squeaked small and broken. She wanted a chance to say that over in her real voice.

"Her body will be released to your funeral home, probably tomorrow," the tan cop said. "Any place you designate."

"They might let you," the dark blue cop said, as if the other cop hadn't spoken. "The examiner's office is just down at the med school on Lovell. We're certain it's her," he added.

The tan cop sighed. "I'm sorry, I don't think so," he said, in a quiet voice. He seemed about to say more on this point but thought better of it. He was significantly older than the blue cop. "Again, I'm very sorry. Please let us leave our business cards with you. We'd like to be in touch and talk more in the next couple of days."

Without looking at the men, she accepted their cards and laid them on the side of her desk. She kept her eyes there until the men went away.

•

She met Ryan at home. He was outside when she pulled up. His eyes desperately wanted her to help him. She got out of the car, and they sobbed in each other's arms on the driveway. Ryan sounded as if something was trying to turn his lungs inside out but he was resisting. Driving together to pick up Nathan at school, in silence, facing forward in their bucket seats, devastation settled across her chest like a drawn seatbelt that kept tightening. *My girl, my girl,* she thought over and over.

Nathan cried over her shoulder, said something in her ear that sounded like "the air will never be long," asked no questions, and, when they arrived home, immediately shut himself up in his room.

She told Ryan what the Kalamazoo cop had said about maybe being able to see Emma at the medical examiner's office. She wanted to go right away.

"We'll see her tomorrow at the funeral home," Ryan said softly. He seemed wrung out, done crying for now.

"How can you think of anything but seeing her?" she cried. His flip response to Emma's absence earlier this morning inflamed her now. "That's your daughter!"

"Not now, Claire, please," he said in a plaintive but rising voice. "Please stop your shit!"

This did stop her. He almost never yelled. They stood staring at each other in the kitchen, both of them breathing deeply. "Your shit" brought her to the brink of an unexplored chasm of accusation she sensed had been opening before this moment. She could not yet step to the edge and peer into what was down there.

"Babe, I'm sorry," Ryan said, though his voice was charged, not conciliatory. "Everything's too much right now. I'm sorry."

She stared at him, felt her eyes brimming again. He had naturally sad eyebrows—at times they seemed to slant down like roof hips, but now they were tensed into a beetling horizontal line. The lack of warmth or contrition in his expression scared her.

"That cop didn't know what he was talking about," he added more calmly, breaking eye contact. "With a hit-and-run, someone's getting prosecuted." He rubbed his hands over his face in a strange polishing motion. He lowered his hands and shook his head, a quick jerk. "They're not going to want anyone else in the room with her. There's evidence they'll be trying to—" He waved away the rest of the sentence.

"Evidence," she said disdainfully, shaking her head.

But even as she said it, she knew she was being foolish, even mean. She was surprised by how out-of-control and animalistic she felt.

Weeping overtook her again. She didn't want to be fighting with him right now. "I shouldn't have said it like that." She could barely get the words out. "I'm sorry."

Ryan didn't seem to hear her. "We'll see her tomorrow at the funeral home," he said, bringing her in for a hug.

She hugged him back, even though he had said "your shit."

5.

Just a few hours after he'd fallen asleep, he was awake again. The pulverizing force of his headache was frightening. His brain was being ground up—his skull a mortar, his spine a pestle. His consciousness felt sick and pressured. He immediately went downstairs where the iPad was charging. He booted it up, grateful to discover Anne and Connor hadn't changed his trusty password, and searched for news. Nothing yet.

He had to figure out what to do about the car. He could not risk coming up with some story and taking it to the dealer for repairs. Not with an unsolved hit-and-run about to hit the news. He thought he might completely destroy the car, disassemble it, and gradually dispose of the parts, and he researched that. He discovered that if he bought the right tools, and an engine hoist from Amazon, and a pickup truck or some other vehicle to drive away the parts and dump them somewhere, he could in fact break his car into smaller pieces and disappear it without a trace. Then report it stolen. Several YouTube videos offered systematic instructions on draining fluids; disconnecting hoses; removing bumpers, windshield, seats, doors, transmission, tires, brakes, axles, and the heavy engine itself. A blowtorch to cut up the frame. This was an option. But it would require a ton of work and many surreptitious late-night drives to the Kalamazoo River or Lake Michigan, where he could sink car parts where no one would ever find them.

This seemed tedious and insane and wrong. But what choice did he have now?

He remembered watching his uncle and his dad replace the water pump in his dad's old Jaguar before he had to sell it. They weren't gearheads but they had figured it out. Maybe he could repair the car himself. Soon he was navigating CarParts.com. A new unpainted 2005 Toyota Camry hood for $195. A new front bumper cover, also unpainted (apparently the only way they sold parts), just $35. A headlight assembly was equally easy to find. There were also plenty of YouTube videos about how to install these parts and paint them if necessary. He learned that each car came with a color code on its compliance plate (whatever that was) that would allow him to get an exact match. He could put in the time to make the paint perfect.

When he tried to find a windshield, things were less straightforward. Carparts.com offered new molding for a Camry windshield, but not the windshield itself. Were windshields generic products and only the fittings for the Camry were particular? He found helpful instructions for removing a cracked windshield and installing a new one. But what he couldn't find was a way to mail order a replacement windshield the way he could mail order a bumper cover or a hood or a headlight. He gathered windshield replacement was big business—cracks were common—and a lot of shops were willing to coordinate with insurance companies. Some websites actively discouraged the DIYer: windshields were tricky to seal; the pros generally didn't charge too much; no good reason to do it yourself. This gave him pause. He had to be able to get his own windshield somehow. There was a shop on Sprinkle Road. He would drive down there and check it out. In the meantime, he ordered the headlight, the hood, and the bumper cover. Then he remembered the grill with the Toyota emblem in it and ordered that separately.

But he needed something to drive to the shop on Sprinkle. He wondered if he should get a pickup truck, in case he had to go back to the disassembly plan. On a hunch, he decided to do a search for the exact car he was driving now. In five minutes he had two options at CarGurus.com: A 2005 Camry LE that the photo suggested was the exact same red as his current car. A seller in Stockton, KS. Only $4979 with

138,000 miles on it. He immediately messaged to say he was interested. Then he found a 2006 Camry LE that from the picture also looked to be the exact same color as his car. In fact, he could discern no difference at all between the 2005 and the 2006. The price was $6700 and it had 105,500 miles on it. South Bend, IN., just 75 miles away. The listing said *Good Deal: $1092 below.* Probably a foolish Catholic low-balling the price so as to not commit a sin. Mike had been Catholic once, but not anymore.

Driving around the neighborhood in an undamaged look-alike car would persuade anyone who thought about it—and of course no one would think about it in the first place—that he was not involved in the accident. In case someone saw the back ends of two identical cars in his garage, he spun out the cover story to himself: He bought this car for Connor. Connor didn't need it right now—the old Civic hatchback was still running with nearly 300,000 miles on it—but he would need it eventually. He would surprise him with it on a trip home for his birthday. He'd bought him a car that looked exactly like his old man's car because this was a funny joke. They could convoy together, drag race each other, swap bumper covers, etc. It would be an excellent ha ha thing. And he could still execute his disposal plan with this car; the trunk was big and he could cut things into pieces. Except the engine. He would rent a van for the night he had to dispose of the engine. Pickup trucks were suspicious in dumping situations anyway.

This car could also be a sign of him overlooking Connor's harsh and angry criticisms, and loving his son anyway. Once the divorce actually happened, Connor had gotten quieter. Mike didn't know if this was good or bad. The replica car could help ensure that Connor was on a good path and not just swallowing anger. This could in turn soften Connor's disposition in general, making him less likely to, say, blow up at his girlfriend or bite off someone's head at work. Could he do this good deed if he were in prison? No.

The idea of having a replica car appealed to him in other ways. It would facilitate imaginative slips and alternative history fantasies in which the accident never happened. A replica car—a replicar—distracted him in a pleasant way.

When business hours were underway, he called the seller and found out it was not an individual but a used car dealer. That was fine. Greyhound sent a bus to South Bend Regional Airport every day at 6 PM.

With progress on the car front, he scrambled some eggs and dispensed a bowl of Special K Red Berries; the dehydrated strawberries were real, or had been real, which had seemed incredible at an earlier stage of his life. This balanced breakfast fortified him to search again for news about the accident. He found a short MLive article about a hit-and-run at Saugatuck Dunes. His dry eyes couldn't focus. Bits came through: two fatalities, searching for the driver, call this number with information.

He thought of the car that had flashed its lights at him. But naturally the search would focus on people in Saugatuck and Douglas and Holland and even Grand Rapids before Kalamazoo. He couldn't believe he'd had the presence of mind to pick up pieces of his car, to clean the paint off the bike. He also had his dinner with Sarah and Dave as an alibi. To be involved, he would've had to drive straight to the park immediately after saying good-bye to them. That's what he *had* done, but what were the odds he would do such a thing?

It took a second pass to grasp the names of the victims. Jeremy Vanden Berg of Gull Lake and Emma Teague of Kalamazoo, both 19. Ryan Teague and Claire Boland lived three blocks away; they had a daughter who very possibly was named Emma, but he wasn't sure. He did not want it to be her. Under a pile of journals and newspapers on the floor, the 2007 phone book was moldering. There were only six Teague listings. Five were from neighboring towns like Paw Paw and Oshtemo. Ryan Teague was the only Teague with a Kalamazoo address.

Mike threw his head back and collapsed in his chair. He'd killed a neighborhood kid. This fact was almost as stunning as hitting the tandem in the first place. He now had a vague memory of Anne once doing a favor and picking Emma up along with Connor after some K Central sports practices. He'd played poker with her father a few times, though he hadn't been invited to a game in a while. Ryan was a Bears fan, and they hadn't really clicked as friends.

Claire Boland was in Anne's old book club. In fact, in the early years after they moved to town, he had gone to some of those book club meetings himself. There were a few husbands who also sometimes showed up, but as they had fallen away and he had gotten busy, he had stopped going as well. Mike had seen Claire over the years at neighborhood parties and jogging past their house. Anne had gone to Emma's graduation party but he had not—telling her, he now remembered with a pang, that he had no intention of watching her get drunk in public for the millionth time.

Killing the daughter of people he knew reinforced both his inability to confess and his inability to deal with not confessing. These two forces leaned into each other in perfect balance, forming an extremely stable arch of emotional pain. The accident would be the talk of the neighborhood. But who would think in a million years that he was involved?

Anyone who saw the car in his garage.

The only plus was that this would allow him to keep tabs on one, and maybe both, of the victims' families. He could make recompense in subtle ways and monitor the levels of distress Ryan and Claire were experiencing. If it seemed their suffering could be significantly improved by his confession, he would confess. In the meantime, living next to the abject pain he had caused would scour his miserable soul far more effectively than time in prison.

His thoughts occasionally jumped to a parallel track: his life here was over. He must find a way out of town. It might take months or years to get out, but this place was no longer tenable. To keep in-state tuition for Connor, which the Promise Scholarship was covering, he probably couldn't go too far, unless Connor established residency independently. He wondered how many other uncaught criminals were hunkered down near the scene of their transgressions, heightening their risk of arrest just to get cheaper tuition for their kids.

He stowed his mini in the dictionary.

•

He showered, ate lunch, and packed his school bag, slipping a change of clothes, some toiletries, and his garage door opener under his books and planner. He walked to campus. It was in the 70s. Sunny. Millions of leaves flashed and fluttered in the faint breeze. Their school was on trimesters, with classes going into the first week of June, and keeping students engaged when the weather turned gorgeous was a perennial challenge.

Young adults roamed free, obliviously crossing the red brick street that ran down the center of campus, eyes on their phones instead of approaching cars. They read sitting with their backs to trees and smoked on the steps of the Fine Arts Center. They beelined between buildings without regard for walkways meant to spare the thick grass. Each of their lives was better than his.

They greeted him enthusiastically—"Hi, Mike!"— because he was a buoyant and friendly teacher, always on his best behavior in the classroom. He responded, "Hey, there," or "How's it going?" because he often forgot their names.

This had always bothered him. So, starting about six or seven years ago, for each class he taught, he used the online student directory to create a roster of pictures of all the students, sized to fit a whole class on a single sheet of paper, easy to consult in the heat of teaching, to help him learn and use everyone's name. Nevertheless, after the class was over, he generally remembered students' faces but not their names. He told himself that now he would review his picture rosters for students who hadn't yet graduated and refresh names, as practice, every time he arrived on campus, until he could properly address any current or former student. These students would feel loved and cared about, they would try a little harder, they would not give up on their young lives.

He took the steps into Bowen Hall two at a time and continued on up to the Econ and Business suite on the third floor. In the hallway, he ran into his department chair, John

Hopper, a bull-shouldered man with a perfectly round bald head and a man-in-the-moon face. He taught Business Stats, Law and Economics, and Industrial Organization. Mike thought John was batshit and had learned to tread lightly around him.

"What happened to you?" Hopper said in his blunt way.

"Doing good, John," he said with a smile, though his heart began to race. Everything Hopper had ever done against him, including the tepid department letter for his tenure review, was forgiven and would always be forgiven.

Hopper stopped and touched his hand to his own forehead, squinted up and under Mike's hair.

"Oh, doorjamb," Mike said. "Do *not* walk around your house in the dark at night!"

"Live and learn," Hopper said sarcastically, and he moved down the corridor.

Instead of entering the suite, Mike headed for the restroom to examine his forehead. It hadn't looked too bad in his bathroom at home, and he had combed his hair down a bit more instead of across his forehead as he usually did. Seeing students he couldn't name on his way in might have prompted him to brush his hair back with his hand, a nervous tic.

In the restroom, there was a student at the sink and a student at a urinal. He had to be careful when examining his forehead in such an environment. He nodded at the student at the sink and quickly approached a urinal and went through the motions while the sink guy left and the guy next to him flushed and went to wash his hands. This guy had to be primping in the mirror or possibly looking at his phone; he stood there an unreasonably long time. Mike discovered his bladder was half-full and urinated angrily, trying to drive the young man out. He had to let up before he tore something.

The sink guy finally left, and he rushed to the mirror, lifted his hair off his forehead. The fluorescent light was revealing. A bright red/purple horizontal bruise. A steering wheel bruise. Right after the accident, he'd banged his head repeatedly with regret. Before it was dragooned into religious iconography, the mark of Cain had probably originated with some ancient remorseful murderer pounding his forehead against a rock.

He rearranged his hair and remembered that Hopper himself had a DUI. He had complained bitterly about it when they'd gone out for beers in the early days when Mike had hoped that Hopper was in the range of normal and they would become friends. Hopper hadn't blown very far over the limit and had finessed it with his chair and the provost.

Mike closed his eyes against the light, took some deep breaths, and headed for the suite.

"Well, good afternoon, Mike," the office coordinator drawled from behind her command center of a desk. "So glad you've decided to join us."

Moira's running joke was that professors never seemed to work a full day, unlike herself, who was in five days a week, eight to five, no matter what. Mike had once hinted that he worked a lot from home, that he could work anywhere, at any time—often around the clock for weeks at a time—but he had given up on getting this point across.

"Great to see you," he said warmly. And then he did what he had once told himself he would never do again but did now because he was trying to love everyone as hard as he could. He asked, "How are you doing?"

Moira trumpeted that she had finally convinced her husband to have a tree cut down. She had been telling him for years that a half-dead oak threatened the corner of their house. Her ultimatum involved leveraging something her husband wanted—at this point Mike's attention began to flag—and the tree had been cut down yesterday, with Moira providing brief supervision during her lunch hour. The tree guys had discovered serious rot within the tree; they assured her that it would have come crashing down in the first heavy summer storm and she had been very wise to have it removed. Moira had thrown this information in her husband's face with great relish.

"Wow, good for you," Mike said. "Glad you got that taken care of."

Which prompted a retelling of much of the story, culminating again with how her husband had finally listened to her about the tree and she had been proven right by the tree guys.

"I said, 'Wait, you've got to tell my husband.' Check this out." For what seemed like minutes, she tapped and swiped on her enormous phone with a shiny finger —"just a sec"—until she called up a video. The gaunt tree guy in John Lennon glasses spoke solemnly about the inner decay. "We had to take it down," he averred. He pointed out a hollow area in a section of the trunk lying on the grass.

"Wow," Mike said. He didn't want to appear as if he were just waiting for her to stop talking so he could walk away. If she figured that out, it would hurt her feelings. Love demanded more of a response. "Hope your husband found his own words to be tasty!" he added.

"Ha!" Moira exclaimed. "Not!"

"Well, sounds like everything turned out."

Which launched her into another condensed version of everything that had happened.

"Well, better hit the rock pile," he interjected, "given how late I came in."

"I hear you!" Moira said, with cheerful implied criticism, turning back to her own tasks.

It had been fifteen minutes since he entered the building. He had given Moira as much love as he could stand to give.

Computer booted, he chose not to look for an update to the hit-and-run story. That would be highly incriminating if the cops ever seized his browser history. Instead, he called his insurance agent and told her he was going to buy a car tomorrow. Without the VIN, she couldn't add it to his policy today, but she gave him a hotline number to call over the weekend so he'd be able to get the insurance necessary to drive it home.

"Nothing in this place can annoy me," he whispered to himself, turning to his email. "Everyone in this place is, and will be, forgiven."

He thanked his correspondents profusely for the smallest actions or bits of information. *Have a great day!* he signed off repeatedly. Within twenty minutes, he was overcome with exhaustion. He closed his office door, pulled a pillow out of the back of one of his file cabinets, and tried to take a nap on the floor.

•

He didn't quite sleep and rose forty-minutes later, loggy-headed. He realized that here he was on campus but he had not reviewed his picture rosters, as he had pledged to do. He dug up old sheets of faces and collected them into a separate folder, then spent some time linking old names and faces, noting Amy Chloris—ECON 305 Intro to Macro, Fall 2014—who he'd just seen on his way in today and had to "hey" instead of offering a spirit-boosting "Hi, Amy!" Sticking to a plan to make others happier made him feel okay for a minute.

He had a sandwich in the student center and headed for the downtown bus terminal on foot, like a hobo.

He hadn't taken a Greyhound in decades and was surprised by how new the breadloaf-shaped coach looked, even as its side was painted to look like a vintage bus from the fifties. The upholstery was patterned with cross-hatched smeary rectangular shapes in shades of blue, gray, and white, apparently designed to pacify passengers by neutralizing all thought and feeling. He hoped it would work. There was a lap and shoulder belt—which he hadn't remembered on buses of old—and he strapped himself in. He opened his air nozzle to the max and pointed it at his forehead, medicating his bruise. He sat ostentatiously close to his window, inviting someone to sit next to him and launch into their pathetic life story. He would listen his ass off. He would listen like no stranger on an interstate bus had ever listened. He would make comments that would reveal how attentive a loving person could be: "You say your mother worked logistics for the National Guard? I bet you could eat off your garage floor." And maybe when he was finally arrested, he would track that person down and put them on the stand as a character witness during the sentencing phase.

But no one sat by him.

Tandem

They rode 131 south at a dreamy speed through a semi-developed, semi-farmy land. Almost every other vehicle passed them. He did not pretend to try to sleep. A Black girl, about five years old, in beaded cornrows, wearing sandals with big plastic daisies blooming between her big and second toes, made pointless trips up and down the aisle, tapping only on seat rows where no one sat. The kid was polite and had a sense of method. "You'll go far," he wanted to tell her, but she never looked at him. He had a smile for whoever wanted one. They were better than he was. He loved them all.

They took I-80 west, into the setting sun. Loneliness poured from the air vents. The bus was like a needle in the concrete groove of a badly warped record, playing elongated sounds. "There's a killer on the road," Jim Morrison intoned in his head. "His brain is squirmin' like a toad."

This journey prefigured his eventual move from Kalamazoo, and that could be a good thing. Socially, he had always been on a demographic island in the Econ and Business department, a stray hire who worked most of his first decade under a well-bonded old guard that hung on longer than expected, then retired almost en masse, over a couple short years. The new hires were friendly and energetic people of color, with hip, behaviorist research fields like reciprocal altruism and microfinance, but they had each other and seemed to put him in the crusty old neo-classical white dude bin. His most likely department buddy was Hopper, who at several years older was now the senior member, but he was insane, with his massive bullet-pointed emails and his tendency to treat department meetings as a gathering of the Supreme Headquarters Allied Expeditionary Force on the eve of D-Day. That was the trouble with these rinky-dink colleges and their tiny departments: odds of simpatico colleagues could be very small. Dave, his best friend at the college, was in the Psych Department.

He couldn't bear going back to his hometown. His father had dementia and had moved with his mother into a continuing care complex in Eau Claire. His siblings were on diagonally opposite coasts: Ed, a software engineer in

Seattle; Barb, a corporate lawyer in Miami. The geographic symbolism was unmistakable. He was the youngest, and he feared each would view his move to their city with cool suspicion. When Mike was six, their stockbroker father had gotten over-extended trading on margin in his own account. When his sure bets went south, the family plunged into bankruptcy and their parents had separated for a time. He had grown up loath to show any signs of neediness, either emotional or financial, and it seemed an unspoken rule among the siblings that they would never burden each other.

The distance from his family only reinforced the sense there was no one to love at the moment. He would not love himself. He could never forgive himself. He wondered about that. Should loving everyone as hard as possible include loving himself? He had read somewhere that hell was hate. He didn't think he hated anyone—now that he had made a point of no longer hating John Hopper—but he was obviously in hell. So maybe that wise, quoted person was wrong about the nature of hell. Or maybe he hated himself for doing the wrong thing, and that was the source of this hellish sensation. So, then, was loving himself going to be the ultimate test of all this? And what would that imply about the question of turning himself in? Could loving himself entail forgiving himself and not turning himself in?

He dimly grasped that his instinct for self-excuse was limitless. He gave himself a sort of credit for this dim grasping. As Dave had explained the distinction years ago, psychopaths were not self-aware; he was, at worst, a sociopath. The only thing he knew for sure was that he didn't want to go to prison and lose all his money.

•

His La Quinta Inn was right next to the airport, only several hundred yards from the edge of the terminal where the Greyhound dumped him. The airport road was winding and sidewalkless, so instead he set out walking across a large green lawn straight for the hotel. He feared he was drawing attention, but the farther out he got into the grass, the less identifiable he would be. Eventually, he surmounted a berm that turned out to be planted on the other side with flowers and ornamental shrubs amidst which was set a huge low sign, fifty yards long, announcing that this was the South Bend Regional Airport. The La Quinta parking lot was not far past the berm.

The lobby was small and low-ceilinged. The desk clerk was a smiley, heavily freckled woman with a sky-blue headband.

The desk was under video surveillance. On a small TV screen set in an upper corner over the clerk's left shoulder, he could see his every move replicated in milky black and white. As the clerk clacked away at her keyboard, he watched himself pat his bangs down over his forehead bruise. He resented the camera. It was intrusive, judgmental, and unfair. Just as he hoped to ameliorate his guilt by weighing acts of love against it, so was he sometimes tempted to ameliorate his guilt by accusing others of acts against him. He resolved to keep an eye on the latter tendency, as he sensed it could undermine his moral development.

She pushed the registration card back to him. "Car and license plate?"

"I came by bus," he said, unable to formulate a lie on such short notice.

"Oh, and what brings you to town?"

He was taken aback. This seemed an egregious breach of hotel desk clerk discretion.

"Business," he said, in a terse voice that was obviously much more guarded than the one that admitted to coming by bus.

"Breakfast is right behind you," she said, her friendliness losing its ease. He had to resist the impulse to wheel around and confront breakfast, bark at it to back off.

•

He lay awake on his king bed far into the night, well after the planes stopped coming and going, scraping the air with the same rumbling sound snowplows made on the streets of his neighborhood. He kept returning to the terrible moment the tandem bicycle had materialized out of the fog; he remembered how surprisingly light his reusable grocery bag of car part slivers had felt; he remembered all the mailbox reflectors as he had driven away.

He wept for an unknown amount of time.

It occurred to him that he might never sleep again. Sleep deprivation was known to be the most effective form of torture.

He got out of bed and set himself the goal of planking for five minutes, an entire minute longer than his best time, which he hoped would both exhaust him and act as a sort of electroshock therapy, clearing his mind. He put his phone on the carpet, set the stopwatch, and assumed the position. As the pain in his abs and back and shoulders and triceps and forearms crested and then slowly got worse, he kept holding, second by second, until he reached five minutes and collapsed. He lay panting on the floor, pulse pounding in his face.

Still, he tossed and turned for more hours.

The planes resumed coming and going. Normal activity in the world calmed him. Just as he felt sleep finally taking over, someone tapped the edge of a keycard on his door.

"Housekeeping!"

Oh Christ!

More tapping.

"Come on!" he roared. "Fuck off!"

The housekeeper made no more sounds, but he could imagine her eye roll as she steered her cart down the hallway.

He realized he had forgotten to put out the "Shhhhhhh" card. He needed to put himself on a ten-second delay. He needed to practice mindfulness or he was going to hurt a lot of people, despite wanting to love them. But he feared he was losing too much of his mind to be mindful.

Before he could forget, he got up and put a ten-dollar bill under the TV remote. For good measure, he took a square of La Quinta stationery and scrawled on it with a La Quinta pen: *I'm sorry! Thanks! Have a good one!*

Tandem

•

The young, bearded car salesman had a way of slowly bringing his hands together as he spoke, as if he were compressing a pillow. Maybe sooner in the process than was natural, Mike offered the information that he was buying this car for his son who was away at college but would be pleasantly surprised when Mike gave it to him for his next birthday. The pillow could not be compressed further; it suddenly expanded back to its original size and, after a hands-at-sides interlude, the compression process began all over again.

He went for a test drive through the unclogged major arteries of South Bend. The car smelled vaguely skunky, as if much pot had been smoked in it and much cleaning had happened since. But the cloth seats were the exact same grey color and plush texture as the seats in his car. The dash controls were exactly the same. And no spiderweb cracks on the windshield.

There was endless paperwork in the salesman's office. The rep on the insurance hotline was confused by the fact that Mike already had a red 2005 Camry on the policy. Was this the same car? Mike had not anticipated this. "Sorry?" he said, making the hotline rep repeat himself. He was afraid to use his cover story about buying a matching car for his son because he wasn't sure if it was fraudulent to insure it under his own name while planning to transfer title to Connor. He turned his back on the car salesman, his face blushing. "No, I just love Camrys," he finally said. The rep said he had just wanted to be sure, and went ahead and processed everything. Mike hung up, wondering if he'd made a critical mistake. When he signed the check on his home equity line to pay for the car in full, his signature was a little shaky.

"I'd like to drive the car home today, if that's all right," he told the salesman.

"That's the dream, isn't it?" the salesmen said. His mud-colored eyes twinkled.

56

He bought a car cover for the damaged Camry from the accessory store.

"A good car is worth protecting," the salesman said, squeezing the pillow.

He felt he was being ridiculed. He wondered if he had exposed himself on the phone. Or had he inadvertently uncovered his bruise? Trying to look up through his eyebrows right now was out of the question. And he could not feel exactly how his bangs were arranged, which was frustrating and surprising. Maybe because of the preponderance of head-butting during prehistoric conflicts, the human forehead had evolved into a desensitized club, oblivious to the touch of an individual's own hair.

Driving the replica Camry back home on I-80 in the middle of the afternoon, he nearly fell asleep at the wheel several times. Some overpowering chemical was flooding his head, making it unbelievably pleasurable to close his eyes for even a millisecond. When he jerked awake to the rumble strip under his right tires, he slapped his own face and shouted: "Come on, you piece of shit, stay awake!"

Would that be his second act: doze off and sideswipe a semi, causing a sixteen-car pile-up with a dozen fatalities? Was trying to evade his crime only going to cause him to repeat it exponentially worse? At this rate, he would never love his way out of this.

He stopped at a Shell station for a plastic bottle of Mountain Dew. Caffeine and sugar battled the sleep chemical to a stalemate for fifteen minutes before the sleep chemical reasserted itself while he was still twenty miles from home.

Luckily, it occurred to him that he might try eBay for the all-important windshield. Anxious to get online to check this out, he perked up and managed to stay awake until he was safely piloting the replicar through his neighborhood. He didn't mind being seen now. And sure enough, a knot of neighbors stood on a corner, conversing with intent faces, among them two dogs tightly leashed. As he drove by, he smiled and waved and caught the eye of Steve, a tall serious man, Clark Gable mustache, on the board of the neighborhood association. His dachshund yapped officiously. Steve waved back with a peevish look on his face, maybe because he was discussing Emma's tragic death with their neighbors and didn't want to be distracted by some clueless, glad-handing bozo.

So much the better. They would just have to conclude he didn't know yet, which could only be the case if he wasn't the killer. Without even thinking about it, they had seen that his car was intact—nothing wrong with the grill or windshield, unlike the perpetrator's car.

He turned into the alley, out of their view, and made a right toward his own driveway. His garage door opened with excruciating slowness—he'd had the foresight to pack the opener for just this moment. He told himself not to look around. The essence of hiding in plain view was to behave as if one were not hiding at all. He pulled up next to the other Camry, hopefully without being seen. He got out and pushed the button on the wall to get the garage door to close. Then he walked around and viewed the rear of each of his Camry LE's. They were the same. The color was a perfect match. The 2005 and the 2006 were twins, as far as he could tell. It was the type of perfect congruence another man in another situation might attribute to divine providence.

He hoped no one had seen his dealer license tag in the rear window. He'd have to order Michigan plates. In the meantime, he unscrewed the license plate from the bracket of his old Camry and put the plate on his replicar. Then he took down the paper dealer license and saved it. This was probably also a crime, but you can't get any wetter when you're already underwater.

He was the only person in the world who would have any reason to look into or go into his garage. Except Connor. And Connor hated him and would probably never come home again. To be on the safe side, he'd have to call Connor and scope out his near-term plans, sending discouraging vibes against any hint of a visit.

Inside his house, re-energized, he accessed his mini and immediately hit the jackpot on eBay: *692.92 free shipping. TOYOTA OEM 02-06 Camry-Windshield Glass 56101AA03083 (Fits: 2005 Toyota Camry).* He wasn't sure he could trust eBay, but he would save the receipt (otherwise, he would *not* be keeping paper receipts for other replacement car parts).

With these qualms resolved, his impulse was to order the windshield right away. But then he wondered whether all of these gigantic boxes from eBay and Carparts.com would set off the suspicions of his UPS person. If all these boxes came the same week, or even separately over several weeks, it would be clear to the delivery person (assuming it was the same person, was it the same person?) that he was repairing a car himself. Why would a person in this neighborhood repair a car himself? Midlife divorce crisis? Maybe. What if the UPS person had heard about the unsolved hit-and-run and longed for a more meaningful life than aggressively piloting an oblong, doorless van in thrall to various efficiency metrics, and decided to talk to the police?

He didn't know what to do. His conversing neighbors had been standing about seventy yards from the murder weapon. The damaged car had to be dealt with as soon as possible. But what if the police were on the lookout for windshields? What if all the auto glass dealers in southwest Michigan and beyond had gotten an email asking them to notify the police if anyone brought in a car needing a windshield repair with above-average crackage? What if the cops had put out an APB for windshields ordered straight from the manufacturer by non-auto-glass shops?

What was plausible? What was noticeable?

It was time to check the news. He saw an updated article with high school graduation pictures of the young couple for maximum pain and guilt. He walked around his study, pulling his hair back on his head, breathing in and out deeply before he could finally read the body of the article. The search for the perpetrator was ongoing. An officer said, *"The vehicle involved in the accident probably has significant front-end damage."* Body shops *in the area* had been alerted. What did *in the area* mean? Was Kalamazoo *in the area*? The article did not mention having just one headlight as something to look for. That might have triggered the memories of people he had passed on his way home. There was no mention of leads or suspects. The article did mention *patchy ground fog* as a possible factor in the accident, which, to Mike, didn't go far enough, however true it was. It would have been much better had they had used the simpler, all-forgiving phrase *dense fog*.

He tried to ground himself in his guiding thought—to be good, perfect, loving. He tried very hard to do this.

He cancelled the order for the bumper, the hood, and the headlight, as well as the one for the grill, and he held off on the windshield as well because they really might be tracking such things. It was just too damn noteworthy to have these car parts show up at a civilian home right now. He probably shouldn't even put the cover over the damaged car. Since it was already in the garage, that, too, would be questionable. From the driveway, someone would just see the back of both cars. If the garage's back door was open, just one of his next door neighbors would be able to look in (the other was down the hill slightly and had a useless angle), but the front end of the damaged car was in the parking space away from that door, and the uphill neighbors were empty nesters who both still worked long hours. Maybe no one would ever notice if he simply kept the car uncovered.

What sort of resources did the cops in Saugatuck have? What sort of patience? Maybe not a lot. Maybe the thing to do was just lie low.

He would play dumb with his neighbors about the death of Emma Teague and then simply show up at the service. Attending Jeremy's funeral would be highly suspicious, a de facto confession; *not* attending Emma's might be suspicious as well. He had to go to Emma's. To pay his respects.

6.

Her sister's family arrived from Cleveland the day before the visitation. Marie taught English at a high school in Shaker Heights. Tom worked for the Cleveland City Planning Commission. Their daughter, Zoe, was fourteen, with braces and a face that so nakedly displayed her distress over the loss of her cousin that Claire had to look away.

Emma and Zoe were too many years apart to really bond, but Emma had loved her aunt Marie, who dressed funkily in paisley scarves, wooden jewelry, and boots of all lengths. She was a fast talker with a big laugh and a natural warmth that Claire envied. In fact, Claire wondered if Oberlin's proximity to Cleveland was a factor in Emma's decision.

It was good to have Marie here, doing the right things in the house, her eyes bright behind jumbo cat glasses. Claire was fine with her sister having a larger and more engaging personality than herself because Marie was also a workhorse. For her part, Claire had been experiencing terrifying moments of inertia. She was capable of going to an appointment with the funeral director or answering the door when Marie's family arrived, but she also sometimes ground to an unexpected halt: half-way through bringing groceries from the car, she might find it necessary to sit on a kitchen chair and stare out the window while a tub of ice cream turned to soup; she left the nose of the vacuum stuck under the sofa and drifted away; she sat on the toilet with her shorts around her ankles, unable to rise again. Her imagination inevitably turned to the crash, or ways she could have prevented it.

Claire and Marie had lost both of their parents within the past ten years, and she missed them. Treating her grief back then as something to fight through, she was all action, looking for things to do, and do well, to prove she could cope with what everyone must endure. Now she felt like the wood her neighbor was always chopping for his firepit: when the axe split the log, the pieces staggered apart and fell over. She found comfort in repeatedly listening to a joint TED talk by a mother whose son had died in the World Trade Center and a mother whose son was serving a life sentence for helping to plan the attacks. They had bonded through loss, found solace in reconciliation, and become friends.

Once he'd made his basic preferences known, Ryan distanced himself from funeral details, and Claire was okay with that. He used his days off from work (he only took a week) to do little household projects: putting down traction strips in the slippery upstairs bathtub, replacing something in the downstairs toilet that stopped it from running, sharpening the blades on the push mower. When she thanked him, he nodded without quite making eye contact. He watched a lot of sports on the basement TV with Nathan. Sometimes she overheard him doing color commentary while Nathan handled the play-by-play.

The autopsy results had been disturbing: apparently, Jeremy and Emma had been high on pot when the accident occurred. In fact, tests on Emma's hair revealed she'd been a regular user for at least the past several months. And in the bottom of her beach bag, squeezed in the tandem's crushed side basket, the cops found a pen-shaped stainless-steel pipe with a glass chamber stained brown inside, as if by cooking grease.

"Did you have any idea?" she'd asked Ryan, who was driving them home from the coroner's office.

"They're nineteen," Ryan had said.

Claire resisted the urge to press him. She didn't want to harass him into admitting there'd been a potential problem they'd missed.

"Maybe she didn't smoke when she lived with us," Ryan added, with a tentative smile. "Maybe she picked it up at that hippie school."

"Like people don't smoke pot at state schools?" she said, more sharply than she intended.

"Calm down. I was joking."

"So I'm too uptight *and* too permissive?" She hated being told to calm down. "Is that *my shit*?"

"Wow. You're *still* on that?" He took both hands off the wheel and pressed his palms to the upholstered ceiling, letting the car steer itself.

"Well, is it?"

Ryan waved this away, his other hand re-taking the wheel.

"It doesn't change anything," he said, almost under his breath.

So they were quiet for the last half dozen blocks until they reached their house.

Mock emotional ball-carrying at your peril, she thought. You'll learn the value of it when no one's doing it.

•

Now she sat with Nathan in front of the Mac notebook set up on the dining room table, going through folders of pictures, including some Emma's friends had sent. He reacted to a few with half-smiles. Occasionally, he narrated:

"Emma and Nathan are happy by a waterfall in Colorado."

"Emma hates me but stands next to me for show."

"Emma and her friend Aisat make disgusting faces."

"Mom, Dad, Emma and Nathan at Jess and Bill's wedding. Everyone knows what's happening."

"Emma is baby know-it-all."

He spoke these captions un-self consciously. She had wondered, when he was two or so, whether there was something going on with him, but Ryan kept wanting to put off testing, and Nathan had grown into a type of normalcy. This was not normal. But was it wrong or bad?

Tandem

Nathan's inwardness had always made him easier to manage than Emma, who had reacted to any sign of a reality that didn't reflect her own ideas and desires with "Oh, my god! This is *sooo* stupid!"

When what she had really wanted with Emma from the beginning, however improbable and absurd it had seemed as she grew up, was a quiet camaraderie. And there had been moments: Emma might come home from volleyball practice or her job at Steak n' Shake and lie on the couch where Claire was reading or watching TV and put her head on Claire's lap and let her stroke her hair. Despite the appalling fry grease smell or the ammoniac sweat odor, this was wonderful. Sometimes all Emma had to say was "good" when Claire asked about her day; she might even nap for a bit. But sometimes she would querulously unspool her complaints and anxieties, and Claire, despite the advice of the better parenting books, had been too intent on solving rather than listening, and too often the conversation would degenerate.

She had hoped that Emma's adulthood would solve everything. Her fantasy had been a "women only" trip to New York City to celebrate Emma's college graduation. They would go to all the museums, see shows, have decadent desserts on metal chairs on a sidewalk in the Village. They would talk like grown-up women, with nothing between them anymore, not like best friends, because she knew it was wrong to want that type of relationship from her daughter, but more like good companions, with opinions and problems and plans to share.

As they continued through the pictures, she began to cry. Nathan acted as if he didn't notice.

"Emma smiles affectionately at the picture-taker," he said.

Who took that picture? It was nighttime. Looked like the fireworks at South Haven. Emma about eleven or twelve. Had Emma once smiled at her affectionately, albeit in the artificial context of posing for a picture?

"Okay," she said, after they'd moved their favorites to a folder, "want to go through and pick the best of the best?"

"No," he said. "I like all these."

Her face flushed, as if she'd been caught paying herself a compliment. "Okay, great. I do, too. Sounds good."

She heard Ryan and Tom coming up the stairs from the basement. Ryan was talking in his sarcastic, exasperated voice.

"So I said, 'You're telling me you have no leads whatsoever?' He goes, 'Well, not really.' They've only got a tiny bit of paint transfer, not enough to figure out the manufacturer. No pieces from the car. They think the bastard cleaned up after himself. Cop had never seen that before." He added with a short laugh, "We're dealing with a criminal mastermind."

"Huh," Tom said, adjusting his Buddy Holly glasses.

They barged into the kitchen, where Marie and Zoe were making dinner, and she heard them rifling through cupboards and opening the fridge.

"Sorry, Marie," Ryan said. "We've got to cramp your style for a minute."

"Do your worst!" Marie volleyed back.

Claire resisted an impulse to insert herself into the kitchen, to assure politeness, but also to nose into the paint transfer conversation. Her own exchange with Ryan on the subject had left a bad taste. Ryan had explained the four layers of car paint: two primer coats, one color coat, and one topcoat, all full of distinctive chemical information that taken together was enough to pinpoint make and model, even the very factory where the car was painted. The primer coats had the most information; the color coat, ironically, had the least, because it was so thin. The problem was that whatever the perpetrator had done to clean the bike had degraded the primer coats on the fragment. They knew the color—some type of dark red—but essentially every carmaker in the world used that shade.

Ryan had mansplained all this until she had to remind him paint was kind of her thing; she'd had training in spectra analysis. She also drove a red Prius, though of a lighter shade—which, unfortunately, Ryan used to illustrate how useless knowing the color was.

Tandem

"How do you want to group the pictures?" she asked Nathan.

He thought for a bit.

"Not in order," he said.

7.

Only the visible needed hiding. His forehead bruise had almost completely healed. No one knew what they were looking at. He didn't mean anything to anyone here.

Mike just had to get through the receiving line and then he could sit on the edge of conversations and talk as little as possible, until there would be an early and unobtrusive chance to leave.

Then he wondered if this was too passive, if this meant he wasn't loving Ryan and Claire and Nathan as hard as he could. If he was just, again, indulging his instinct for self-preservation. What would be the loving thing to do?

The lobby of the funeral home was overrun by dewy-skinned young people, their vibrancy muted by blank or distressed expressions, their high school graduation suits and dresses recalled for grim duty. They streamed and clumped in inscrutable ways, like ants interacting in the heart of the colony. Amidst Emma's friends and relatives were a few neighbors he knew, or thought he should have known. He nodded but kept moving to avoid conversation. The tail end of the receiving line extended into the lobby and he attached himself to it. There were so many people, because of him. Guilt lapped at his ears, spilled into his mouth—he couldn't keep his breathing holes above it.

Just in front of him in line, two couples from the grandparent generation talked quietly in the old and true ways about how a parent should never have to bury a child. A passing person touched his arm and he jerked in that direction: Randy Shepard, the man down the street who had rebuilt a retaining wall of large stones next to his driveway all by himself. Randy squeezed his forearm with one hand and patted his shoulder with the other. They'd had four conversations in ten years, but his wordless gesture of solidarity almost brought Mike to tears.

A few of his colleagues from the College who lived in the neighborhood sat together on couches in a corner. More neighbors on the upholstered row chairs. A large group of young people standing by the receiving line spoke more animatedly than they probably should have. Some of the little black dresses were too short for the occasion. But who was he to judge?

The line passed a small flat screen TV showing images of Emma and her family and friends that faded one into the next. He looked, partly to see if he could take it, partly to see what it would tell him about whether he should confess. He compared these smiling, happy faces—Emma sitting at a birthday cake-lit table, with teammates in front of a volleyball net, by a waterfall with her brother—to the inward but expectant expression he'd seen on the bike in the instant before impact. What struck him in contrast to these pictures was the terrible unposed intimacy of that glimpse: a palpable sense of the private consciousness he was about to snuff out.

He turned away from the pictures, closed his eyes, only to see her bloody face in the road, that geyser of hair. He flexed his face, trying to restrain an outburst. The edges of his body softened until he felt a sharp grip under his left armpit, a hand clasping the back of his suit jacket. He opened his eyes and stiffened his faltering knees, regaining his balance. "Whoa there," the man behind him said. He half-turned and murmured, "Thank you, I'm sorry." "You all right?" "Yes, thank you," he said, unable to look at the man. Feeling sweat condensing on his forehead, he stared down at his shoes and took deep but restrained breaths. He sensed a few nearby gazes let go of him one by one.

He wiped his eyes, composed himself. The line had not stopped moving. Someone began weeping behind him and now people had that to ignore.

Then it was his turn to approach Nathan, who was in a suit, with his hair slightly gelled and combed off his forehead. He looked handsome, his face open and shiny, like a seed inside a green bean.

"I'm sorry for your loss."

Nathan shook his hand, said thank you, and abruptly sawed his forefinger against the side of his nose, readying himself to dispatch the next person in line.

"I'm so sorry," Mike said to Ryan, looking into his weak, slate-gray eyes. He clasped his hand firmly and, with perfect timing, cupped his left hand against Ryan's shoulder. Ryan moved into a brief hug, which surprised him. They weren't close. But that's evidently what Ryan needed, and maybe Mike's focus on being loving to Ryan had done something to his body language, which had brought out a reciprocating loving response from Ryan.

As he stepped in front of Claire in her short-sleeved black dress, he tried to focus on what she needed now. He made brief, acute eye contact. Her irises were a bright yellowish brown—gold, really, her eyes were golden. He had never even heard of a person with golden eyes, much less seen them. He had talked to Claire a few times before but never noticed.

"I'm very sorry," he said and looked down. She did not hug him. She said, "Thank you," softly but clearly. His eyes swelled again. He stepped away and childishly knuckled his right eye with his fist.

He stopped by the open coffin, but he looked at the cream-colored lining past Emma's head, not at her face. He didn't know what would happen if he looked at her real face. He touched the side of the coffin. "I'm so sorry," he said in his mind.

He bowed his head and drifted through thick air, past people he couldn't look at, until his shoes were clicking across the funeral home's parking lot.

8.

Claire's director, Teresa Banks, offered her a month. She took two weeks. The original Rita Bowman reception had not happened as planned. Teresa had cited various reasons for the rescheduling—Rita's sudden chance to meet with an elusive artifact collector in D.C., Rita wanting to pair her travel to Kalamazoo with a lecture at the MoCA in Chicago, key KIA trustees couldn't make it. Claire suspected her often morose and erratically empathic director had rescheduled because of Claire's absence.

But Claire wished the opening had simply passed by without her. Worst of all, Teresa seemed to have picked up on Claire's feelings, or had come to the same conclusion herself, and had apologized to Claire shortly after her return to work for "having to deal with" the Bowman reception. Teresa was now insisting on emceeing the gallery talk instead of Claire. Claire found herself dreaming of Teresa taking a different job, far, far away.

During her talk, Bowman directed the audience to look behind themselves at a four-foot by five-foot photographic self-portrait on a far wall that represented her assuming the character of a conjure woman—Rita disapproved of the term "voodoo doctor"—in whose persona she had produced the pieces in the exhibit.

A man watching the talk from the back happened to be standing in many sight lines to the photograph, though he wasn't especially close to it. He stepped to the side so he wouldn't block anyone. She recognized a neighbor— Mike Kovacs.

His ex had been in the book club and he himself had shown up a few times in the club's early days, but they had never been out together as couples. He taught something like econ or poli sci at the College. Tall and athletic-looking. Short brown hair. He'd made peculiar eye contact in the receiving line, as if peering into her pupils allowed him to see little people performing tasks in her head.

When the talk ended, she went over to him. "Glad you could make it out, Mike," she said.

"It's a cool show," he said, nodding, looking away. He had a striking, Easter-Island sort of head, strong-browed, with deep-set, hooded eyes and an unusually tall, smooth expanse between his upper-lip and nose—a bit like Will Ferrell with narrower cheeks.

Then he abruptly swung his eyes toward hers. "So what's your role in all this?" he asked more brightly.

She dutifully outlined it. He nodded, made small interested sounds, one hand tucked under the opposite armpit. He raised his other thumb to his lips where it bounced slightly. He listened with a weird intense benevolence.

"What was your toughest choice," he asked at last. "I mean, with the layout?"

"Well," she said and paused, trying to remember. "Well," she started again, "she has a story in mind for all the work, and it would have been great to have a room big enough to do everything in a clearer sequence, but we had to put it in these two galleries, so—"

"Ah," he said. He surveyed the space, giving the problem its due. "Two rooms."

"The pulpit, over here, probably," she said, intent on answering his question. "It ended up a little bit out of the way, when it's one of the more important pieces."

They walked over to face it.

"Oh, I don't know. It seems pretty snug back here." He smiled warmly, loosely, as if now they were in on a joke together. He was handsome in an unusual way. "Framed up pretty nice!"

"Eh, it works okay," she said, with a shrug, but now she was half smiling.

He fairly peppered her with questions: How long had she been at the museum? Was she an artist herself? What was her favorite period of art history? It all made her a bit dizzy. She couldn't remember such intense interest from any person she'd talked to, in any context, for years, much less from a tall, dark, and handsome type.

"So, jeez, what's a poli sci prof like you doing in a place like this?"

"I teach econ," he said reluctantly.

"Oh, I'm sorry!" She had hoped to impress him by guessing right.

He waved a hand. "This is very cool. Haven't been to a museum for a while, but it just seems like a nice space to work in. Do you like it?"

His focus on her was starting to feel like a move of some kind. Or maybe he was just going out of his way to avoid talking about Emma.

"I do, I do like it," she said, but felt she must change the subject. "So what are you up to this summer?"

"Oh, god," he groaned, "the work of macroeconomic analysis is never done! A tricky paper on monetary policy, to be honest. Probably should paint my garage, too. Don't want to drag down the neighborhood! Well, I'm sure you have a lot of other folks to meet and greet. Nice seeing you!"

"Thanks for coming!"

After he walked away, she found herself facing the portrait of the conjure woman, whose eyes looked past her, as if focused on something approaching from a distance.

9.

As the term was winding down, Mike went to Bowen Hall on a Saturday afternoon to score the last problem sets for his international trade course and put the finishing touches on his final exams. On his way to the Econ and Business suite, he passed the glassed-in lounge where a single student sat in the corner of a couch, his feet flat on the floor, a large textbook open on his lap. The student looked up and waved to him. Mike didn't recognize the student, but he waved back.

    The suite was open. He passed Hopper's closed door, behind which he heard the man himself talking urgently, probably on the phone. This didn't necessarily mean anything was urgent—it was just Hopper being Hopper. He left his own door open, because he had nothing to hide, and began slogging through the problem sets. Slowly, he immersed himself and forgot about the accident for seconds at a time.

    "Hey, Professor Kovacs."

    He jolted upright. The student from the lounge. A white kid who held his thin but broad-shouldered upper body very stiffly, like a sail blown taut.

    "Sorry, didn't mean to scare you," the student said, his eyes darting to the side.

    "Oh, you didn't scare me. I'm glad to see ya."

    The student slowly took a seat in a chair opposite the visitor leg of his L-shaped desk. His high shoulders made it seem as if he were perpetually inhaling or preparing to speak. Mike rolled his own chair to face him directly.

"How are you?" Mike added warmly, just in case they had a longstanding relationship, though he still didn't recognize the kid.

"Pretty good," the student said.

"How's your quarter going?"

"It's all right. My psych class is kicking my butt."

"Which is it?"

"Abnormal."

"Oh, I've heard that's a great class." Dave was teaching it this term. Maybe Dave had suggested the student ask Mike whether one could go into marketing with just a Psych major, or was a Business double major expected.

"It is," the student said. His hair flowed forward in an amazing thick pile that covered his forehead and extended well beyond it, before curving up like a backwards ocean wave. "So how's your quarter going?"

"*My* quarter?" Mike pretended to consider this. "You know what?" he said, turning arch. "I'm going to stick it out. I'm going to finish this quarter because there's still some learning to be done!"

The student smiled at this and scratched the back of his neck. "Yep," he said. "Same."

The student looked out of the corner of his eye again in a nervous way. He had no upper lip whatsoever—face surface, then mouth hole, without transition. He might state his purpose at any moment, and Mike prayed to the universe that this information might help unlock the secret of his name. But Mike couldn't bring himself to ask what the student was doing in his office. That would be rude and might somehow reveal he had no idea who the student was, which would erase the student's personhood and undermine his will to live.

"Well, I hope things are going well for you," Mike said. "Are you thinking about grad school?" Virtually every student at the College considered grad school.

"Yeah, but not like I talked about before."

"Oh." Had *they* talked about grad school or was the student referencing another conversation with someone else? He hadn't said *we*. "So what are you thinking now?"

"Maybe the Peace Corps. Or Teach for America."

"Really." He associated such plans with directionless humanities majors. "What would you be looking to do in the Peace Corps? I mean, do you have to offer some sort of skill?"

"I'm not sure." The student looked down. He smiled to himself, shook his head, as if to dispel a thought.

Heat gathered in Mike's face. "It's a lot to think about," he offered.

The student looked up. "How's the class?" he asked, as if Mike hadn't just spoken.

"The claaaass," Mike said, drawing out the word in an ambiguous tone that combined asking a question with considering an answer. He felt checkmated. Or maybe this was the kid who only sporadically attended his International Trade course and hadn't turned in a problem set, the one who sat in the top tier and chewed pen caps. Maybe he was about to apologize for his lapses, or was waiting to hear Mike's judgment on him for same. "I don't know," Mike ventured. "What do you think?"

"What do *I* think?" The student raised a hand as if he were going to scratch his neck again, but only got as far as his ear, where he delicately fingered cartilage, before, just as carefully, lowering his hand to his knee.

Mike had fucked up. The student wasn't the pen-cap-chewing backbencher. He would have remembered this absurd torrent of hair. Plus the kid was a genius of awkwardness. Hard to forget on a number of counts. Yet somehow Mike *had* forgotten him. He blinked as hard as he could, twice. He hurt the top half of his face with the violence of his blinks. But that was better than reaching across the desk, taking the student by the throat, and screaming, *Who are you? Why are you doing this to me?*

"You know,—" Mike began aimlessly. "You know, I'm just about... I don't know. The term is getting to me, the term is getting to me. Is the term getting to you?"

"A little bit."

"I hear you," he said, nodding. "I hear what you're saying."

"Ohhhkay," the student said, darting his eyes left and right, as if to signal to some onlooker that this had gotten very weird. "Well, let me know if you need a TA for something," the student said, slowly standing up. "If that would help."

"Oh, okay, I'll do that. You'd be great at it—I bet."

"Take care, professor," the student said. He self-consciously waved one hand around hip level, which Mike answered with a wave of his own, and stiffly walked out of his office.

Mike immediately rolled his chair to his file cabinet to find his folder of picture rosters. There were about forty sheets, one per class, in no particular order. He sorted for courses within the last four years and found one to be missing. This cast the whole process into doubt. Nevertheless, he systematically scanned the ones he had. No match. Maybe the hair was overwhelming his impression of the student, but what if his hair hadn't always been that way? He made another pass, trying to control for the rolling tide of hair. No match. Why hadn't he just asked the student how he could help him? He found himself nearly panting with incredulity and frustration. He slapped the sheets on his knees. In one clean strong motion, he gripped and tore the rosters in half.

•

His failure to identify, much less love, the mystery student seemed to mock one of his main justifications for living outside of prison. The young man had left his office worse off than when he arrived—more bereft, more confused, less confident in the care of authority figures. Mike questioned whether such indirect attempts to address his crime could have significant impact, no matter how well executed. Maybe it was time to engage Claire herself more substantively. On the KIA website, he noticed an upcoming reception for a new exhibit.

He remembered a key aspect of the MLK speaker's description of restorative justice: victim and perpetrator met face to face, and the perp tried to understand what they'd put the victim through and worked to make amends.

Of course, he knew he wasn't ready for a formal process, with a trained facilitator and a full acknowledgment of what he'd done, but it would be loving to see how she was doing; it would be loving to support her and her life's work by attending a museum event; it would be loving to at least give himself the chance to confess to her, right then and there, even if he didn't think he could; it would even be loving, albeit in a more roundabout way, if he could somehow gauge through the encounter whether helping her was possible.

Hesitating under the Chihuly chandelier in the museum's vestibule, he had a vertiginous feeling not unlike what he imagined ski jumpers experienced just before they spurred themselves down a sheer ice ramp—yet he, too, mustered the will to jump. And by concentrating on loving Claire to the best of his ability, he landed without incident, despite her unexpected approach and his completely unnecessary reference to painting the very garage in which the murder weapon was hidden. He asked her so many questions about herself she couldn't help but feel she was valued and cared about and her life was worth living in spite of her grief. From one angle, going to see her had been impulsive and perverse and insane, but from another it just might have been his first step, after the obligatory funeral, on the torturous path of loving her while being extremely guilty.

The only recent news about the hit-and-run was a MLive article about the stalled investigation and the scrubbed accident scene. Embedded in the article was a video from the evening newscast. He never watched the local news. He wondered if there had been other stories. As the Latinx female reporter stood next to the bank of bushes in broad daylight at the state park and spoke about the status of the investigation, his nerve endings burst into flame. It had all happened. It was loose in the world. The cops were closing in.

Or they weren't. The gist of the story, after all, was that there were no viable leads. But he wondered what the consequences would be if that in itself became a thing. Would it somehow make the story bigger and draw more police resources to it? Or was it a prelude to giving up?

The reporter urged viewers to phone the newsroom's anonymous tip line. Mike jotted down the number. Maybe he could use it to mess with the investigation, throw them off the scent. But then he realized that might be more likely to create a scent where none existed, and he thoroughly crossed out the number.

He threw the iPad mini aside, closed the curtains, and collapsed on the sectional in his TV room. A few weeks ago, the news report might have triggered mewling and weeping, but today that switch flipped on a dead circuit. Instead, he felt squeezed and squeezed by anger, frustration, self-pity, guilt, and hopelessness. The fear of being trapped in these feelings forever made them unbearable.

His resolve crystallizing, he lay prone on the longest side of the sectional, set his face squarely into a seat cushion, and put his right hand on the back of his head. His nose bent painfully—some cartilage or bone nub was getting pinched— but it smooshed closed. His cheeks ballooned to the sides, helping to seal his face to the fuzzy cushion. He pressed his head down as hard as he could. Almost immediately, he felt the burgeoning ache of not enough air, but it resembled the suffocating discomfort of planking before the endorphins kicked in, and he gutted through that. Dense carbonated bubbles increasingly pressed against the inside of his skull; growing alarm threatened to buck off his resolve. He was losing strength in his arm; his neck was resisting, though he wasn't asking it to. But he had killed two people, so with a final thrust of effort he pushed into the exploding stars—then his face was off the cushion, gasping for air.

He sat up, let his mouth hang open. His chest went up and down. He pushed a hand over his forehead. Who was he kidding? Not only was killing himself that way physically impossible, the thought of putting that on Connor was too incredibly sad. Yet not having that way out was also incredibly sad, and he did end up crying in a brief and frustrated way.

He decided to go on a giving spree.

The Teague-Bolands had directed memorial donations to MADD (a reasonable guess as to what had happened, he had to admit) and he had already given a hundred dollars—more, he'd decided, would have drawn attention. Now, for the Econ and Business Department, he shouldered an extra senior thesis for next year, one nobody else wanted to supervise. For Planning and Budget, he volunteered to research and write over the summer a white paper P&B had promised to the Faculty Executive Committee, positing the optimal size of the student body given the current tuition discount rate; housing, dining, and classroom capacities; and possible student/faculty ratios. He made a $500 donation online to Ministry with Community, the service center for homeless people downtown.

He chastised himself for not thinking more about the Vanden Bergs. He needed to do something for them, so he looked up Jeremy's obituary. They also wanted donations to go to MADD; the general presumptuousness on this point felt over-done. The contribution in Emma's name had to be typical, but he felt the Vanden Bergs deserved something more significant. Of course, he couldn't contribute in Jeremy's name. Even sending a second donation to MADD, especially a big one, could look like Lady Macbeth repeatedly washing her hands. The whole idea started to seem pointless and even risky, but then he realized these thoughts were simply the machinations of self-excuse. He ended up making another donation to Ministry with Community—this time $1000—even though giving that amount felt like pulling off his fingernails. He wrote "For WK" in the comments box—Jeremy's initials backwards and shifted one letter in the alphabet. The least he could do would be to stress his life as much as he could stand by loving others with his time and money.

He wasn't a conscienceless psychopath, he told himself; he just didn't want to go to prison and be poor, which was completely rational. Similarly, just because he refused to donate blood didn't mean he was a hopelessly selfish person; he just hated needles, especially needles stuck into his veins. Was he a horrible person if he didn't do every possible good thing? Of course not. No one could do every possible good thing they could do. Wouldn't it be good to donate a kidney, or take in foster children, or give $5,000 to a bunch of starving people? Yet instead people watched TV, or whacked weeds, or took vacations at all-inclusive resorts in Jamaica with swim-up bars and unlimited seafood—and no one accused them of crimes against humanity. Confessing would be a good thing, no doubt, but maybe also it could be one of the possible good things he wouldn't do. There were an infinite number of ways to do good, so he had to pick and choose.

·

Whether he dismantled the car or simply repaired it, the one thing that seemed right and safe to do was remove the cracked windshield. YouTube videos and supplemental Googling apprised him of the tools he'd need. The fact that Amazon "frequently sold together" a windshield removal tool and a urethane cut-out knife told him maybe there was more civilian repair of windshields than he'd imagined—or maybe the pros just had to get their tools from somewhere, or maybe it was just another nefarious upselling strategy. He decided acquiring such specialized instruments wouldn't be quite as suspicious as he'd feared.

But this would not lull him into rash moves. The problem with the windshield removal tool was its product name—Windshield Removal Tool—and it was designed solely for that purpose. Therefore, he needed to purchase these tools locally, in cash, and in disguise. No credit card paper trail or revealing store surveillance video. He was painfully aware of the risks of not being in disguise when he purchased his disguises, but he consoled himself with the fact that several disguise items could go through checkout in an inscrutable folded-up state.

At three different stores, he bought two ballcaps (one Nike, one Detroit Tigers), a Hawaiian shirt, and two pairs of sunglasses (one wraparound, one aviator). The riskiest item to acquire would be the false mustache, but he felt it was essential since the unusually large span between his upper lip and nose was too distinctive. He could get a theatre-grade mustache from The Timid Rabbit Costume and Magic Shop blocks from his house, but it was dark inside the store, tipping any sunglasses-wearing from curiosity to red flag, especially when buying a false mustache.

He decided to buy the mustache under the pretext of putting together a Mike Ditka costume to wear while attending a preseason Bears game in Chicago. That was one sly layer of misdirection; it would be sacrilege for a rabid Packers fan like himself to dress as the hated Bears player and coach. But how would the mustache-seller know what he was attempting? He considered first driving to Chicago to purchase a 1980s Bears sweater in person for cash, but maybe he had discovered one limit to his OCD. Instead, he ordered the sweater from Etsy using his credit card; after all, it would only be worn to acquire the mustache, not while purchasing the tools.

Once the sweater arrived in the mail, he printed an old sideline photo of Ditka wearing the same style of sweater and aviator sunglasses, then wetted and combed his hair straight back as Ditka did before walking over to the costume shop with those items in a plastic Meijer bag. Hiding behind the shop, he donned sweater and aviators—one of the most anxious moments he'd had since the night of the accident itself—and then entered the range of The Timid Rabbit's security cameras (if they existed) already in disguise, assuring an unbroken chain of concealment moving forward.

Behind the counter was a smiling middle-aged woman in a pink leather vest. Her front top teeth were prominent, suggesting she was the timid rabbit herself in human form.

He told her he was attending a Bears preseason game in Chicago and needed just the right false mustache to look like this guy, at which point he brandished the sideline photo, rendering the absurd sweater and indoor aviator sunglasses suddenly not noteworthy at all.

"Gotcha," she said.

Soon he left the shop with a convincing false brown mustache made from a combination of synthetic fibers and actual human hair, plus bottles of spirit gum, and spirit gum remover for sticking on and taking off. He stripped his sunglasses and sweater behind the shop, and by the time he was approaching his house, his heartbeat was almost normal.

He had moments during this outing when the lengths to which he was going produced a plunging sadness, a sense of free-falling into paranoia on the scale of a mental illness, but Timothy McVeigh had not taken the trouble to disguise himself before renting the Ryder truck, and he had ended up executed by lethal injection.

For purchasing the Sawzall and three-inch scraper attachment at Lowe's, he wore wraparound shades and white Nike cap, bill backwards. Low-key disguise for nominally risky purchase. The stakes were obviously highest at AutoZone, where he would buy the blatantly named Windshield Removal Tool and the urethane cut-out knife, so he pulled out all the stops: Detroit Tigers hat, aviator sunglasses, Hawaiian shirt, Ditka mustache.

The older white man at the register smirked, "Hey, it's Tom Selleck."

Mike's face flushed. Having inadvertently costumed himself as Magnum, P.I., he felt shady and memorable. He grinned sheepishly against the hybrid bristles, then fired a finger-gun of acknowledgment at his tormentor.

•

He chose an overcast Friday afternoon to actually do the deed, when fewer people would be around to hear his Sawzall or notice him working in the garage—both potentially suspicious activities because he wasn't handy. He'd walked past the busted windshield dozens of times while getting in and out of the replicar and had waffled between leaving the original covered or uncovered, but he hadn't had to *really* look at it. Now he did. Jeremy's single crack in the upper corner was hardly noticeable, but Emma's cracks on the right side of the windshield formed a slight depression in which it was too easy for him to see contours of her death mask.

"I am sorry," he said aloud, calming his breathing.

The exterior molding came off easily. Breaking the urethane seal on the underside of the windshield was more difficult. The Windshield Removal Tool worked well on the upper edges when he added some elbow grease. The tricky part was wielding the Sawzall and jamming its reciprocating scraper attachment to free the bottom of the windshield where it met the space between the dash and the hood. He had to get in the front seat to do that. He chose the passenger side, to keep the memories at bay as much as possible.

He had not been in the front seat since the night of the accident. As if he were about to dive underwater, he sucked in a deep draft of air, then got to work. He spritzed water down into the crevice as a rudimentary lube. The Sawzall made a terrific high-pitched grinding racket inside the car. The spatula-like scraper thrust in and out of the crevice like a meth-crazed chipmunk. His brain rattled like a screw in a soda can, but through it all he sensed the breaking of the seal. He leaned over and extended his reach down the base of the windshield. He went all the way to the left edge, to avoid sitting in the driver's seat and getting the view he remembered too well.

He bailed out of the car and set down the heavy Sawzall. The silence was like the aftermath of a scream. His fingers were trembling from something besides residual power tool vibrations. The glass was probably too compromised to lift off by hand and suction cup, as he'd seen in one video. The cracks revealed the windshield was in fact a plastic and glass sandwich, with tough but super-thin layers of plastic holding the glass between them. He didn't know how all this would come apart when he started to lift the windshield out.

With fingers still not completely steady, he cut the side seams of a thick black trash bag, so the plastic lay in a single-ply rectangle he would tape to the interior of the car under the windshield to catch any falling pieces of glass during removal. He soon realized that just one splayed bag wasn't quite big enough. He'd have to go back into the house and get another one and tape them together.

Tandem

This was frustrating, but it wouldn't be bad to get away from the murder weapon for a little bit. Just like the people who pasture-raise livestock, kill the animals as quickly and painlessly as possible, butcher the meat themselves, and eat it with reverence and knowledge, he was humanizing and dignifying the experience by personally performing the awful mechanical processes. But such integrity and awareness were stressful, and he needed a break.

He locked the garage door and headed into the house.

He poured himself a glass of ice water and wandered past the kitchen island into the dining area, up to a front window, where he rested his forearms on the sash. He focused on each breath. He was alive. His life was no worse now than it had been when he woke up this morning.

A huge, perfectly symmetrical maple tree dominated his small front yard (a plateau carved in the gentle hillside), spreading itself to fill the entire airspace, from house gutter to sidewalk, retaining wall to retaining wall, one wall up to the neighbor on the right, one down to the left, and a third fronting the sidewalk. The clouds were coming apart, and looking beneath the maple's limbs he could see an unsteady play of light and shadow on his opposite neighbor's large lawn, and in the grove of tall trees down the block standing in a remnant space between the curving streets. Two small birds flitted and alighted repeatedly on the post lamp next to his front walk. It seemed as if they were looking for the best grip to lift the lamp and fly away with it. They gave up and left, just as an unfamiliar car—a new-looking royal-blue compact—pulled up to the curb.

He was always on guard against a plainclothes detective, and this would be a very good disguise car for a hard-bitten gumshoe. The person inside did not immediately emerge, which further piqued his anxiety, as if the detective were unpacking his binoculars, or activating a listening device, or simply executing a classic naked-eye stakeout.

But the delay also reminded him of Anne, who always had much to do whenever she docked a car: stow (or put on) her sunglasses, reapply her lipstick, put in eyedrops for her allergies, finish the texting she'd been doing while driving. If she was heading into an especially challenging situation, she would rummage in her bag for a talisman to clench: a miniature sour-faced Peruvian man with one botched eye wearing a smock, a jade elephant from Thailand he'd picked up for her when he'd boondoggled a visit to the College's study abroad site in Chiang Mai, or—if she was feeling nostalgic—a silver cross.

The driver finally exited. It was a woman. It was—Anne! She stepped around the car in a high-waisted fuchsia dress and gladiator sandals. Lifting her large rectangular brown leather bag onto her shoulder made him think of someone saddling a horse. She rose up the steps from the sidewalk—spine straight, shoulders square. Her broad mouth, naturally pulled down in the corners, which gave many of her expressions a gasping or shark-like quality, was set in a determined frown. Her slender calves, her substantial hips, her margarita belly, her tremendous chest—Anne! Headed straight for his door.

Was she coming for a relationship do-over? And would that also somehow revise his trip to Saugatuck Dunes State Park?

She rang the doorbell. He was un-showered, wearing filthy jeans, work boots, and a ratty yellow T-shirt. But she knew what he was better than anyone. He flung open the heavy wooden door.

"Anne?" he said, breaking a smile that ruined a poker face he never quite put on. He leaned out the glass storm door.

She smiled, too, squint-eyed, though the stoop was entirely in the shade. Actually, it wasn't a smile at all. It was a wince.

"Yeah, wow, Mike, it's you." She pulled the storm door all the way open, separating it from his hand, then walked right past him and into the living room. "I knew it would be you, but shit, here you are."

"Yeah, good to see you. I didn't expect this."

"Well, why not," she said. Her eyes flew around the room, as if she were sizing up the place realtor-style. He had not changed a bit of the furniture; the room hadn't been dusted or vacuumed since she moved out seven months ago.

"Have a seat. Want something to drink?"

Offering a drink might have landed awkwardly, but she gave no sign. She held on to the strap of her big purse with two hands up by her shoulder like a paranoid subway rider.

"I didn't want to bother you, but I was on my way to see Connor." Her eyes finally rested on him. "And thought I'd say hey."

"I'm glad you did. Yeah, I should call him, see how he's doing!" Mike had tried to check in regularly with Connor since the divorce—no matter how terse the conversation, Mike knew it was important to do. But he had only called him once since the accident, to make sure he wasn't coming home any time soon, and they were far from having a regular texting relationship.

"He's better, doing his thing, not as pissed off." She was looking around again, inching toward the two-way staircase leading to the TV room.

"Go ahead and sit." He gestured to her favorite soft chair where she used to drink and Facebook for hours.

Her eyes fastened on him. "Look, I don't have much time," she said. "It turns out I left something I really need. I think it's in the garage."

"The garage?" His pulse abruptly switched speeds, like a turntable going from 45 to 78 rpm.

"Unless you've cleaned out the garage," she said warily.

"I haven't cleaned the garage. I haven't cleaned *anything*."

"You're blushing," she said. "Not cleaning is nothing to be ashamed of. It just means you're a human being. I'm actually glad."

"I'm just...surprised you're here."

"Great! Just give me a minute, okay? And then I'll get out of your unwashed hair."

She walked up and over the two-way stair landing and into the TV room, evidently on her way to the back door.

"Hang on a second," he said, following behind. "This isn't cool."

"I know, nothing's cool. I'll be gone in a minute. You won't even remember I was here." She gripped the back doorknob, but it wouldn't open. He always threw the deadbolt even when they were in the house, for security purposes, and she had hated that he did this.

She growled with frustration.

He caught up to her and grabbed the arm that was reaching to turn the deadbolt.

"You can't just be like this!" he said. "What's in the garage that's so important?"

"It's none of your business." She tried to shake off his grip, but he held on, feeling her forearm muscle ripple under his hand. "Oh, *come on!* I should have just broken in there without saying hey, but, no, I'm always polite and friendly, no matter how shitty people treat me."

"It's in *my* garage!"

"Because I left it there when it was *my* garage! And I'd appreciate you not assaulting me, and just staying here and letting me get it."

He moved to get between her and the back door, then let go of her arm.

"Anne, no."

"Oh, Christ."

They were chest to chest. He was just a few inches taller. Her face was tan and soft. Crow's feet accented her eyes. A hint of the chili powder smell of her armpits, which he loved. This moment could have played out so differently if he didn't have to hide the murder weapon.

"I'm sorry," he said, calmer now. "I can't let you go back there. On principle. This is a boundary violation, Anne, and you know it."

Anne was quick to trace interpersonal problems to one boundary violation or another. But like someone more comfortable with maps than actual terrain, Anne lived a life wildly confused about boundaries, as far as Mike was concerned.

"You're the one who grabbed my arm!" she shouted.

"And I let it go."

"Like that undoes what you did!"

"This isn't your house, Anne. I have every right to stop an intruder."

The word "intruder" hung in the air. He could see her recalibrating.

"You're so lost," she finally said. "My God. Listen to yourself."

"We're divorced," he said coolly. "That's what you wanted. You left, and this is my space now, and you're just crapping on my boundaries. Thinking you can get anything you want here without my permission..."

"It's not *yours*. I left something, and then you moved the border—all right?—but I can still get it, because it's mine."

"Tell me what it is, and you stay here, and I'll go get it for you. Those are my terms, in my space."

"That's ridiculous!"

"I've got to protect myself," he said.

"Don't be a control-fuck asshole, Mike," Anne responded heatedly. "You *don't have to be* a control-fuck asshole. You can be something else—oh, like a normal decent person."

"It's a boundary violation, Anne," he said with a killing calmness. "And you of all—"

"Oh, just stop it!" Her broad shoulders slumped. "You win, asshole. Good for you. Mike fucking wins! I'll tell Connor, 'Asshole says hi,' from you, because you're a fucking asshole. I don't care what you think about anything, so fuck you." She reversed course for the front door.

Having her so angry at him pulverized what was left of his soul. He wanted nothing more than to go upstairs with her and lie together on their old bed in silence. Even as deprived as he was, he didn't think he was capable of having sex with her—something would have to be rebuilt in him for that to be possible—but physical closeness with her would be good medicine. It might even make him strong enough to confess. In fact, he realized that if he had her back in his life, he could confess, even if it put him in prison, because all he would have to do to get through prison would be to count down the days until he was back with her.

He also thought Anne would understand if he told her every detail. She would call him a raging hypocrite, a soulless fuckup, a moral black hole—yet on some level she would understand. She made no pretense to being a moral exemplar. She had done sketchy things on their taxes for years, driven drunk plenty of times, lied to their friends and relatives more than was probably necessary, and who knew what else.

Nevertheless, he could not let her see what was in the garage.

She walked briskly out the front door, her shoulder bag nearly catching on the handle of the storm door.

As he watched her jolt down the steps to the sidewalk, it occurred to him she might make another attempt on the garage from the alley. He ran through the house, out the back door, and down the walkway.

Though he'd just been working in there, the back door to the garage was locked, thanks to his careful nature, but he had never made her hand over her keys. For months after she left, this had fueled a fantasy of her coming home some night and crawling into bed with him. He could physically bar the door now, but she might look through a side window and see too much, or simply come back when the garage was unattended. His best hope was to find whatever she wanted, grab it, and bring it to her, outside the garage. He would have to look behind things, probably against the back wall where everything was piled. Anything out in the open he would have noticed by now. Besides, if there was something Anne wanted hidden, she would probably stuff it in the most convenient and obvious place.

He unlocked the door, flicked the light switch, and looked behind the shelving unit right on the back wall. He peered at the floor, and because he was looking for something, he saw the different degree of darkness that might mark an object. He reached behind the unit, and his hand closed on a black umbrella. He straightened up and backed out as a car pulled into the driveway. He tucked the umbrella under his arm, fumbled with his keys again, and relocked the door. A car door slammed.

The umbrella was closed, but its ribs were unsecured by the Velcro-tipped band. He glimpsed raised red lettering on the canopy folds—a monogram. Hearing footsteps down the pebbly dirt on the side of the garage, he opened two folds, saw the crimped letters, PRG. The umbrella was snatched out of his hand. Anne instantly tucked it behind her back—though not before he'd glimpsed an address label on the handle. Anne would never purchase a black monogrammed umbrella.

"Whose is that?" he asked.

"Mine!" she said. "What's with the two cars?"

She must have seen through the side window. This jarred him violently.

"It's for Connor."

"He has a car."

"It's old. I'm giving him a new one. Don't try to distract me. Who gave you that umbrella?"

She whirled and headed back down the narrow path between garages.

"Whose is it?" he shouted. He followed her but he was moving in slow motion, because realization weighed heavily on his limbs.

"None of your beeswax!" she yelled back. "We're over!"

He pictured some rainy day, his wife in dalliance with a chump who actually owned a monogrammed umbrella. "Here," Chump said, "take my umbrella." "Why? It's only two blocks to my car from your office, where we secretly fuck after hours." "Just take it, to maximize your comfort—and get home quick, so your husband won't be suspicious." "Wow, your concern with protecting me from the rain is a sign of your chivalrous nature, and a big contrast to my uncaring, self-absorbed husband. Love you, Partner in Adultery!" She gets home, sees his car, finds herself in the garage with a wet monogrammed umbrella. What to do? Hide it in the garage, in the most naïve hiding place imaginable. Enter house. Begin drinking, or probably, rather, continue drinking. Plan to deal with it, but forget. Plan to return it, but wracked by guilt, decide to never see Monogram Man again. Drink more. Forget. Or hope Mike finds it, so his accusations and her perfectly reasonable explanation will enrage him and he'll blow up their marriage once and for all and she can leave.

She opened her car door, threw the umbrella on the passenger seat, and flashed a smile.

"Bye, Mike," she said with cheerful sarcasm. "I'll tell Connor you send your best, such as it is."

"Don't tell him about the car, please. It's a surprise."

She looked into his eyes. "Your secret's safe with me." Maybe she knew he suspected her of an affair he could tell Connor about. Mutually assured destruction. Maybe he could trust her.

"Great to see you," he said. "You're welcome any time."

He could envision her betrayal, yet not get super angry. Whatever she had done, he had done worse. He was a walking billboard for restorative justice based on indirect communication.

"Hah!" she said. She slammed the car door and backed out of the driveway.

As he re-entered his house to finally get the second black trash bag, he wondered if this was exactly how Anne wanted this to play out, to tell him without telling him. She was a shit-starter, unlikely to take the trouble to foresee consequences—which, against his better judgment, he had always found irresistible.

When she was safely gone, he made curtains out of crudely tripled sections of an old bedsheet and nailed them over the garage's two dirty side windows. Why hadn't he done that before? Then he removed the windshield and the front bumper cover and sawed them into small sections. All of the pieces fit in one large black trash bag. With the hood up and the bumper cover removed, he had easy access to the bolts and clips that held the broken headlight assembly in place. He pulled off the four lamp connector tabs and put the headlight in its own trash bag. He would need a blowtorch to cut up the hood, but so far, in some ways, it was almost too easy.

10.

Six weeks after Emma's death, Ryan declared a family movie night: streaming *The Big Lebowski* on Amazon Prime. The Tigers were also scheduled, and Nathan blanched when Ryan made the suggestion over dinner.

The meal was tabbouleh à la Claire, with separate dishes incorporating either grilled chicken strips or fried tofu. She had amassed a repertoire of recipes with single-ingredient variations to make her vegetarianism work for the family. When she'd renounced meat, Ryan had demurred, proclaiming bacon his "only true friend." In his family, the favorite dessert was double-stuff Oreos coated in peanut butter and Nutella, placed in a pan, covered with brownie batter, then baked, cut into pieces, dipped in pancake batter, and, finally, deep-fried.

It had been more complicated with Emma and Nathan. Despite reassuring scientific evidence, she could not bring herself to deny meat and fish to the growing brains and developing bodies of her children. However, when Emma turned thirteen and was menstruating regularly, Claire took her aside and explained why she was a vegetarian, emphasizing that Emma was free to make her own decision. Emma angrily claimed that Claire had "ruined food forever." For two sullen meals, Emma had slapped the vegetarian version of dinner on her plate, until at the third she burst out with "Oh my god, can't I just eat what I want?" Opposing currents of repulsion and sympathy formed a whirlpool in Claire's head. "Yes, of course," she said. From then on, meat-eating seemed an integral part of Emma's mother-resisting strategy.

When his time came, Nathan nodded solemnly during The Talk. He seemed to comply for months until he confessed he had been eating "every single meat" at friends' houses or fast-food outlets. For Nathan, every single meat meant cheeseburgers, chicken nuggets, and pepperoni pizza. Thus began years of high-stakes drama for Nathan, alternating proud vegetarian streaks with guilty meat-eating sprees.

Claire did not feel great about sparking this moral struggle in Nathan, but sheltering children from reality was not tenable long-term. Since Emma's death, however, Nathan had been a strict vegetarian.

"Hey, bud, your family needs you on that couch tonight," Ryan told Nathan. He was having a beer with dinner, which either meant work had been brutal or he was intent on fun. "How about DVR the game, make your call with the mute on, then watch it again, per usual?"

Nathan sat abstracted and still, as if listening carefully to a distant sound.

Ryan cuffed Nathan on the shoulder. "Hah? Works?"

Nathan finally bobbed his head, suppressing a smile, apparently pleased to be wooed by his dad.

"Wow, that sounds fun," Claire said and grinned broadly at Ryan.

Ryan gave an ironic, self-approving head waggle as he rose to clear some dishes.

•

Aside from a few flare-ups, lately they had been polite and somewhat cool with each other. They hadn't had sex since Emma's death. Claire had apologized for lashing out over the pot smoking, and had eased off in general, half-hoping this would draw Ryan back to her while maintaining her resolve not to carry the emotional ball.

Ironically, Jeremy's funeral had been a rare occasion for their old closeness. Jeremy's mother, Suzanne, had a narrow, hard, protruding chin like the toe of a shoe-stretcher, strikingly veined and muscular arms, and a knack for bitter asides. A beefy man, Richard Vanden Berg wore a near-constant close-mouthed smile, which when combined with his apparent absence of a sense of humor, gave him an unsettling sarcastic affect. He owned a business in Comstock that sold cement, sand, and gravel in mass quantities.

The Vanden Bergs were conservative reformed Protestants, so Jeremy's funeral was very spare and simple. The minister's sermon was mostly dour bits from Deuteronomy and 1st Thessalonians, laying down strictures on sorrow and hope, and there was no eulogy for Jeremy, in contrast to Emma's gathering with its personal speeches and music and lack of religious texts.

Heading to the car, Ryan had said, "Well, at least we dodged a bullet on the in-laws front."

She had surprised herself by throwing her head back and ejecting a shard of laughter from her throat—"Ha!"—as if the joke were a sort of Heimlich maneuver for someone choking on grief. Their hands came together—she gave his a squeeze—before they parted to get in the car.

•

The Big Lebowski was funny, though more funny to Ryan and Nathan than to her. Ryan was into his third beer and clearly enjoying himself. She was aware that in the past Movie Night had often functioned as foreplay. But honestly, John Goodman's character—Walter, the mercurial Vietnam vet—bothered her. She'd finished listening to *The Submission* and was on to Denis Johnson's *Tree of Smoke*, so Vietnam sorrow was fresh in her mind. Plus she'd been outraged by what she'd recently heard on NPR about treatment delays at the VA, and the number of vets who suffered from PTSD or committed suicide every day.

In one of the movie's many bowling scenes, an opposing bowler's toe crosses the foul line on his first ball, yet he insists on recording eight pins. Walter pulls a gun to force the bowler to record a zero, because of his foot fault.

"I wonder how Vietnam vets feel watching this sort of thing," she blurted.

"They laugh their asses off," Ryan said sharply. He picked up his beer and drank the last swallow, as if to forestall any further discussion.

"Do they? All of them?"

Ryan let it lie.

Nathan shifted where he was lying sideways on the couch, between the two armchairs where she and Ryan sat. Subsequent jokes drew no audible laughs from any of them.

Then a scene in which Walter ties another petty bowling thing back to watching his buddies die "face down in the muck."

Claire tried to control herself, but she still made a sound. It probably seemed like a dismissive sound. It was a dismissive sound.

Ryan turned off the TV and whipped the remote control at the window. A pane of glass broke.

"Dad!" Nathan exclaimed. He sat up and put his hands to his ears, though everything was very quiet all of a sudden.

Ryan stood and wheeled on her: "Do you have to find a way to make every instant suck?"

"Ryan..." She tried to protest but found herself trembling.

"What are we doing here? We're watching a *comedy,* for fuck's sake! But you have to turn it into a tragedy, because everything's a tragedy, our whole life is a tragedy!"

Nathan got up off the couch, scooted awkwardly around the coffee table and his father's back, and headed upstairs. Catching the fear and anguish in her son's eyes made her hate Ryan very intensely.

"I'm sorry. It was just a thought. I'm just—"

"It's *The Big Lebowski*! It's *the most laid-back movie of all time!* And you found a way to ruin it. Congratulations! Didn't think it could be done."

Anger and remorse battled within her.

"I'm sorry," she repeated miserably.

She bit back other words. She had to keep things from spiraling further out of control. Why did she have opinions?

Tandem

Why did she have to express herself? Why couldn't she just let things be?

She got up and went into the dusk-lit kitchen, but she felt she was still somehow in Ryan's space, so she went upstairs. Darkness seeped into the hallway. There was light coming from underneath Nathan's door. She heard him say, "Cabrera takes a slider, low and outside. Ball one."

She paused outside Emma's dark bedroom. The door was open a couple of inches. She found that having it completely shut created a tantalizing sense that Emma was in there, because she always kept her door closed; leaving it wide open, on the other hand, exposed too much. She was tempted to go inside and sit on the bed. But this was not likely to make her feel better in any way. She heard a downstairs window sliding up, then back down, glass pieces faintly clinking. The TV came back on. She decided to get ready for bed and listen to *Tree of Smoke,* to remind herself that her dismissive sound had come from a righteous place.

An hour and a half later, in the spaces between the narrator's voice, she heard the bathroom door close. She had left their bedroom door ajar, the same amount she left Emma's door open, a distance intended to create a sort of speed bump, not a stop sign. She turned off her book, removed her earbuds, and listened—toilet, teeth-brushing. It was Ryan not Nathan, she could tell, because, even in grief, Nathan couldn't resist modulating the sounds his brushing made by opening his mouth in various patterns, creating a musical range of rhythmic echoing or muffled mouth tones that reminded her of a kid burping the alphabet; whereas Ryan brushed mostly closed-mouthed until he spat a foamy wad at the drain plug, rinsed his brush, re-brushed briefly, spat, rinsed the brush again, and tapped it three times on the edge of the sink before placing it in the ceramic holder. These Ryan sounds now ran their course. She held still. Heat prickled her neck. She did not want him to come to bed with her; she was afraid he would not come to bed with her. The bathroom door opened—an abrupt sound. She closed her eyes. The crackling shift of floorboards. Steps receding down the hall. The guest bedroom door creaking in, creaking back. Clicking shut.

•

Ryan must have gotten up earlier than usual, because when she went to take a shower, she found his damp towel wadded over the rack. Nathan's door was closed. Since school had let out, she suspected he rose only just in time for his lifeguarding job at Kik Pool. She assumed Ryan was bent on getting out of the house before she came down.

She kept herself from rushing through her own shower—she wasn't going to chase him—dressed, and went down to the kitchen, somewhat surprised to find Ryan still there with his suit jacket over the back of his chair, hunched over his bowl of cereal, a banana skin nearby, his laptop open on the table.

"Morning," she said, as neutrally as she could.

"Morning," he said, and kept reading.

He would not apologize, which pissed her off, but she'd slept badly again and didn't want this argument hanging over her all day at work.

"I'm so sorry, Ryan," she said. "This is bringing out my worst, my worst..." She couldn't finish the thought.

He looked up, nearly flinched when he seemed to grasp the distress on her face.

"It's tough," he said quietly, looking down again. "It's really fucking tough."

He swallowed another mouthful of his cereal, then did a repetitive bowl-scraping thing to get the last bits. She thought of the soggy sweet mush passing down his throat and almost gagged. She wished he hadn't said "fucking." There was menace in the word.

"Do you want me to call about the window?" she asked.

"Of course not," he said, as if her offer were a passive-aggressive move, and it probably was. "I'll handle it," he added. "I'm sorry." He finally looked up, but not exactly at her.

"I don't want us to end up like a lot of the families that go through something like this," she said. "We're better than that."

"Yes, we're an excellent family," he said drily. He got up, grabbed his banana peel and his bowl, and went to the sink. "One of the better families I've come across."

"I love you," she said, reflexively. "I want us to stick together."

He gave her a lengthy, straight-lipped, appraising look. He seemed to consider and discard several possible replies. Then he walked to her, his hands drawn up slightly at his sides like a gunslinger about to draw, and hugged her lightly, then more firmly. "Hey, come on, don't worry," he said past her ear.

He patted her back twice and let go.

"Justice calls," he said, his voice sliding almost smoothly into the track of everyday sarcasm as if nothing had happened, and headed out of the kitchen.

•

She was grateful to work at a museum. She did believe that art could heal—just as she believed in most of what emanated from the *New York Times* or NPR or the TED stage—though not in a simple or inspirational way. Lately, she liked to go down to the Ahn exhibit on the lower level. He was a South Korean artist who put lights and mirrors into boxes to create illusory spaces in which patterns of bright lines repeated themselves, receding forever into the wall. In an accompanying video, the artist, a soft-spoken young man in a gray T-shirt, said he wanted his mirrors and light to create a sense of calm, infinite space.

Emma had come to see the exhibit. She didn't say much about it, of course, but she stood longest in front of a piece, *Forked Series #7,* where the square was bisected by a diagonal green fluorescent bar. The lower right half of the box curved away into a long bending tube; the upper left half curved the opposite way into its long bending tube. Maybe, for Emma, it was a light box version of "two roads diverged in a yellow wood." Or maybe it was just a trippy effect.

The most affecting piece was *Tunnel*. A box of cinderblock bricks rested on the floor and stood two feet high. There was a plate of glass across the top. On one inner wall, the rungs of a ladder. On the opposite wall, vertical sets of fluorescent lights. The passage seemed to go straight down for a hundred feet before it curved away. It was not as calming and spiritual as the others. Who would want to imagine descending into that dank abyss?

Still, she found herself standing before it most often.

Now she peered down the illusory shaft and wished Ryan had said more than just "don't worry." She wished he had said he loved her, or at least affirmed they'd stick together. She wished he hadn't acted as if he'd won when he'd left the kitchen. He'd broken a window in anger, so how did he end up winning?

Because you let him, she thought, and a bolt of rage stiffened her spine. If she were to crack the top pane of glass on *Tunnel*, right now, her curatorial career would be destroyed instantly and forever, yet where were the consequences for Ryan?

She had given away too much and gotten too little in return. People who gave were supposed to be happier than those who took, but she couldn't remember where she'd read that.

She stepped away from *Tunnel*. She needed some air.

Someone entered the gallery and went to the left, clockwise, which was her and Marta's intent and expectation. She went around the other way.

As she was about to leave the gallery, she noticed that the person staring into the first piece was a tall, broad-shouldered man, wearing dark straight-leg jeans, a nice grey dress shirt, and expensive high-top tan leather shoes. Short brown hair.

She hoped he wouldn't turn to look and she could escape without even having to nod hello, but another part of her, something traveling with her but independent of her will, like a dog or a child, turned her head and called back:

"Mike?"

11.

Over the weekend, he suspended work on the Camry because neighbors might be nearby doing their own chores. Instead, he waited until Monday morning to put on his fake mustache and sunglasses, part his hair on the opposite side, and head to Goggin Rental for a blowtorch to cut up the damaged hood. Then he drove the replicar a few blocks to the College and walked home. He didn't want his own car parked in his driveway, because that would be so unusual a passing neighbor might head for the garage's back door to ask about it, see sparks through the side-window's bedsheet, find the door locked, and call the police just to be sure everything was okay.

Having reviewed numerous YouTube videos, he arrayed his tools on the cracked and oil-stained concrete floor and set up two mirrors so he could see any sparks that might land behind him or otherwise elude his peripheral vision, which was limited by a welder mask. Then he left the garage and turned the cold garden hose on himself, soaking his long-sleeved cotton shirt, jeans, and old high-top work shoes to make them as fire-resistant as possible.

Back in the garage, dripping wet, he checked his pressure settings one last time, then fired up the odorless flame of his torch and held it near but not directly on a section of the hood resting on the garage floor. The paint bubbled, acrid smells rose, sparks sprayed at every angle, and the metal miraculously liquefied. With a boost to the jet of oxygen, the molten inch of the hood blew to the concrete below, leaving a cut gap.

Mozina

He worked exceedingly slowly, stopping periodically to make sure no spark was smoldering on his jeans or the wall or, God forbid, on the red and green tubes leading from the tanks. He dutifully checked his mirrors. Heat and fumes built up quickly in the closed garage and soon his face was running with sweat, but he kept to his disciplined pace.

When he was about to start his second slice, his phone lit up with a call. Connor.

Yesterday had been Father's Day, but he hadn't heard from his son. He cut the torch and ripped off his mask.

"Hey, Connor," he said, in a breathless voice. He turned 360, looking for smoldering sparks. His wet feet squelched in his shoes.

"Hey, Dad," Connor said languidly. "Did you get it?"

"Get what?" he asked warily. Was Connor asking if he'd really gotten him a car? He walked to the back door, opened the dead bolt, and gulped fresh air.

"I sent you something. For Father's Day."

"Oh, oh. No, I don't think so."

"Sorry about that," Connor said. "Mom was visiting and it was hard to do anything. You'll like it," he added.

"Right. Definitely. I'll be on the lookout for it."

He knocked down the thought that Anne had chosen Father's Day weekend to visit Connor in order to sabotage their relationship somehow. When Mike had called his own dementia-wracked father, the old man accused him of stealing his watch from his golf bag. Mike apologized and promised to return it the next time he came home. Not hearing from his own son had stung a bit, but he was glad to let that go now.

"How's everything?" Mike added. "How's the job?"

"Ah, pretty wild. But I'm hacking it."

"What do you mean by 'wild'?"

"I'm working hard. It's good. I think they're going to want me next year."

"That's good," he said. The kid's optimism reminded him of his dad's; somehow it had skipped a generation. "How's Denise?"

"She's chill."

"Have you been out to see her?"

Connor's girlfriend had an internship with an international aid agency in New York City, and Mike was slyly pointing Connor's road trips away from Kalamazoo.

"Not yet. But I will. Maybe this weekend. I don't know."

"This weekend? Well, let me know if you need a plane ticket or something."

"I got it, Dad." Connor laughed.

Mike couldn't tell whether that meant he was going to cover it himself or he understood his dad was an open checkbook whenever a whim struck him.

As Mike was realizing he'd run out of the standard parent questions, Connor said, "Well, I've got to get back to work here. Good talking to you, Dad. Like I said, Happy Father's Day."

"Thanks, Connor," Mike said. "Have a good one."

The conversation had been brief and missing sincere connection, but Mike appreciated the lack of overt rancor. He was pretty sure Anne hadn't told Connor about the car.

He pulled his welder's mask back on and finished cutting the hood of the murder weapon into disposable pieces without accidental fires or explosions or spatter burns.

Soon after he put out the bagged-up hood, he happened to see the mammoth trash truck lumber by, completely filling the narrow alley. The truck's mechanical grabber hoisted and over-turned his bin, lid aflap, then awkwardly slammed the empty can down on his cement driveway—not unlike a drunk with a twenty-ounce glass. No sanitation engineer ever touched the can. The driver couldn't see what fell into the compactor—though maybe there were cameras, which seemed to be everywhere these days.

Now all the damaged parts of his Camry would reside soundlessly in black trash bags in a landfill. Someone looking at his hoodless, bumpercoverless, headlightless, wind-shieldless sedan might not automatically think "accident." Everything about it looked neat and intentional, more undressed than damaged. They might just ask, "What's up with your car?"

For days, he had no answer, then it came to him: he'd picked it up dirt cheap for Connor at an impound auction. They were going to finish the repairs together, bonding over the dying art of men fixing their own cars. Wasn't it funny that father and son would have virtually the same car?

With this new story at his disposal, he no longer considered disappearing the entire car. If he disappeared the car, he'd have to buy a whole other vehicle so he could still give the replicar to Connor in case Anne actually did tell him. Besides, he needed to save his money to donate it to other people.

Soon Mike realized he might even be okay waiting another month or two before ordering the replacement parts; by then the cops would be more likely to have given up. In the meantime, he drove the replicar around town—to get groceries from Meijer, to go golfing or drink beers with his buddies, to take nature walks in the College's arboretum far from the reality of what he'd done—enjoying extended reveries in which the accident never happened. He was back to his one-beer limit (two, if it was a prolonged gathering), so everyone could see how routinely he passed when others pounded another.

On one outing Dave took Mike aside and said Sarah had a friend Mike might want to get to know, a woman who had lost her husband to cancer and was maybe thinking about dating again. She was a doctor, with two teenage boys.

"She's pretty special," Dave said. "Seriously."

"Tell Sarah thanks, but it's a little soon for me," Mike said soberly. It was bittersweet to be rehabilitated in Sarah's eyes but unable to risk a relationship right now, as badly as he wanted one.

"One day at a time, brother," Dave said, patting Mike's shoulder. "You'll get there."

•

But despite these interludes of normality, toxic ruminations piled up in his head far faster than he could empty them onto his legal pad. The itch to see Claire again had been growing. He wondered whether he could traverse the tightrope of love stretched across the pit of his guilt—and whether there was something solid and good and morally revolutionary on the other side. He had been surprised at how composed she was at the exhibit opening, as if she weren't carrying unimaginable grief. He imagined that seeing her without so many people around would be more revealing in every way. He went back to the museum.

Keeping his peripheral vision on a tight leash, so he wouldn't see her first and blunder over, he went gallery by gallery, acting as if he were enthralled by the art, and for seconds at a time he was. He soon exhausted the entry level without an encounter, despite gratuitously crossing the main lobby several times. He considered leaving—really, what was he doing here? what would he say to her?—but headed down to the galleries on the lower level.

In one that was full of contemporary pieces, he spotted a security guard, and his skin sizzled with guilt and paranoia. But as he came closer, he realized it was only an amazingly lifelike sculpture of a security guard.

He fairly reeled out of that room and into a sponsored gallery of East Asian art. A video was playing on a wall opposite the entrance, but he couldn't focus on it. The first piece hanging to his left was a box with fluorescent lights and mirrors in it, so the bars of light receded into the distance. He liked the magic of it. He imagined climbing into the frame and walking down the infinite corridor, which was strangely both lit up and dark. No one would follow him into such a stark space.

"Mike?"

He froze, as if someone had said, "Drop the gun and put your hands up." Then he slowly turned around. But he had wanted to run into her, and here she was.

"Hey!" he said, smiling big.

Claire wore a dark jacket and a colorful scarf hanging straight down around her neck.

"Back for more?" she asked. Though her eyes were tired, her smile was pleased, which calmed his racing heart.

"Can't get enough of this place." He thumbed at the nearest light box. "Pretty freaky."

"Yes, well, we aim to please," she said.

He'd said the wrong thing. "How're you doing?" he asked too brightly, over-compensating.

"Oh, I don't know," she said. "Hey, how's the tricky monetary paper going?"

"Very badly!" He laughed because the paper had never existed in the first place. "The Fed's balance sheet has been so insane, but there's no inflation, and I thought I had something really cool to say about that, but—" He flexed his chin despairingly.

"Well, don't look at me!"

"So, really, what's going on with these things? I don't mean to be so boorish." He nodded toward the screen where the artist was explaining. "What's this guy trying to say?"

"Oh, gosh, well—" She took a deep breath, but then just exhaled. "I'd rather hear about the Fed." She laughed weakly.

"Hah! Who wouldn't?" He clapped his hands like a guest trying too hard on a late-night talk show.

"I'm serious," she said. "Give me your elevator pitch for monetary policy."

"Are you kidding me?" He raised praying hands up to his nose.

He couldn't stop over-acting. What if he broke the fourth wall? What if his conscience took the wheel, right now, and drove smack into the bridge abutment of confession?

But he was already saying something else, having an almost out-of-body sense of listening to himself, as sometimes happened in front of a classroom when he was very tired, which of course he was right now beneath his manic nervousness: "Because everything, I mean, *everything*—or at least the possibility of material well-being, which is everything to most people—depends on how much it costs to borrow money, and the Fed sets the cost of money. Janet Yellen is probably the most important person on the planet."

She spun a finger encouragingly.

Tandem

"And no one talks about how Ben Bernanke saved civilization! Man should have a national holiday!" His hand gestures were getting way too big. "All right, I'm going to stop myself, because I don't want to be your typical macroeconomist at a party, going off about the yield curve or whatever. You're already carrying so much right now, I don't want to annoy you."

Her expression sank, her eyes welled with tears. She seemed about to speak but only shook her head, as if to say she hadn't been annoyed. The generosity of this gesture threatened whatever poise he had left.

"I'm sorry, that's my own crap..." He trailed off, looked away, took a big breath. "Okay! Not that I have to explain myself, but I guess I do want to, because this is one of the things I'm doing, going to the museum, doing different stuff, just to get out again, get back into life after my stupid divorce. So, sorry to use your world for that. I hope it doesn't look weird or coincidental."

He lifted his eyes, performing fear and hope for her good opinion.

"No, no, you're fine," she said, waving a hand back and forth in front of her face. His outburst seemed to have given her the chance to master her own feelings. "It's just that what you said kind of got to me, because—" Her voice trembled. "How do we deal with things? I have no idea how to deal with what's happening. No idea."

He compressed his lips, nodded at the floor, made himself breathe so he wouldn't falter like at the funeral.

"Have you seen the tempera paintings?" she asked, pulling them out of their nosedive.

They were in an adjacent gallery. Portraits of beautiful young women representing the signs of the zodiac. He thought of Emma and, for a knee-weakening instant, everything heat-shimmered. Was Claire staging the whole museum as an elaborate tell-tale heart?

He took his time looking at the portraits, mastering himself instant by instant, delaying the dangerous moment when he would have to speak. He mimed great interest in the artist's technique, avoiding the eyes of the young women. He observed lustrous cream or honey skin clothed in striking blues, subtle oranges, and rich greens. Distant backdrops of gold-leaf or indigo skies speckled with stars, the horizon light of sunset blooming from the bottom of a frame. Every woman seemed barely legal. The paintings were very well-done, but in their sundresses, night gowns, and clinging bodices, the subjects came across as high-brow pin-up models. The name of the exhibit was "Eternal Beauty." *Only in Humbert Humbert's dreams*, Mike thought.

"Creepy," he finally blurted.

"I think so, too!" Claire lit up. "I hadn't thought that exact word, but yeah."

Claire went on to explain that the director had lobbied hard for this artist, in part because he promised to come to town and do a tempera workshop, which did end up over-subscribed. She granted his technique was amazing, but during his gallery talk Q & A, he had said he only painted women because their "rounder forms" were "more conducive to molding," which Claire recounted with an eye roll. She didn't seem to at all associate these portraits with Emma.

Mike felt great relief at this turn in the conversation. As Claire vented, he dipped his head and nodded empathetically, regaining natural control of his gestures.

Could he have helped alleviate her professional frustration from prison? No. Was it beyond excruciating to cause and endure these moments with her? Of course. But maybe braving this ordeal wasn't a sign of his own creepiness, but of the intricate and unconventional form of love this terrible situation required.

"How's your son doing?" she asked, abruptly changing the subject.

"My son?" Did he have a son? "Oh! Connor. Yeah." He stuffed his hands in the pockets of his jeans and rocked back on his heels, looking at a low blank space on the wall. "He's good. Not terrible. He's spending the summer in Ann Arbor. Got an internship with Google." He turned to her and gave her a proud, million-dollar smile.

He knew he had good teeth. Anne had complained that he smiled strategically to charm people with his impressive array—"Like Obama!" she'd accused.

"Oh, that sounds wonderful," Claire said warmly.

"How's Nathan doing?" he asked, a far less innocent question, but she'd invited it.

"You know, he's hard to read. Actually, what am I saying, he's *not* hard to read. He's really upset, of course... but he's coping. He's got his ways of coping."

"What can you do?" Mike said softly.

"Can I ask you a question?" she said, peering up at him. "You don't have to answer, but I'm curious."

"Sure," he said carefully. He instinctively removed his hands from his pockets, as if preparing to ward off a physical attack.

"I guess I need some perspective on this," she said. "What's your sense for how prevalent pot smoking is these days among high school and college kids? I mean..."

Mike exhaled, looked away, shrugged. "Connor's a drinker, like his mother. I don't know how much he smokes weed. He probably does. I think they all do, really. But I don't know if I can worry about that stuff anymore." He gave a short laugh. "He's functioning pretty well. He doesn't seem to ever want to live at home again, so he's motivated to keep his act together. Is that bad?" He tilted his head and squinted at her. "Let him have a bunch of addictions—as long as he's got a job!" He laughed more.

Now who was he trying to be? Self-deprecating dad? Random imbecile?

"That's interesting," she said, as if trying to determine whether or how much he was joking. "You know, I would have never thought of my Emma as a pot smoker, but apparently she was. She was high when she was killed."

"Oh, I'm sorry," he said, caught up short, as if hearing about her death for the first time. But he didn't panic. He was getting used to hiding right in front of her.

"Maybe I shouldn't," Claire went on, "but I always associate that stuff with sadness, with compensating for being sad. It's...I don't know. Not knowing something like that about your daughter is..." She choked up.

"It is," he said sympathetically, agreeing with whatever she couldn't formulate. He risked looking into her golden eyes, which were so sad they suggested tremendous powers of forgiveness.

She put a hand over her eyes, as if to block his gaze. She sniffed. Her tears seemed to be finally taking over. He was so deep into his role, he felt the impulse to hug her, but he was restrained by the sense he was wearing a suit of spikes.

"Well," she finally said, running a finger under one eye. "I need to get back to work."

"Yes," he said. "I'm very sorry. If you guys need anything, anything at all, just let me know."

"You should come back to book club some time," she said. "You're quite the critic."

"Maybe," he mumbled. Then he added in a stronger voice: "Take care."

12.

In the Sunday *Times* Claire read a review of a book that described how, during the financial crisis, astute and magical coordination between the heads of three central banks—the Bank of England, the European Central Bank, and the U.S. Federal Reserve (yes, Ben Bernanke)—prevented another Great Depression. It was her habit to email friends about books they might like. She believed a well-read citizenry was the backbone of a healthy democracy, and it was up to individual citizens to promote intellectual curiosity and knowledge of current events. She was not above adding a smiley face emoji to show she meant no harm.

She debated whether to email Mike with a link to an online version of the review. It had been a few weeks since she'd seen him last.

After she'd left him in the tempera exhibit, she'd gone upstairs and could only work for fifteen minutes before needing more coffee. When she crossed the main lobby, she happened to see him just leaving the museum. He looked preoccupied. She'd sensed a tug, as if she should follow him out the door.

Though she had been hit on by visiting artists and museum donors over the years, she'd never been tempted beyond recognizing the idea. She was married, and that was that. Plus she simply didn't trust attractive or highly accomplished men. They tended to reveal themselves, eventually, as assholes. Even, sadly, the ones who seemed different at first, like Mike. He wasn't as cool and collected as he looked. Maybe his wife leaving him had knocked him off his perch. Maybe tiptoeing around her grief made him awkward.

She was aware that a single partner couldn't provide everything one needed to be happy. A book review she'd read about biological imperatives had addressed this. Mike just made the world seem a little friendlier than it had been feeling lately. And he had done so in spite of his own burdens, which was admirable.

Though he had doubtless seen the book review himself, he would appreciate the support. She had to scan the massive roll of recipients for a neighborhood association list to find his email address.

Hey Mike, Someone gets it! she wrote.

She dithered over her sign off before settling on a simple *C.*

He wrote back within the hour: *Hi Claire, Looks like a great read! Thanks for sending! Take care, Mike.*

It had been a warm but chaste exchange. Just what she'd hoped for.

The after-effects were unexpected. She had a sudden urge to bake bread for dinner.

She laid the table with spaghetti and salad and a loaf of homemade Italian. Ryan and Nathan thickly buttered piece after piece. After everyone had been asked how their day went, including herself, and gave relatively cheerful but vague responses, including her own, Ryan announced he was taking Nathan on "a tour of the Ohio Six," a group of liberal arts colleges in, yes, Ohio, one of which was Kenyon, her alma mater. Four days in the first week of August.

"So this is all set?" she asked. She carefully set down her fork.

"Yeah, I've made all the arrangements," Ryan said casually. "I've got vacation."

"But that's just two weeks away. I'm hosting book club. I have to work." Her pressing tasks ran the gamut from a collection inventory, to mounting a new exhibit in an upstairs gallery, to evaluating prospective additions to the permanent collection. She was still catching up, and on top of that, still working sluggishly.

"Doesn't matter," he said, lifting a mallet of twirled spaghetti off his plate.

She leaned back in her chair, both hands wringing the paper napkin in her lap. Noodles slithered into Nathan's mouth like a small octopus.

"What?" Ryan asked, chewing. "We talked about this back in April. You planned things for Emma, so I did it for Nathan."

She realized he was right—they'd talked about it in a general way but hadn't done any specific planning. "I know," she said, trying to be as conciliatory as possible, "but when I was putting things together, I talked to you about it, and you said you couldn't go anywhere but MSU—and we all went there together."

"Gotta warn you, Claire." Ryan shot Nathan a smile. "This is going to be the Ohio Six *unplugged*. Only one change of clothes, right, Nate? Like being stranded in the wild."

Claire did not smile. Nathan rubbed his mouth with his napkin, ignoring his father's appeal. Then he asked to be excused. They let him go.

"Are you really doing this?" Claire asked.

"I thought I was helping." Ryan sounded aggrieved. He tonged a heaping salad onto his plate. "You're always complaining about how you have to organize everything."

"I don't complain about that!" In fact, she had made a point of *not* complaining about it, though she frequently did think it. Had she actually said something? Was her body language giving her away?

"I thought I might bond with Nate. Pretty soon he's going to go, and I'll miss him."

She was surprised Ryan said this so directly.

"And if you can come," he went on, poking randomly at the leaves of his salad, "that's great. Are you sure you can't make it?" He looked up with his naturally mournful eyes.

"Yes, I'm sure. I can't ask off so soon."

"That's when the schools do it." He shrugged. "I'm not *choosing* to go then. That's when it is. You had book club on the calendar, so I assumed you weren't planning to go."

Since when did he check the family calendar? She was forever having to remind him of events plainly listed there. But why had she agreed to host book club during the Ohio Six tour? Why hadn't she seen that coming? Maybe she was blocking out Nathan's college search because the options were too depressing.

"Come on, Claire," he added quietly. "Are you saying he shouldn't go if you can't go?"

"I just wish you'd told me."

"I guess I was thinking you knew."

"All right, I get it."

She needed to stop over-reacting to things. Ryan taking Nathan on his college tour was just a natural extension of their highly gendered parenting roles: he had primary responsibility for Nathan, she for Emma.

Still, she decided not to help Ryan clear the table. Instead, she went to listen to her book club novel.

13.

On a Wednesday evening, nearly two weeks after talking with Claire in the downstairs galleries at the KIA, Mike walked to a modern-looking Catholic church tucked on a street near the College. St. Thomas More. From 6:30 to 7:30 PM, they offered the Sacrament of Reconciliation—confession.

He showed up around seven, hoping to avoid any opening prayer service. The sanctuary was open and airy, spanned by exposed roof trusses, with a wall of large windows at one end through which the evening sun angled. There were no fixed pews, no kneelers, just arcs of wide padded chairs orbiting an altar in the round. A few yards into the sanctuary squatted a hot tub-like pool made of rectangular stones and lined with blue tiles. The pool contained a few feet of water fed by a trickle from a pile of rocks. At his boyhood church in Eau Claire, there had been a half-bowl of holy water on the wall by the ornate wooden door, and a marble basin the size of a bird bath near the altar for baptisms. In the meantime, New Age culture had apparently made inroads with church architects, which he thought augured well for today's purposes.

To maintain his cover, he dipped two fingers in the hot tub and made the sign of the cross on his chest. He spotted the portable wooden confessional box parked against the wall opposite the windows. Its dark varnished wood was carved in Gothic style, its side panels inset with lancet arches. Contrasted with the spa vibe of the rest of the church, the box was a sobering throwback. Someone was sitting behind the left wing—he could see the back of a tight navy shirt.

The handful of people in the church were seated on the opposite side of the room from the box, and he spaced himself behind them, as if to acknowledge his place in line.

The sanctuary was perfectly quiet and still. He folded his hands in his lap and looked down as if he were praying. Then he acted as if he were finished praying.

The navy shirt rose from the booth. It was an older man, wearing wire-rimmed glasses, cargo shorts, and gym shoes as white as his calf-high socks. He walked back to his seat with his hands pressed together, as if he had just clapped them around a fly. A middle-aged woman in blouse and blue jeans, with a bowl haircut faded below the ear line, immediately shot up and went to the confessional. Somehow everyone knew what the order was. He counted three more people to go before it was his turn.

Bees in his gut, sweaty palms, an exact form of nervousness he hadn't felt since he was twelve. As a child he had been told the "seal of the confessional" meant the priest couldn't tell anybody what you said, no matter what.

It occurred to him he was about to speak to the Wizard of Oz, but he'd already seen behind the curtain and knew the absence of real authority in the priest. Then again, it was maybe the first time since the accident he felt he was in the right place.

Then it was his turn. No one had arrived after him, so he could hog the rest of the time without feeling bad. His soft-soled shoes made no sound against the flagstone floor. The chair was still warm when he sat at the confessional. There was also a kneeler. He slid to his knees, feeling the old tightening of his hamstrings.

"Hi," he said into the screen, and then added the remembered formula: "Bless me, Father, for I have sinned. It's been a long time since my last confession, probably thirty-five years."

"Well," the priest said with a dry chuckle, "what's the occasion?"

The priest sounded roughly his age, maybe a little older, his voice more reedy than resonant, surprisingly like that of Yale economist Robert Shiller, who was always on CNBC talking in a studiously open-minded way about housing prices and stock market valuations.

This was a good thing. Mike admired Shiller greatly. He took a deep breath.

"About eight weeks ago," Mike began, "I went out to dinner with some friends, and I got drunk. After dinner, I was driving, and I—I accidentally hit some people with my car. They died. Two people."

It was thrilling to say this, an incredible relief. It was also awful beyond bearing.

The priest was silent for a bit. Mike waited him out.

"And are you—sorry—for what you've done?" the priest finally asked.

"Yes, I'm terribly sorry. I wish I were dead."

It was true. And the point was to speak nothing but the truth to this stranger. It was a breathtaking freedom, no doubt the secret sauce in the Catholic confession ritual. He wondered what he would say in the name of truth, and what he might learn about himself in the process.

"Okay, I hear the guilt you're feeling," the priest replied, "but, please, don't harm yourself. Don't even consider that."

"I won't," he said politely.

If the priest was really serious about keeping Mike alive, all he had to do was perform an absolution marked by deep empathy and state-of-the-art forgiveness, recasting this relentless horror in a more bearable light. Even back in the day, white-haired Father Hoffman, who hobbled side-to-side as if he had broken glass in his chunky black shoes, had told his eighth-grade religion class not to worry about Hell. "That's not the point," he'd said. Father Hoffman had to be dead by now, but hopefully this priest was cut from the same spiritual cloth.

"Do the police know what happened?"

"Uh, yes and no. Basically, no."

The priest said nothing.

"When I saw they were dead, I drove away."

A deep nasal breath from the priest. The screen was a metal grill of interlocking scalloped shapes; behind it was a fuzzy filter like the one on the air-return for his attic air-conditioning unit. Mike put his fingertips against the metal edges of the grill. He thought of cell bars, of speaking by phone through Plexiglass with Connor.

"How did it happen?"

He emphasized the fog, the going out through the in lane, the surreal jack-in-the-box suddenness; how Emma and probably Jeremy were high; how his ex-wife was the drinker, and he didn't usually drink at all.

"I know it sounds like I'm making excuses," he said. "I need someone's help to get me past all the excuses."

The priest considered this for a time.

"Can you say more about making excuses?" he finally asked.

As he did when standing over a putt on the golf course, Mike tried to steady his mind, the way a needle could float on a bowl of water if it was placed perfectly level, so he might continue to speak the truth. "I don't want to consider anything that's not legitimate," he said. "I don't want to excuse myself, but—I guess—I want to be fair to myself, too."

"Okay, hang on, you said you were terribly sorry. Do you not know what you're sorry for, why you're seeking absolution?"

He was actually glad the priest was thinking carefully. He wanted to weed out the weak excuses in the hope of—he had to admit it now—finding an excuse or two that would stick, morally. Or, barring that, maybe they could agree on a spiritual accommodation: maybe he could wear a hairshirt for a set period of time, or otherwise earn the modern version of an indulgence. (Mike assumed the practice had undergone some degree of re-branding, given past criticisms.) But if the truth was that no excuse could stick, or nothing could be done to mitigate things, he would accept that.

"I don't know what to do," he said calmly, without defiance or whining. "I want to confess, but I don't know what to do."

"Well, confession, as far as saying something to a priest, is really just a small part of it. This is about reconciliation. 'First be reconciled to thy brother, and then come offer thy gift.'"

Mike didn't like the sound of that. It suggested that turning himself in was a necessary part of the process. Certain aspects of restorative justice were hard to enact. He fell silent, trying to imagine a way around this.

"So you said drinking is not an issue for you?" the priest asked in a delicate tone.

"Right, that's the thing. It's not." Mike raised both fists and set their heels against the screen. He closed his eyes hard. "I usually never have more than one drink. I was just celebrating one night, I swear."

"Okay, I understand that," the priest said, in a calming voice. Mike lowered his fists, but he didn't open his eyes. "Anyone might have done that," the priest went on. "You're not a monster. If you turn yourself in, you'll feel better, you'll begin to heal your soul, and God will be with you whatever happens to you legally. God's law is higher than the court's."

"Yes, I know. I've been thinking that."

He was suddenly so tired he couldn't open his eyes. Why wasn't this priest an obtuse prig, or a pervert whose manipulative way of framing things made it clear that he sexually abused minors—someone he could dismiss? Why did he have the same nonchalant aura of authority and common sense as Nobel-winning economist Robert Shiller? Shiller had actually attended the College for a time before finishing at U of M. Maybe his brother (Roger Shiller?) had also gone to the College, and had stayed and somehow become a priest, and was now on the other side of this Gothic air-conditioning filter.

"Do you want to change your life?" the priest suddenly asked.

He opened his eyes. His nose had drooped within an inch of the screen. "Yes. Yes, I do."

"Are you ready to come back to God, not just to get absolution for this sin, but permanently? It sounds as if you've been separated from the church for a long time. Sin is a separation from God. That's why we call this sacrament 'Reconciliation.'"

"I don't know," he said. "I don't know if I can, to be honest." What he had meant by wanting to change his life was that his life was awful and he wished it were different.

"You want absolution, but you don't want to be a member of the church?"

Anger flared in the back of his brain. This smacked of the upselling tactics of his aggressive dentist.

"I'm having a moral crisis," he said. "I just need to talk to someone."

"I'm glad you're here, but I'm not a therapist," the priest said curtly. Then he sighed. "Look, I pity you and wish God's mercy for you. And I strongly urge you to go to the police. You need to be reconciled with the people you've hurt."

Uncanny vocal similarities aside, this man was not fellow economist Robert Shiller, or even his more religious brother, Roger. This man had grown, root and limb, in a different part of the world from where Mike had been living, far from Mike's imaginative constructs. Mike wanted to reply, but his own voice seemed to have slipped away, out of reach, like a quarter dropped between the emergency brake and the driver's seat in the replicar.

"And I know God will absolutely forgive you," the priest went on. "I believe there's real contrition in you, I believe that, but I can't absolve you today."

This was a bitter pill, but he must be reasonable and mature, to show that he was not usually the selfish and impulsive man who hit and ran.

"I understand, Father," he said. "But can I ask you something?"

"Yes, of course."

"I know that confessing to the police would be a good thing to do. And I know that giving most of my money to the poor would also be a good thing." He paused to gather himself. "And I know that giving up my guest bedroom to shelter a homeless person would be a good thing to do. But I don't know if I can do *all* those things. So is it okay for me to not do *every* good thing I could do?"

There was a long pause behind the filter. Mike didn't even hear breathing, as if his unassailable Jesuitical reasoning had struck the priest dead.

"Why are you asking me this?" the priest finally demanded.

"Because I'm trying to figure out how to do what's right."

"You need to be reconciled with the people you've hurt—and with God," the priest replied with implacable calm.

"But you haven't answered my question!" Mike's voice rose.

All of a sudden it was like the Planning and Budget meeting when he was trying to explain to a colleague from the English Department why the rise in the tuition discount rate was going to hurt the College's Moody's rating which was going to raise their borrowing costs which would ultimately limit their raises. The colleague had refused to make eye contact. That's what happened when you put humanities people on P&B!

"I know it's hard," the priest said. "But God will forgive you."

Mike drilled his eyes into the screen. He raised both fists over his head, gathering his strength. He understood now that the screen was not there for confidentiality, but to protect the priest. And wouldn't the priest be surprised when the screen crashed against his head?

"Look, don't confuse yourself," the priest continued. "The only thing to do is to reconcile with the people you've hurt—as soon as you can. Everything will be wrong, and *feel* wrong, until you make it right."

Mike's boiling rage turned to simmering resentment. The priest could never be made to answer his crucial question. He lowered his fists and forced himself up from the kneeler before he could commit another crime.

He peeled away from the confessional, making a quick move to avoid running into the back of a padded chair. He found the aisle and beelined for the hot tub, as if he wanted to douse his flaming head in it. By the time he reached the water, he understood what he needed to do to maintain his cover, though there was no one left in the church but himself and the priest. He dipped two fingers in the tepid bath and crossed himself.

•

When he got home, he wandered the first floor of his house, replaying his conversation with the priest. He hadn't realized how much he'd been relying on talking to the priest to bring some sense of progress or clarity to his situation. But, ironically, the whole experience made him need to talk to someone even more. Maybe he could simply go to a priest in a different parish and take a less-blunt approach to asking his question. But why stop at a second opinion? There wasn't a priest in Michigan, or the world, who would refuse to talk to him if he showed up during scheduled confession time. Their jobs trapped priests into such absurd exposures. And not all of them could be as judgmental as this St. Thomas More priest. Thomas More, of course, was a famous stickler, and this priest could be following his lead. Maybe he would only visit churches named after Mary, where the outlook might be more merciful.

Even with that limitation, he would never run out of Catholic churches. He could use the mini to create an itinerary. He could hit the road in the replicar, drawing travel funds from his home equity line. "A Pilgrimage for Penance," he wrote on his legal pad, and underscored it three times. It was a real possibility. He would either learn a lot, or learn how little there was to know. If he talked to enough priests, a constructive consensus might emerge. Each confession would raise the possibility of hearing what he needed to hear. Maybe he could do it for the rest of his life, perpetually engaged in the process of becoming moral. After all, the journey was more important than the destination, wasn't it?

Meanwhile, on the edges of his awareness, intense feelings of shame darted like mice along the baseboards of his ramshackle soul. He had no choice but to open a beer and Netflix an episode of *30 Rock*. No more *Breaking Bad*—that show was brutal. He needed to watch comedies from now on, because laughter was better for the world. All of his toil as a teacher and scholar of macroeconomics, not to mention as a stalwart committee member, had left him with a lot of TV to catch up on. When *30 Rock* was over, he paused the TV and went for another beer. Another episode, another beer.

Eventually, he shipped his oars and drifted in his drunken boat, borne along by the show's little waves of talking and zany transition music, until he finally felt the big wave coming. *Holy Mary, Mother of God, pray for us sinners, now and at the hour of our—* He turned sideways on the sectional, curled, and sank.

He dreamed he met Emma and Jeremy on foot at dusk in the parking lot at Saugatuck Dunes. They seemed solid and alive until they moved and came apart briefly before their molecules could regroup, like a cloud of bees in the shape of a person. They weren't mad at him. Their tandem bike was nowhere in evidence. They wanted to walk the trail through the woods toward Lake Michigan, but they dawdled behind him, huddled in wraith conversation. He went back to get them, but he couldn't draw their attention, could only walk forward again and hope they would follow. To the right was a broad forested ravine, which the path skirted without a railing. He knew they had disappeared into the ravine, which was crisscrossed with long, fallen trees, but Emma had become Claire and Jeremy had become himself. He saw Claire and himself flying through the trees on the other side of the ravine. Following them into the ravine seemed like diving into a bottomless lake. He couldn't make himself do it. He kept waving them to his side, so he could be one person with Claire, but they wouldn't come. Then he lost them altogether.

•

She was on his mind so often, it seemed they were in the early stages of developing a single, shared consciousness. Her email about a financial crisis book, the first time she ever reached out to him, seemed a watershed moment, like the collapse of Lehman itself. Who signs off with just a single letter for their name? An intimate acquaintance. He replied in the most innocuous way possible. Meanwhile, his imagination sprinted like a dog released into a field: what if she liked him?

Reviewing their encounters, he realized one man's exploration of someone's receptivity to a life-shattering confession could look a lot like another man's flirtatious interest in a grieving and vulnerable woman. Why had he focused his restorative love on Claire, rather than Ryan or Nathan?

His guilt bucket already runneth over, so he tried not to think of her in romantic terms.

Yet marriages often blew up over the loss of a child.

He imagined he still knew, deep down, the right thing to do.

Yet questions were said to be more productive than answers.

Wouldn't the person who facilitated her escape from a sinking relationship be doing her a service? Wasn't doing her such a service a form of recompense for killing her daughter? Wouldn't that good be a better good than confessing? If he felt love for her, and she felt love for him, and she no longer felt love for her husband, weren't they, in fact, *morally obligated* to consummate their love, even though he had accidentally killed her daughter?

She conversed like a normal, well-adjusted person, with a sense of give and take; she did not monologue until he could feel his face sliding off his head. She did not carry herself with attitude. She was smart and had a cool job. Physically, she was the opposite of Anne: petite where Anne was bodacious, pretty where Anne had a fulsome, broken-nosed beauty. He did also notice that Claire's slightly hunched shoulders and brisk efficient movements sometimes seemed to wring the sexiness right out of her. Her hair was conservatively bobbed and unabashedly going gray. Though she dressed well, she didn't seem bent on promoting her own attractiveness, which intrigued him. Granted, he wasn't drawn to her to the degree he'd been drawn to Anne, but she was interesting and sensible—a good contrast to Anne. If she were not married and if he had not killed her daughter, yes, he would be perfectly happy to ask her out.

But she was married and he had killed her daughter.

And yet...

•

He cut back on his drinking and started exercising more. He increased his plank time to six minutes, then seven. Planking for so long was amazingly uncomfortable, a proverbial ecstasy of pain. He started to wonder if the ex-Marine who set the planking record had been unhappy about something.

Near the end of July, on a day of thunderstorms and tornado warnings, Connor called to ask for airfare to visit his girlfriend in New York. The Father's Day gift, which arrived over a week late, had turned out to be a five-pound drum of "gourmet" chocolate-covered almonds. From one angle, a crass gift, possibly an insulting gift. On the other hand, the chocolate-covered almonds were the best thing in his life at the moment.

As if he felt guilty for avoiding his dad all summer while sponging off him to spend time with someone else, Connor also made a point of announcing he was coming home the last weekend in August to see friends and pick up some stuff before the new school year started.

He should have seen this coming.

There was no plausible way to talk him out of this, and Mike didn't even try. Since his burst of activity after Anne's appearance, he'd gotten lax about the car again, hesitating over the potential exposure involved in ordering the replacement car parts. Now his plan for a father-son repair of a wrecked Camry from the impound seemed as idiotic as waiting this long to deal with the car. Connor would literally smell the difference between the replicar and the original. He would be irritated by having to repair the car instead of hanging out with his friends.

So instead Mike would finish repairing the murder weapon himself and tell Connor to take the train from Ann Arbor instead of driving his rattletrap Honda. If Connor protested, Mike would ham-handedly tease the gift by saying he "had him covered."

Mike immediately ordered the headlight assembly, choosing expedited shipping, and charted a schedule for the bumper cover, the hood, the little grill at the tip of the hood, the rearview mirror, and the windshield. He had no choice but to put the headlight on his credit card. This was a particularly dangerous thing to do. Of course, a paper credit card statement could be destroyed—if he was willing to forgo his sacred monthly reconciliation process, which, shamefully, he'd let slip since the accident—but destroying statements might only induce a false sense of security, since every credit card transaction lived forever on computer servers. At least he would be sure to destroy the itemized receipts. With a few taps on his mini, he summoned incriminating evidence toward his front door.

14.

Ryan and Nathan threw their black cloth luggage in the back of the old Forester. Claire would see them off in the driveway, per family tradition. She chattered to Nathan, "Be sure to ask a lot of questions. Ask the questions *you* want. You can really go anywhere."

She did not believe her own words. Nathan hadn't taken the ACT in May because of Emma's death. He had to buckle down on his prep over the next month and ace his one chance.

It was unlikely.

Nathan barely nodded at her encouraging words. His thick chestnut hair arced from its side part in a strange bed-head wave, though she knew he had showered this morning. He texted furiously by the open hatchback.

Kenyon and Oberlin were out of reach, but maybe there was a respectable Ohio Six institution that would open its doors to their sports-broadcasting-obsessed son and give him a decent liberal arts education.

Deep down, though, she knew the solution was right in front of them—or just up the road, in Grand Rapids: Grand Valley State was a Division II sports powerhouse, an "easy" school to get into according to an uncomfortably blunt online rating site, where Nathan would probably get the chance to call some games. The Promise Scholarship meant free tuition. Nathan himself had never brought it up—he was so sensitive to her standards in all things that maybe he was afraid to—but she knew he'd received a packet of info he had opened and saved on his dresser. Maybe he wasn't even aware of how perfect it would be for him. All she had to do was accept its low status on the great totem pole of higher ed, stop helicoptering, and let Nathan live his own life.

In the meantime, she just hoped he would notice the hatchback needed closing. But he kept texting, now drifting toward his side of the car.

Stay. I give up, she almost said. She slammed the hatchback closed and moved in to hug him.

"Bye, Mom," he murmured, briefly separating his thumbs from his screen so he could embrace her almost without touching, as if she were coated with wet paint.

"Bye-bye, dear," Ryan said, with something like pre-Emma irony, ducking into the car without looking at her. She waved back, making a lopsided face. She surmised he was sick of her and needed some time away. Doors slammed, the brake lights came on. She had to get out of the way so they could roll down the driveway and proceed to Ohio.

They made the turn that took them from her view.

It was early Sunday afternoon. Like something played on a synthesizer, the electronic buzz of a cicada rose up, plateaued, slowly thinned, stopped. There was no answering buzz, no symphonizing of many rising and falling buzzes. She couldn't remember ever hearing just one cicada before. In all directions up and down her street, the old trees and the newer trees stood perfectly still, their leaves inert, as if they had nothing to do.

The urge to sit in the grass by the driveway was very strong, but she worried if she lowered herself, she might never rise again. Nevertheless, she sat. The grass was short and thick. Ryan had been obsessive about the lawn this summer, watering and cutting more than usual. She lay back on the grass and crossed her ankles. Gravity pulled her hair down past her ears. She stared at the unstirred leaves well above her, some hunter green, some India green; saw clouds through branches almost unmoving against a bright sky. Her goals were 1) to not cry 2) to get up as soon as possible. She held off crying, but she couldn't move. *Don't be the crazy bereaved mom,* she told herself. *You're in public. This looks like a melodramatic cry for help.* But she resisted the lurching frantic desire to scramble to her feet and escape the clutches of public shame and possibly endless stasis. She closed her eyes, as if to blanket herself in privacy.

Ryan and Nathan would arrive in Springfield, Ohio, this evening. They would visit Wittenberg first thing Monday morning, then arc up through the heart of the Buckeye state: Ohio Wesleyan, Denison, Kenyon, Wooster, Oberlin, doing two schools a day. Then they would stop in Ann Arbor on Thursday on their way back. The house was hers until then, with book club Wednesday night. All she had to do was get up and get back in there.

She had let things get to a very tenuous place with Ryan, and now here he was, headed for Kenyon, her alma mater, which, amazingly after all these years, happened to be the last place she'd experienced the disintegration of a long-term relationship.

Kevin—rich, witty, tall, dark, and handsome poet from Oxford, Mississippi.

Prizewinning Kevin. Fucking Kevin.

She had never known a man with so many clothes and shoes and glasses, which he assembled into coherent costumes: preppy, punk, glam, hippie. In winter, he wore a bushy mustache and a black snowmobile suit, like an aspiring Bond villain. They met in Classical Mythology fall of her sophomore year. He wrote poems about her and encouraged her to write as well. He made a big deal out of her golden eyes, nicknaming her Hattie, short for Hathor, after the Egyptian goddess who was the female counterpart to the sun god Ra, often depicted as a yellow eye, helping him rule and create. She loved Kevin's tight chest. She even loved how he smelled.

Aside from his lying and cheating ways, what had ultimately bothered her most about Kevin, and which stuck like a splinter in her self-concept even now, was his trick of turning whatever she cared about into a personal problem she was having. If she went to an anti-apartheid rally, he asked her if she felt alienated, set apart. When she wondered what could be done about the poverty she saw in the little towns around Gambier, he asked if there were things she lacked but felt she deserved. If someone pissed her off, he might observe: we are often most critical of others when their faults remind us of our own. Insidious prick!

Still, she couldn't end it herself, which bothered her to this day. In their early days, he had seemed perfect—talented and mesmerizing—and why couldn't she have that again?

Ryan had been an antidote to Kevin and the other tall, dark, and handsome men she'd dated. She'd met him during her first year of art history grad school in Champaign-Urbana, on a coed Ultimate Frisbee team. He could be sweet, seemed wholly guileless compared to Kevin, had a good sense of humor and no designs on Parnassus.

But maybe the love and comfort she felt with him took the edge off of her own ambition. She had been working in the Krannert Museum on campus, and when she graduated, she stayed on, moving from Assistant Curator to Curator of Contemporary and Modern Art. That job could have been a springboard for a position at a big coastal institution or an even better university museum, but she'd gotten intrigued when the KIA job came open. She would be in charge of all the collections, yet still get to do the hands-on work she loved. Kalamazoo wasn't exactly the center of the art world, but she knew there were thousands of art history majors and PhDs who would kill for a job like this.

For a long time, that had been enough. But that was a side of grief people rarely talked about—how it pulled back the curtain on other losses, mistakes, regrets, until you found yourself lying half-dead on your front lawn on a Sunday afternoon.

She heard the sound of dog tags approaching on the sidewalk. She sat up. Thank god, she didn't know this woman with her enormous, cream-furred dog. The dog looked at her frankly, then looked away, sniffed at grass on the edge of the sidewalk.

"Gosh, what a beautiful day!" she managed to say to the woman, as if she were so overcome by it she was lying in the grass like a six-year-old.

"Lovely," the woman said brightly, but her eyes slid by. She was a little older. A woven sun hat sent dots of light swimming across her sturdy face with a disco ball effect. She dangled a huge load of dog shit in a blue plastic Sunday *Times* bag. Claire looked away as woman and dog made their slow progress past the neighbor's box hedge. When they were out of view, embarrassment helped her to get up and go into the shadow-cooled house.

And a good thing, too, because it was time for the book club reminder email. She hadn't attended the June meeting, but she had assured everyone she was looking forward to hosting her turn in August. Asking Mike had been in the back of her mind since she'd last seen him at work.

It hadn't been an easy conversation but it had been a good one, different than her conversations about Emma with Ryan and her female friends. Somehow she found herself being more honest with Mike. Getting him back in the book club might revitalize the group, might convince Ryan to attend, as well as some of the other husbands who skulked on the book club's periphery. It would signal she wasn't going to shrink into her grief and show Mike that the neighborhood didn't hold his divorce against him. He must have worried whether Anne had aired any of their dirty laundry at book club. She hadn't, except once when she'd said Mike was turning into a "temperance crusader." No one had responded, maybe because the amount she drank had been noticeable for years. For Claire, this only confirmed that Mike was a good egg.

She consulted last month's email to refresh her sense of the list. Anne Kovacs was still there. She deleted akovacs@gmail.com and added mkovacs@gmail.com. She doubted anyone would notice, unless Mike showed up. Then they would understand the substitution: the old divorced-spouse switcheroo.

After sending the group email, and a separate personal invite to Mike, she felt free. The relief over not having to cook was significant. Eating leftovers was the least she could do with a famine raging somewhere. She had things to catch up on at work, but she wandered into the TV room where pieces of the Sunday *Times* sprawled across the coffee table. In the Business section, a market strategist warned that the bond market and the stock market were sending mixed signals. The Fed was looking to "unwind its balance sheet." She remembered Mike talking about that.

She investigated the broken window. The jagged remnants had been cleared, but a new pane of glass had not been installed. It didn't matter, it was just the start of August. She ran her finger along the edge of the frame, expecting to be cut by an unseen micro-shard.

"Emma, I'm sorry," she said aloud.

No emotion welled up. She didn't know why she'd said it.

When she didn't hear an answer, she lay on the couch and, like a bum on a park bench, pulled the Business section over her for a blanket and took a nap.

15.

Her follow-up email said it was okay if he didn't have time to read *Tree of Smoke;* the book club was a welcoming group, and it was "good social time." Mike thanked her for the invitation, said he hoped to make it. He didn't say he would go for sure because he saw how insane going would be—yet he knew he would go.

Immediately after he sent his reply, Mike drove the replicar to This Is a Bookstore and bought a copy of the novel. He believed shopping at an independent bookseller banked him only a speck of redemption against his mountain of guilt, but he needed constant positive offsets to tolerate being with himself.

His emotions careened pitifully as he braved *Tree of Smoke*. Vietnam was a moral and human catastrophe that dwarfed his accidental killing of two people. How did LBJ and Westmoreland and McNamara and all the rest live with such tsunamis of blood crashing over their heads? And yet, sadly, he could no longer read history with a pure sense of moral righteousness. It was another unfortunate consequence of committing a hit-and-run.

The only major female character in the novel so far— Kathy Jones, a Canadian nurse and aid worker in the Philippines—made him think of Claire: her missionary husband disappears and ends up murdered under mysterious circumstances. Except the novel suggests Kathy has suffered some kind of profound world-historical wound, whereas Claire was merely the victim of *him*. Maybe Claire would make a telling comment about Kathy Jones, revealing her attitude toward bereavement, sacrifice, or life's random shittiness, and he could use this remark to culture some kind of resolve, to confess or take some other step towards her.

The night before book club, it took a third beer to spill him towards sleep on the sectional. He was avoiding the master bedroom ever since a week ago when he'd hallucinated a person hitching themselves up on their forearms on the ledge outside the window as if preparing to climb in, accompanied by scriffling sounds like a mouse rooting around in the wall. He chalked the vision up to extreme sleep deprivation. Exercise, a beer or two, and TV comedy helped him to drop off, but usually he woke up way too early and couldn't get back to sleep.

He was lucky to be on summer vacation. He couldn't function, but looming Planning and Budget white paper notwithstanding, he didn't have to accomplish anything today. All he had to do on this particular Wednesday was get dressed, get some cherries from the grocery store, get caught up in watching the garage out the master bedroom window in case Anne or some stranger attempted a break-in, get caught up in watching out the front bedroom window in case a detective pulled up, and get his ass three blocks to Claire's by 7:30.

While he was watching out the front window, a UPS truck raced to a stop at his curb. An incredibly fit and tan man bounded out carrying a large, rectangular box, and ran up to his front porch. He rang the bell, but by the time Mike opened his front door, the truck had roared away.

It was the headlight assembly. He was glad he had seen the driver. Now he could monitor whether it was the same one every time.

He had time to install the assembly, but instead he imagined being outed and stabbed to death by a ring of highly literate women wielding shrimp forks.

•

Carrying a glass bowl of cherries on top of a paperback copy of the book, Mike walked to Claire's house. The sidewalks were a luxurious distance from the street and

Tandem

undisturbed by the roots of massive oaks and maples growing in between. Shadows had climbed high up the trunks, but sunlight still blazed the top leaves and made long glowing stripes across a few large lawns. The temperature and light breeze were perfect. He passed well-kept hundred-year-old Craftsman- and Colonial-style houses, most of which had third-story windows.

He had scored a valuation coup by getting one of the smallest houses in a generally upscale neighborhood, but his cedar shingles needed a paint job even more than the garage, his tiny lawn was afflicted with weeds and mysterious bare patches, and his cramped attic was a no-man's land of calcified bats and blown insulation; he resolved to pull his meager spread into shape. He dreamed of belonging to his neighborhood again on clean terms.

In the front yard of Claire's bungalow was the usual dark-green-and-yellow sign: *One Human Family: We Support Refugees and Our Muslim Neighbors*. On the porch stood a tin paper box with a sunflower hand-painted on it.

He rang the bell but no one came to the door. He let himself in.

It turned out Claire was just detaching herself from the gathering in the living room and welcomed him. "How lovely," she said, taking the bowl of cherries. Rather than join the women chatting loudly, he went the opposite direction, following Claire into the dining room where the table was crowded with potluck offerings ranging from a veggie platter to a bowl of M & M's. Three bottles of wine were running low and reinforcements stood behind them. He hadn't wanted to be one of the first to arrive, but maybe he had taken that too far. Claire set down his bowl right next to another glass bowl of cherries and burst out laughing. "That's me with the cherries, too!" she said. She invited him to help himself and went back to the living room.

After filling a glass of red wine past a decorous level and stocking a small plate of cheese cubes and M & M's, he took the last seat in the living room, on a dining room chair wedged between a sofa and the fireplace.

Mozina

"Hey, everyone, it's our prodigal son, Mike!" Claire exclaimed. "Let's welcome him back to the Boiling Waters Book Club!"

People laughed and said hey. "Boiling Waters" was apparently one translation of the Potawatomi word for "Kalamazoo." Colonialist appropriation or proper land acknowledgment? Mike couldn't tell, but he sensed a hardcore earnestness that was vaguely frightening.

He was embarrassed to be the only man present. His brow wrinkled when he realized the odds of him making a "fox in the hen house" joke were not zero. The women seemed to range from their early forties to their mid-sixties. Claire performed some introductions and he realized he had seen some of them around, even vaguely remembered a few from book club meetings of yore. They were mostly professors from Western, the state university near his little college, mixed with a few other neighbors. He nodded his head and smiled at everyone.

A free-for-all of conversations rattled and spun in twos and threes around the circle. Mike was partnerless. The woman to his right, Betty, the owner of Betty's Bakery, was tete-a-teting with her neighbor on the other side. Mike observed the iron fireplace tools hanging in a rack at his left knee. Of course, no one was saying anything about Emma—or maybe things had been said before he arrived?—but people were probably watching their words with Claire. He had blundered across another Rubicon of awfulness: should he be caught or confess, all of these women would have an irresistible story to tell about how he'd socialized on false pretenses with the mother of the young woman he had killed. He was silently stupefied by the fact of his presence in Claire's living room when she spoke up: "So what'd you guys think of the book?"

The responses broke into two camps: those who grooved on its sterling literariness and profound subject matter—Mary, an English prof, declared it "a cross between Conrad and Pynchon," and explained why—and those, including the baker, who complained about having to keep track of so many different characters and times and locations. Everyone acknowledged its unremitting sadness, which led to a pained debate about whether books needed to be so sad.

After twenty minutes, discussion evolved into stories of relatives who fought and even died in the war. Cheryl, a svelte older woman in a dress plus leggings, had been an undergrad at Madison during the Sterling Hall bombing, and her anger over the war, which seemed somehow preserved in her many waving metal wrist bangles, was undiminished. Claire recited PTSD statistics for Iraq and Afghanistan vets and decried the poor data on Vietnam service people. Mike's general knowledge of the war turned out to be irrelevant. He knew male silence was always a good strategy in a group like this.

Once they decided on the October book—Eula Biss's *On Immunity*—things shifted back to general party mode. Mike asked any woman who tripped into range what was going on with her. He was relieved when no one asked him about himself. Somehow he felt this would play in his favor if the truth came out: *We didn't think he had anything to say!* Before he knew it, people were taking off. He didn't want to be seen lingering. Beyond Claire's introduction, no one had said anything about his sudden return to Boiling Waters, and he didn't want to foment gossip as Claire's book-club boy toy by staying until the end or offering to help clean up, especially because it had emerged that Ryan and Nathan were away on a college tour. So he abruptly said his goodnights—making a point of thanking Claire with just a little nod, his hands behind his back—and slipped out.

•

He was into his third episode of *Parks and Recreation*, nursing a goodnight beer, and beginning to see Claire as a Leslie Knope figure (all of her book comments had amounted to some form of veterans' advocacy), when he heard a knock on his front storm door.

He convulsed like a clumsily worked puppet until he was sitting bolt upright on the edge of the sectional. It was the police—who else would knock after dark?

Mozina

He headed into the dark living room, stepped around the headlight assembly box, which he hadn't yet moved to the garage, and peered out a front window, bracing for a parked cruiser. He spied no vehicle and had no view of whoever was on the porch slab.

He heard the telltale sounds of someone opening the storm door. It might be a burglar, but he didn't have a peephole. He threw the deadbolt and opened the door. Crouched over, his nearly full bowl of cherries balanced on her thigh as she placed his copy of *Tree of Smoke* on the threshold, was Claire.

16.

"Hi," she said, straightening up. "Sorry, but I didn't want to steal your things."

"Oh, not at all," Mike said. "It's a Hungarian custom to leave behind personal items, as a tribute to the host. My great-grandfather left his dentures if he had an especially good time."

"Ha! Well, I guess it's an Irish custom to return them too late at night."

"No, it's very nice of you. Thank you! Come on in!"

Her hesitation melted quickly. There was no foyer, so she stepped straight into the living room. He took the book and cherries from her, set them on an end table, and turned on a floor lamp, revealing thick dust on every surface. Beyond the living room, on the other side of a two-way staircase landing, there was a dimly lit room filled with a brown sectional. The house had otherwise been completely dark, a miasma of loneliness drifting between the rooms. She had been right to invite him to book club.

"Hey, thanks for including me," he added. "It was a fun night."

"Yeah, it was a pretty good discussion."

"That's a tough book—I mean, I haven't read it all yet, but that's a tough war to think about." He gave a head shake.

"Oh god, they're all so bad."

"And it's even worse when they don't have to happen. The big mistake was in '56."

"'56?"

"Yeah, you know, when the French left, there were supposed to be unification elections, except they didn't happen. Eisenhower could have finessed it, but he punted when the Soviets opposed the American plan." As he got going, he rotated his hands forward in a sort of dog paddle. His fingers were long and knuckly, with poorly kept nails that needed a trim. "When Ho got screwed out of the elections, which he probably would have won, he had no choice but to unify the country by force."

She was touched by how awkward he was delivering this speech, yet she craved substantive discussions of significant events.

"But what about the Domino Theory?"

He explained how Ike could have leaned into his military credibility, played Ho as more of a nationalist than a communist. "But, yeah, like you said, once Ho started fighting under the banner of socialism, the Domino Theory meant we had to get more involved." He shrugged.

"I thought you said you're an econ prof?"

"Well, economics drives everything, but history's even more mind-blowing. The twentieth century was such a catastrophe!"

"It's like modernity made the human race crazy for a while, right?" she ventured. "But have you read Steven Pinker?"

Claire loved talking about Steven Pinker, because he showed that things had gotten better in so many ways over the centuries, even though we didn't realize it. It'd been too long since she'd had a chance to talk about him, and maybe now she went overboard describing how the feminization of culture had decreased violence. Mike was such a good listener.

"I'm sorry, do you want to sit?" Mike asked. "I've been so into talking."

"Me too. Um." She visored her hand on her forehead and looked down. She wanted to stop noticing his shoulders, but it would look strange to cover her eyes altogether. She had already been reckless talking herself into returning his stuff tonight. Who knew what would happen if she sat? "You know what? I really should be getting home. I have to work tomorrow."

"Of course."

"I just wanted to give you your stuff," she said, looking up into his eyes, which were calm and focused. They had the weird benevolence she had noticed before. The sincerity made her nervous, but in a good way.

"Well, let me walk you home." He stepped into some loafers sitting next to a large, unopened box on the floor. She sympathized with his inability to take care of basic things.

"Oh, but then who will walk you home?"

He laughed. "We should talk game theory some time. But tonight I'll take the risk for making you come over here."

She checked her phone. It was 11:45! They'd been talking forever.

"Sure. Thanks," she said, feeling shy.

Outside, over the soft sparkling trills of crickets, another insect made raspy calls, like a pepper mill twisted back and forth. The medley was like something from a meditation CD. Claire wondered if her feeders meant the birds ate fewer insects, with the survivors helping to make this natural music.

"What's that sound, besides the crickets?" she asked.

They listened for a few steps.

"I think those are katydids," Mike said. "Katie did, Katie didn't—that's how the sound made the name, according to my dad."

Claire could imagine the scene—parent and child outside in the backyard on a summer night—and it choked her up a bit.

"It's kind of a beautiful neighborhood," Mike said. "I didn't give it enough credit for years, but it's damn nice."

The air was pleasantly warm. There were not many lights burning in the large-but-not-too-large houses on Grand. The half-moon—bright white against the black sky—posed over the middle of the street. She didn't know if it was waxing or waning.

"If you could live anywhere in the world, where would you want to live?" she asked.

"Oh gosh, right here is fine. What do you mean?"

He had such a wicked deadpan, she almost doubted he was joking. "I mean, god forbid, if you couldn't live in Kalamazoo."

"Ah, well, probably D.C."

"Where the Fed is."

"Yep. Or New York City. Or Thailand. Some place with elephants. How about you?"

"You might like India. My friend and I went to Kerala, way in the south. There're wild herds not too far from where we stayed, but we didn't get out there."

"That sounds awesome. So India for you?"

She didn't want to bring up Ayurveda. She didn't want to admit how much she had hoped the India trip would change things.

"Oh, no, it was just for my friend. She was getting some training to open a yoga studio. I know it sounds super privileged and white and everything."

"Oh, I don't know, travel with the right attitude is good for the world. We need to get to know each other."

For a second, she thought he was talking about the two of them and not about all the citizens of Earth.

"Actually, in the mountains or on a coast," she said, returning to the question.

"And yet here we are."

"Talking like college freshmen. I know, I know—I started it!"

It wasn't as if she wanted to do her college years over. She had been immature, just figuring things out, and Kevin and the other men were assholes, just figuring things out, and she had gotten over it, mostly.

They turned up Prospect, her street.

"It's not *bad* to talk like this," he said. "Just some possibilities."

"Like we have any left?" she joked, but she couldn't resist glancing at him. He didn't look at her. She felt an old itch to be out in the world in a bigger way, the way Kevin was, with all of his books on Amazon; she checked periodically, hoping for signs of faltering that never appeared. Maybe he'd soured her on ambition too soon, made her think grander dreams were only for jerks. There was a sudden dizzying feeling that she had misled her life, didn't belong in her own family, had fallen into a stupor, only to have Emma's death awaken her.

"You never know," Mike said brightly.

Her heart was accelerating, as if they were in a boat skimming down a river: the sense of speed was irresistible even as she sensed a precipitous waterfall up ahead. She couldn't speak.

"What a fun night at book club!" he finally exclaimed with mock exuberance. He had already said something similar, and she wondered if he was getting nervous.

"I think so," she said. She was growing more nervous herself. Up ahead, she saw the dark bay window on the side of her empty bungalow. Mike was too kind. She needed to keep her head.

They stopped at the walk leading to her front door, just outside a cone of streetlight.

"Thank you for putting that up, by the way," he said, pointing at her pro-refugee sign. "I really should have one up myself."

"Oh, just go to the website!" She gestured toward the bottom of the sign.

"I should do that." He looked down at her and smiled a perfect smile.

"Well, thanks, good night." She moved to hug him. Men and women hugged hello and good-bye in their social circle, and Mike was definitely in her circle now. He bent down and hugged her back. He was lean; his broad back had no softness to it. The momentum of some inner current intensified her hug—maybe it was her way of saying they were both going through something, sharing their burdens and their lives in constructive ways. But her sustained hold on him seemed to pry loose a deeper hold on herself. Tears sprang to her eyes. She let Mike go and took an abrupt step back.

"Are you okay?" he asked.

She shook her head and let herself cry.

"I'm going kind of crazy," she said, looking past him up at the Browns' house across the street, at the dark second-floor windows.

"Oh, oh," he murmured. "I'm sorry."

She reined in her tears, but her thoughts zoomed everywhere at once. "We *did* have good times together, Emma and me," she said with a plaintiveness that embarrassed her as she heard it. "I only remember the tough stuff. Why?"

She looked up at him. A deep vertical crease had formed between his eyebrows. He squinted like someone experiencing a splitting headache. Then his face relaxed.

"Maybe you're protecting yourself?" he offered.

"I wish I could," she said. He wasn't teasing or appraising her from a remove, as Ryan often did. He seemed to be exactly where she was.

She wanted to be held so badly, she embraced him again in the almost blind way a child throws themselves into the arms of a parent, assuming intimacy and affection. He accepted her embrace, holding her firmly. He felt so strong and steady and alive, enough to carry her to a whole other life.

She pressed against him, lifted her face, to say something, to kiss him. He lowered his head toward her, but then he straightened up and pulled away.

"Claire—you're an awesome person." He spoke with a strange choppiness. "Do you really want this?"

His question only confirmed he cared for her and wanted what was best for her. She pulled him back to herself. This time, when she raised her lips to him, they kissed.

"Let's go inside," she murmured, taking his hand.

They floated up to her front door. The starfish of keys in her palm pulsed like a living thing. The tip of a key was its most accessible part but not what you wanted to hold in order to use it. She dropped the whole ring.

Finally, they were inside her house, the door closed.

In the dark foyer, Mike took her in his arms.

She jumped up and scissored her legs around his waist, wrapped her arms around his neck.

Tandem

Mike laughed and they kissed.

She cupped Mike's Easter Island face with her hands, and he held her up with apparent ease. Soon it was time for a bed, but she couldn't take him upstairs. She spread a quilt on a couch in the living room where the book club had gathered. Mike was tender and attentive to a fault, until she couldn't wait any more and pulled him on to herself.

17.

They sat at the small kitchen table in the back of the house, sharing a bowl of vanilla ice cream. The house was still dark, but an alley light beyond the backyard cast a bright window on the hardwood floor.

"What's your favorite ice cream?" Claire asked.

"Häagen-Dazs, Vanilla Swiss Almond," he said, though this wasn't true. "What's your favorite music?"

"Impossible."

"Beatles vs. Stones?"

"Beatles."

"Pink Floyd vs. Led Zeppelin?"

"Neither."

He laughed, but it was excruciating to be in her presence. He felt like a bank robber waiting for all the money to get stuffed into the bags before he could start running.

"I've thought about you for a long time," he said.

"Same," Claire whispered.

They didn't talk too much longer after they finished their ice cream. When he said he should probably get going, Claire nodded. "Yeah, we have to sleep at some point."

She led him to the front door, where they hugged and he kissed the top of her head.

"I'll email you," she said, holding one of his hands. Then she laughed. "That sounds strange! I don't know why."

"New things are always strange."

"Good night, Mike."

Even if Ryan and the cops were waiting for him outside, he would always have the way she just said his name.

Tandem

There was piercingly naïve love in her voice, of a kind Mike had never expected to hear again. He wondered if it was possible to freely accept that love.

"Good night," he said. He squeezed her hand and let go.

He walked home slowly, listening to the crickets and the katydids. He remembered the campfire near the Boundary Waters in Minnesota, just after his father got in financial trouble, on a vacation they could no longer afford, his father saying, "Hear that? Katie did, Katie didn't. Katie did, Katie didn't." Katie did, and everything was different.

By the time he stepped into his house, he had a ferocious case of the munchies. Claire had put so little ice cream in the bowl, he first thought she was just serving herself. Then they'd shared it, and she hadn't been shy about getting more than her half, which had been annoying. But he had tamped down his annoyance. In fact, he decided she would never annoy him. He had been too easily annoyed by Anne, which had driven her to drink and ruined everything. While a frozen pepperoni pizza baked, he sat on the sectional with the remote in his hand, unable to resume watching the *Parks and Recreation* episode Claire's arrival had interrupted.

Having sex with his victim's mother did seem pathologically shitty. But when she had pressed against him in her sleeveless top and shorts, none of her sexless tics were on display; it had simply been too long since he'd been with a woman. Maybe there was no way out, he'd thought as she'd led him to her front door—only a way elsewhere. And maybe not all was lost. Maya Angelou wisely said people won't remember what you did, just how you made them feel, and maybe making Claire feel loved could atone for what he did.

In any case, he no longer had a choice. Confessing was no longer possible. If she found out now, she would probably actually kill him, Steven Pinker be damned. At least he was finally done agonizing about that.

He had his first reasonable night's sleep since the accident.

18.

The day after her stunning night with Mike, work was busy, which she welcomed. She was wired, not tired. Chul Hyun Ahn himself was in town to pack up the light box exhibit. Normally she would just work with Marta or Scott, their trusty preparator, to deinstall a gallery, but Ahn always traveled to personally assemble and disassemble *Tunnel*.

While she crated pieces with Scott and ran them to the loading dock on a flat truck with rubber wheels, Chul Hyun and his lithe assistant Dan took *Tunnel* apart, cinder block by cinder block, leaving only a clean blank space on the floor where even she had almost come to believe a hundred-foot shaft into the ground had been.

Mid-afternoon, the U.S. Art truck was loaded and gone, Chul Hyun and Dan were on the road in their rental car, and Claire returned to the empty gallery. The only remains of the exhibit were the outlets and hooks on the walls; Scott would take care of those.

Now the walls were as bare as the walls in Emma's room. The museum had hosted the Ahn exhibit long enough for Emma to have attended the opening over spring break. She had lingered in front of *Forked Series #7* in her flat sandals and jeggings, with her long straight hair flowing down her back, arms crossed on her chest, as she seemed to lose herself in the slats of light that layered away into opposite corners like stairs or the panels of blinds.

Now it was just a blank wall.

She had dreaded this moment for weeks. This exhibit had been a place to find respite in the lighted empty spaces that always dimmed into the illusory distance. She hadn't known what she'd do without it.

Fuck your moment of ritual sadness—the thought flamed through her mind like a Molotov cocktail.

She raised her hands to her face and then extended them overhead, reaching as high as she could, squeezing her eyes shut.

Then she looked across the room where Mike had faced *Forked Series #23*. Maybe she had come together with Mike just in time.

"I'm sorry, Emma," she whispered. She headed upstairs to email her lover.

Easier thought than done. She composed various drafts—some effusive, some chatty and familiar, some just checking in—but couldn't figure out the right tone.

A text came from Ryan: *Going well. Home for dinner. Great*, she texted back. *See you soon!*

She had become complicit over the last few years in the ridiculous exclamation point inflation over-running all communications. This particular usage seemed especially offensive, but for now she had no choice but to perform her role. She couldn't concentrate. She packed up early and headed home.

•

Making dinner was necessary and involved her hands and a less addled part of her brain. Red beans and rice.

She chopped onion and green pepper and celery, bracing herself for Ryan's return.

He should not have called out her shit the day their daughter died. That was inexcusable. He should not have thrown the remote. Who did he think he was, with his reluctant apologies and his sarcasm? In the end, he'd backed her into an emotional corner. She'd had to stand up for herself.

And even if standing up for herself felt more like careening down a steep hill on the front seat of a tandem bike, with her heart in her throat and Mike riding shotgun, that didn't mean she had to lose control, or even that her marriage was necessarily over. She would have to research what third-wave feminists said about extra-marital sex. She would listen to some TED talks on the subject. She doubted it was as cut-and-dried as she had once thought.

Still, there had been moments today when she was overwhelmed by what she had done. She was tempted to ingest a deadly amount of her yoga mat disinfectant spray and end it all. She couldn't figure out how to email her lover.

Then Nathan came through the back door into the kitchen, heedlessly biffing his rolling suitcase around corners and on each step going upstairs until she called his name in a way that made him stop that. Ryan hung up his Cubs hat and put his keys in a bowl on the counter.

"The Ohio Six have been deep-sixed," he announced wearily.

"Good to see you," she said, smiling. She hugged him as if nothing were between them.

"Same here, oh wife of mine."

He seemed surprised and pleased by the warmth of her welcome. She was afraid she'd overdone it.

•

Dinner conversation was all about the trip. Nathan didn't offer much. People were "nice," tours were "good," food was "pretty good." "They're all down with being vegetarian," he explained. It gradually emerged that only Michigan had a real broadcast journalism department.

Nathan's report suggested the Ohio Six had been a useless detour, an exercise in appeasing his parents, especially Claire. Even though Ryan had planned the trip behind her back, she felt responsible for it. She was Ms. Liberal Arts College. It was like forcing Emma to go to KAMSC all over again.

"What about Grand Valley?" she asked. "Have you thought of that?"

"Sure," Nathan said tentatively.

"Maybe they'd let you call some games?"

He barked a laugh. "Wow, Mom, I can't even—they'd *never* let a student call a real game. Dick Meredith's been doing their football and basketball for 20 years!"

"They were pretty encouraging at U of M, weren't they, Slugger?" Ryan pitched in. He lifted his dark beer bottle.

"I'll never get in there," Nathan said into his plate.

"Don't say that," she murmured.

"But, yeah, Grand Valley would be great—if I don't get into U of M."

"Sounds like good choices," Claire said. "For sports broadcasting," she added, flaying her own soul. But let her soul be flayed—sports play-by-play was what he cared about, as depressing and inexplicable as that was.

Nathan replied by shoveling food into his mouth at a rate that suggested he couldn't be more at peace with the direction of his life. He had served himself the meat version of the red beans and rice, maybe by mistake—she'd diced the andouille sausage into tiny bits, like someone making confetti out of a damning document. She couldn't remember the last time he'd tucked in like that, but it had to be before Emma's death.

She had been so focused on Emma and Mike and her crumbling marriage that it took a moment for it to dawn on her that she was essentially done with Nathan as his mother, this very instant. The big moment had snuck up on her, but it was unmistakable. She had let go. And maybe, in a roundabout way, Mike had helped loosen her grip on her family, and that wasn't completely awful, for she had always annoyed them. She put her spoon down and sat back in her chair. The napkins in their holder became a blurry white square. She picked one out, held it against her eyes, then wiped her mouth. These transitions were like skydiving: one instant, you were in an airplane; the next, you were plummeting, hoping your chute would open. No one seemed to notice her tearing up. Around their house, crying had become as routine as dinner itself.

After Nathan went upstairs, Ryan made quick work of the dishes between slugs of a second beer. He seemed to be in a pretty good mood. She wondered if he'd reflected favorably on his life, on their marriage, while on the tour, or if he was simply displaying the surface affability that was his default personality, while inside he was as disdainful of her as ever. She wandered into the open space near the front door, where she had climbed Mike, scissoring her legs around his waist. A wave of guilt came toward her, but she raised her hand like Wonder Woman, and it broke around her.

In the TV room she stood by the window with the missing pane. Any reminder of Ryan's flaws helped her stay strong.

"Yeah, that's next on my list," Ryan said, entering the room.

"I wasn't thinking about it," she said.

This was obviously a lie, but Ryan chose to call it out with only a beat of silence.

"I missed you," Ryan said, in a different voice. "Every school, I was thinking, *Claire could sell this so much better.*"

She made herself smile.

He studied her with his sad slanted eyebrows. "Come here, you."

She went to him. He held her and she put her cheek on his shoulder.

"We've got to stop beating ourselves up," he said.

"Yes," she said. She assumed he meant "beating each other up" but couldn't say it.

"You don't deserve that," he added.

"You, too," she said.

"I'm gonna take a shower. Want to come up?"

•

After the sex, Ryan sighed and turned onto his back, like a man who had passed through the Valley of the Shadow but nevertheless gone on to reach the mountaintop.

He lay on his pillow with his hands locked behind his head, and she lay against his side. The windows were open. It was not too warm. The sun was going down. She listened for birds.

Tandem

She didn't chastise herself for having sex with him—it was the price of the hiding place she still needed—but she told herself to notice how false and awful she felt right now. She loved another man more, and that changed everything.

"Thank you for taking Nathan on the tour," she said. "I feel OK with everything."

"Grand Valley?"

"Yeah, maybe the legendary Dick Meredith will take him under his wing."

"Oh, God, I'd hate to see what's actually under the wing of a guy like that."

He draped his arm around her, putting her under his own wing, apparently without irony.

"Mites, probably," he continued. "Or a lot of dander."

She made herself laugh. She could sense his answering smile through his shoulder.

"It's good that he's focused on what he wants," she said.

"Yeah, you're right." Ryan sighed.

Her ear was resting on his chest but not the side his heart was on. Still, she could hear it. Her eyes began running. She felt sick to her stomach.

When she felt a tear slide onto Ryan's chest, she started up, turned from him and wiped her cheeks. "I'm sorry," she said, "but I've got to go back to work."

"Right now?"

"I'm really behind on something." She stood up facing away from him and began dressing. "I'm still catching up and Teresa is not happy."

In minutes she was out of the house, and in a few minutes more she was unlocking the door to her museum, and a few minutes after that she was pressing send on an email which simply read: *How can I see you?*

19.

The Monday after making love to Claire in her living room, Mike drove the replicar to the KIA. He paid his five dollars and headed to the downstairs galleries.

He didn't cross paths with any other visitors. 3:54 PM and the museum was as unpeopled as the sky. He found his way to the last gallery, as instructed.

He heard the rapid clicking of approaching heels across the parquet floors. Claire entered the gallery without acknowledging him, projecting an aura of mania and distress. She passed through wide-open fire doors and out of the space. Mike followed her down a white cinder block hallway.

She walked so quickly her bob lifted off her neck, low pumps tattooing the concrete floor. She was wearing a long purplish-black velour jacket over what seemed to be a black one-piece outfit with leggings of a type Mike had never seen before. Was it a sex suit? Trailing behind, Mike smiled, a last moment to himself. She shook out her key ring and unlocked a random black metal door. She stepped inside and out of the way.

"Quick, get all the way in," she said with some asperity and a frantic hand motion. Mike felt scolded, but she was relatively new to the stresses of guilt and secrecy, so he forgave her.

Motion-activated florescent lights rippled on across the ceiling. The left side of the room: a long line of close-packed rolling walls hung with paintings; the right was cabinets and drawers. Panicked beeping emanated from a keypad. Claire closed the door and punched in a code. The beeping stopped. She took a deep breath with her back to Mike. Then she turned, her face transformed into silent glee. Mike laughed without sound and embraced her.

There was an old, cushioned gallery bench. They sat on it and made out for a while like teenagers. When it was time to get undressed, the bench made cuddling harder and other positions easier, which seemed fine with Claire.

It was strange to be in this bright space that smelled of old paper, getting intimate with someone he had hurt so badly and still hardly knew—strange enough to undermine his arousal. Yet eventually her pleasure swept the strangeness aside, until for several delirious moments, he almost believed only he could comfort her, because he had been the one to hurt her.

After they had dressed, Claire said, "Can I show you one of my favorites?"

From a locked cabinet, she removed a black hinged box like a slim briefcase. Inside was a plainly matted photograph.

"Georgia O'Keeffe and Eastborn Smith in Twilight Canyon," Claire said. "1964."

She placed it on an easel on top of the cabinet. O'Keeffe, in a spear of sunlight flying between dark canyon walls, stood facing the camera, reflected full-length in a pool of water. She was wearing a long pleated skirt, wide as a chest of drawers, a blouse, and a light jacket, dusty dowdy, like a nun in mufti. Smith stood in darkness, silhouetted against his sunlit portion of cliff, in the tip of the spear, wearing a backpack and hiking boots, facing away from her.

The picture seemed composed for maximum visual drama. He wondered if Claire saw herself as the hero of a would-be grand life, like O'Keeffe.

"It's like she's saying, 'I'm never out of place,'" he suggested. "'I live wherever my imagination lives.'"

Claire slipped her arm through his and leaned against his shoulder.

The touch of her head against his body made him think of Emma's head. He shivered and wanted to squirm away, but he didn't.

"Are you okay?" she asked.

"It's a dramatic picture," he said.

"She was seventy-seven. A year later, she finished her last great painting, *Sky Above the Clouds*. Then her eyesight went bad and she more or less stopped."

"Hmm," Mike said.

Claire was having some kind of moment. He knew a good lover would ask about it, but he was experiencing a sort of performance fatigue and couldn't quite make himself do it.

Attached to the wall in a plastic case was a measuring machine with two horizontal styluses inscribing lines on a vertical drum graph. Mike found graphs to be deeply comforting. The line had jumped slightly for both measurements.

Mike pointed. "Did we do that?"

Claire frowned. "Maybe." She stepped away and peered at the readouts. "I should have thought of that. If Derek asks, I'll figure out something to say."

"Maybe we can use my office some time? I've got a comfy chair."

This did not cheer Claire up. Mike considered it his job to make Claire happy, but that was not always easy; she tended to take things hard, it seemed.

"I love your world here," he said.

"I do, too. I just hope I don't get myself fired." She finally laughed.

Who might be passing in the hallway when they left the storage room? It didn't matter to him. Let him be known as a homewrecker; that would be a significant step up from drunk-driving murderer. But gossip mattered to Claire. How could he help her?

"I need to gather my strength before telling Ryan," Claire said, staring at O'Keeffe in the photograph. "Is that okay?" She braved a look at him.

Tandem

"Of course," he said, alarmed she was already thinking that way. What had he gotten himself into? Why did every action have consequences? "No rush."

Claire stowed the photograph, locked the cabinet, and straightened her scarf.

"Time to go, Love," she said quietly.

•

Mike was getting to the point where simply encountering a wheel-shaped object could remind him of his damaged Camry, which in turn could make his shoulders twitch and his hands reach for things that were not there.

They had agreed that going to each other's houses under any circumstances was out of the question for now. That gave him time. But Connor would be home in nine days, and the murder weapon needed to look once again like an old sedan mainly used for transporting groceries or taking road trips to Wisconsin to visit family.

Mike had cycled through so many possible lies about his Camrys that he had to write out on his legal pad *The Final True Histories of the Two Camrys* to get his latest stories straight: 1) he would tell Connor he bought the replicar from a used car dealer because he thought it would be funny if father and son had the exact same car; 2) he would finish restoring the missing parts to the murder weapon and then take it to a Toyota dealer in Battle Creek for the paint job. He would tell the dealer he had acquired the car through an impound auction, repaired what he could himself, but needed their painting expertise. Back when he'd first researched his impound lie, Mike had discovered that used car dealers and freelance car flippers did this all the time. But this story wouldn't fly at the dealer where he'd originally bought the car. Plus he wanted to get another county further east from Saugatuck, in case any police notice had gone out only to body shops in counties immediately adjacent to the one where the accident happened.

The day after he first made love to Claire, he'd unboxed the new headlight and found the two bolts in a sealed plastic

156

bag. He attached the tabs of the four circuit connectors to the back of each lamp in the headlight. He pushed the assembly into place, hearing the left clip catch right away. With a whap of his palm on the right side, the other clip snapped closed. After he screwed down the two bolts with a socket wrench, he felt an upsurge of mechanical bliss.

The rest of the parts had arrived in due course, and he affixed them to the Camry, paired with Claire trysts: custodian's closet at the KIA before the front bumper cover; after hours in his office in the Econ and Business suite, then hood and grill; after hours in his office in the Econ and Business suite (including a narrow escape when Hopper had shown up to make alarmingly intense phone calls with his door open), followed immediately by windshield and rear-view mirror. The windshield was tricky as a one-man job, but, thanks to the instructions of a generous YouTuber, he had used a suction cup and levered his other palm on the glass, laying the windshield precisely into place from one side.

That was quite a moment: the damaged Camry whole again, a mere ninety minutes after cuddling naked with Claire in his office comfy chair.

•

Later that night, after the narrow escape from Hopper's gaze and setting the windshield, at 1:17 AM, he got behind the wheel of the Camry he hadn't driven since he struck the tandem bicycle and its riders over four months ago. He started the car. It was the same tank of gas. The stale gas might not be good for the engine, but he admired its salient properties: cool and quiescent for as long as necessary, then perfectly volatile when sparked inside a cylinder. He had to resist the urge to rev the engine. People didn't appreciate gasoline—they were numb to it, in a way. But he did.

Once he made it down Grand and merged onto West Main, he felt safe and anonymous. He avoided I-94, taking M-96 past a massive metal recycling operation; a strip club; small, low-slung factories; and more than one truck rental operation. On such a blue-collar road, unpainted replacement car parts were almost *de rigueur*.

As he drove below the speed limit, his eyes bounced from tree line to tall weeds to bushes to ditches. He slowed at intersections, not trusting his right-of-way, scanning for the tell-tale flashes of something about to dart unexpectedly into his path. He wasn't surprised this little outing was aggravating his guilt. In his own defense, he reflected on how even the Catholic Church hadn't come close to the confession and atonement necessary in its centuries-long global sexual abuse scandal. Was guilt only for chumps? Maybe so. But he still couldn't shake it.

He fantasized about what he would do when he finally went berserk from the moral and emotional strain. He would scope out the Pope's next open-air mass in St. Peter's Square—maybe midnight mass on Christmas Eve. He would fly from Kalamazoo to Rome, his luggage stuffed with brand new sets of socks, underwear and dress shirts still in their plastic packaging, plus a note to be read afterwards by *la polizia*. Without claiming his bags, he would Uber directly to the Vatican and slowly elbow his way to the front of the crowd, apologizing for his rudeness the whole way. During the consecration of the host, while Francis directed his eyes heavenward, he would break through the rope line and charge the altar, bent on literally and figuratively grappling with His Holiness, only to be gunned down by the Swiss Guards before he could get close enough to whiff Francis' austere, incense-inspired cologne. The authorities would find the note in his luggage donating the new clothes to the poor, *courtesy of Pope Hypocrite*.

Suicide by papal security detail was full of the grim ironies Mike now favored, though it was possible the Swiss Guards were unarmed and would instead have to chase him down in their blue-and-orange jester outfits like stadium security guards corralling a streaker on the field. Either way, if the Vatican was the farcical face of confession and atonement, it was hard to believe he had ever been tempted by it.

No, fuck all that. Next stop on his moral odyssey: Cereal City. Kellogg's corporate. Tony's town.

•

After Mike checked in at the downtown Baymont, he slept very little, if at all.

At 5:00 AM, his next-door neighbor got up and took a shower while playing a country music station at a volume that allowed Mike to identify the genre but not make out a single lyric, or even if the singer was a man or a woman. When the shower ended, the tinny music kept playing. He began to suspect the person had nowhere to go at this hour. Maybe this was their idea of an awesome vacation? Wet hair neatly combed, they were probably sitting cross-legged in the chair by the window, wearing one of their favorite casual outfits, listening to music, pondering the complimentary breakfast buffet, which opened in eighty-three minutes. They would eat several bowls of Frosted Flakes, then tour the very factory that had manufactured them.

Mike decided that each minute that went by without this person leaving their room to do something that would justify getting up at 5:00 meant the universe wanted him insane. He laughed to himself at how angry he might be at his neighbor, at just how close he was to pounding so maniacally on this person's door they would never consider opening it; instead, the police would show up while he was still pounding and arrest *him* for disturbing the peace. Just as he was on the brink of putting this whole crime behind him!

Maddening.

He remembered how badly he'd felt when he'd yelled "fuck off" at the La Quinta housekeeper, and told himself to just hang on. Just don't mess up today. You're very close. To give his anger an outlet, he got out of bed and planked for seven and a half minutes, a new personal best. Then he opened his laptop, cued up "Let It Be" on Spotify, put in his ear buds (was he the only considerate person on Earth?!?), and played the song on repeat. It was a great song, and though Paul McCartney had written it, he felt it was his personal anthem. The Beatles also had a White Album and he had a White Paper—there were more connections between himself and Sir Paul than he had first imagined. Maybe he could deal with his life if he could exercise and play "Let It Be" on repeat all day, every day, starting at 5:00 AM.

•

    His vehicle approached, and the Sunshine Toyota service garage door magically lifted. A friendly person took his mileage and his keys and placed a paper mat on the floor of the murder weapon. He approached the Gold Team's desk and there was Marcia herself, looking just like her phone voice—young, no-nonsense, the build of a competitive powerlifter. When he had made the appointment over the phone, she had just asked him for the VIN. There were no prying questions, and it took all of his discipline not to work into the conversation all he had learned about impound auctions. He just wanted the paint to match as well as possible. Marcia assured him their experienced technicians shared his desire. It was a two-day process; the paint chemistry was non-negotiable, but who was arguing? Mike once again marveled at the marketplace's seamless provision of goods and services. They were doing exactly what he needed for a reasonable price while respecting his privacy. A classic arms-length bargain. It almost made him cry.

    Mike walked all the way back to the Baymont, crossing over a creek (*the* Battle Creek?!?) and a river along the way. He fell into a fantasy of writing a book about walking and Buddhism: *Strolling the Buddha*. Since the Buddha was always (usually?) depicted as seated, this would be a game-changer. All he had to do was research whether in fact the Buddha was never, or almost never, depicted as walking. Once he figured that out, the book would write itself.

    Other pedestrians, Buddhist or not, were sparse downtown. A shabby shoe repair shop, sandwiched between two sets of storefront windows lined with brown paper, infected him with a forlorn feeling, but he was not suicidal right now, which was interesting. Why wasn't he suicidal? Because he was loving Claire and building a new life with her.

Though he was hungry, it was still too early for lunch, so he returned to his room, and, at long last, felt his mind was free enough to work on the White Paper for Planning and Budget. His neighbor was still listening to country music— unless Mike was imagining that sound with help from the constantly running fan on the air conditioner? He pressed his ear to the wall and heard an underwater vacuum sound that could have been an external sound or some internal personal head sound audible only when his ear was closed against a wall in a room with a whirring air conditioner vibrating everything. In any case, he did not hear country music more clearly and wondered if he was hallucinating the whole aural assault.

But on the plus side, his phone didn't ring; no one knocked on his door with a few questions about the car he'd dropped off. The parameters of the White Paper, long shrouded in mystery and wrapped in neglect, came to him all at once. He outlined the whole thing in about ten minutes, made a list of elements he'd have to research and plug in, and then was so excited he couldn't sit still. He went back out on foot looking for a lunch spot and almost had to laugh when he spotted a cavernous but mostly unoccupied brew pub on Michigan Ave. He had a half-pound bacon cheeseburger, string fries, and two pints of a Black IPA brewed on the premises, which got him drunk. Claire loved him! His plan was working!

Back in his room, he napped until a phone call woke him up. It was Claire herself.

"Hey, Mike."

"What's up?"

"Where are you? Can you come by?"

Mike was a little taken aback. They had just been together yesterday evening. He knew he was taking a risk by having the paint job done in Battle Creek, because it would necessitate two nights away, which he didn't want to have to explain to Claire, but he had hoped he'd bought some time apart.

"Sorry, I'm getting my car serviced."

"You sound like you were asleep."

"This waiting room is super comfy. They pump new-car smell into it."

"What's wrong with your car?"

"Hopefully nothing. They've got it. It's just a routine service."

"Can I see you tonight?" It sounded as if her voice was breaking.

"Yeah, I meant to tell you last night that the next few days were going to be hard for me." This was true, but Hopper's appearance had thrown everything off. "What's up? Are you okay?"

"Every once in a while I lose it, Mike. Everything just seems so...out of control."

"Well, you're dealing with a lot."

Silence from Claire. He pictured her with her hand on top of her head, elbow akimbo, paused mid-hair rake.

"You don't have to do anything in particular," he added. "I want you to be happy—that's the most important thing. I hope you feel that."

"But what about you? Don't you want to be happy?"

"I am happy. I'm happy with you."

"But what if I can't be with you?"

"It'll be bad, it'll be super bad. But it'll be worse if you're not happy, so take it easy. I mean, we can take it easy. I mean, this is easier for me! I'm not trying to tell you what to do!"

"Can I see you tonight?"

Hadn't he just told her it was a rough week for him?

"Well, I'm supposed to be going out with my friend Dave to drink and work on this freaking White Paper for the Planning and Budget Committee; I've put it off the whole summer."

"Drinking and working?"

"This is how liberal academics operate."

"We've got family movie night tomorrow night—it's a Ryan thing—and Thursday is a bad day at the museum."

"We'll get together when we can and it'll be great. Talking is fun. It's a good thing to just talk, right? Connor's coming home for a few days, but I hope we can get together before that. My office or yours?"

"How about we get a room at the Radisson, early on Friday morning, before work?"

"Great idea!"

"I'll reserve a room for Thursday night. I can check in after this KIA event, but then sleep at home, and meet you there at, like, 7:00 AM?"

"Dang, that's genius. Let me give you my credit card info, so it won't show up on your bill."

"Oh, of course," Claire said.

He'd probably saved her from a rookie mistake. Mike found his wallet on the nightstand and read her all the numbers, as well as his street address, just in case.

"Oh, thank you," Claire said. "Thank you. Better go. Bye, Love!"

"Love you, Claire."

Her emotional turmoil, not to mention her investment in their relationship, was more than he'd bargained for, but that was simply the burden of love. Her happiness was his happiness. *Tu felicidad es mi felicidad.* What if we all treated each other as if we'd really hurt each other and were trying to make up for it? What if we all treated each other as if we owed each other some great debt? And weren't we always in each other's debt because we hurt each other so often, even when we didn't mean to? Yes, he was onto something. He was fusing economic and moral principles in a way that very possibly was revolutionary.

He knew his fellow macroeconomists would not accept the idea unless it was expressed in mathematical terms, so he scrawled an equation on a piece of Baymont stationery:

$$B*G = L$$

Bad Faith multiplied by Guilt equals Love.

It didn't capture everything—no series of equations could, of course—but it was a start.

Tandem

•

On Thursday, he checked out at the last minute, ate lunch at a McDonald's, and walked back to Sunshine to pick up the car. He knew it wasn't supposed to be ready until late afternoon; he just wanted Marcia to know he'd be in the waiting room. He found a cubicle away from the TV, pulled out his laptop, and toiled on the White Paper.

At some point, Marcia's voice roused him from his work trance: "Mr. Kovacs, your car is ready."

His skin hummed. His vision tunneled.

Waiting for them at the Gold Team's desk was a pony-tailed technician with tatted up arms and earlobes portaled with white gauges as big as quarters—you could see right through.

"Brandon did the work," Marcia said.

The firmness of Brandon's handshake suggested he considered himself an artist.

The three of them walked out to a lane next to the service garage. There was the murder weapon, gleaming in the sun. Mike knew exactly where to look to find contrasting color tones, but he could not tell.

"My god, how did you do it? Wasn't the rest of the car faded?"

"The sun leaches out yellow ochre," Brandon explained, "so you go lighter on yellow ochre. That's most of it."

Mike pulled out his wallet and gave Brandon a sixty-dollar tip.

"Great job, man! Amazing job!"

Marcia looked away.

"You're welcome," Brandon said.

Marcia had to stop Mike from getting in the car.

"Mr. Kovacs, we still need to settle up. Just wanted to make sure you're satisfied."

Mike felt tears swell behind his eyes. He could only nod. Yes, he was satisfied.

•

Mozina

Mike took the freeway back to Kalamazoo. He listened to an NPR story about Donald Trump and Hillary Clinton accusing each other of bigotry. They had a sound bite from Hillary at a rally in Reno, Nevada, but her slow and measured voice sounded as if she were speaking in a conference room. Mike couldn't put a finger on exactly what was a little off with Hillary's personality, but he respected her and thought she got a bad rap from too many directions. Claire was more into Hillary than he was, but talking politics with her was one of the most enjoyable and normal things about their relationship. It gave him hope for their future.

Soon he was thumbing his garage door open and then thumbing it closed, just as he'd done the night of the accident, but now there was no sign of the accident.

There was no sign of God, either. Mike was alone in the world with his actions. That was all.

20.

Ryan was getting suspicious. Or maybe he wasn't.

He started inviting himself on her evening walks. He sometimes wanted to hold her hand as they strolled, which she would submit to until she could use skirting a sidewalk puddle or crossing the street to break the clasp, which neither she nor Ryan would try to re-establish.

There was more silence than conversation. Ryan's father's health was declining, and she commiserated. Nathan was about to start his senior year. He was apparently dating a girl named Amanda, a fellow snare drummer in marching band, his first-ever relationship as far as Claire knew. Ryan reported on the efforts of a maniacal young Allegan cop who apparently took solving their hit-and-run personally. Since it was all they had to go on, he'd had a color swatch made from the paint transfer fragment, which he'd distributed to cops in Allegan, Ottawa, Van Buren, and Berrien counties. Ryan said he'd also offered it to Kalamazoo and Grand Rapids, but those were much bigger population centers and the reception had been cool. Claire remembered how at first she had been on the lookout for salsa-red cars until she counted about two dozen in a single day on the streets of Kalamazoo. It quickly became a useless torment, and she'd tried to put it out of her mind. "It's still an open case," Ryan assured her, but Claire suspected every unsolved case stood open in perpetuity.

After their walks, occasionally it would be time for a shower and sex. In her heart, having sex with Ryan was cheating on Mike. Of course, men had done this with impunity since the beginning of time, but, as was often fruitlessly pointed out, there was no male equivalent for "mistress," which was infuriating. Claire felt best when she considered herself an insurgent in the long-running battle of the sexes.

She felt worst when she thought of Nathan. Could she keep her relationship with Mike a secret until Nathan went off to college and he'd had another year to deal with losing his sister? That was a long time. Studies suggested staying in a marriage for the children didn't have long-term benefits.

As she and Ryan neared the end of one conspicuously quiet walk together, passing the grassy triangle of Henderson Park, Ryan asked jokingly, "Was it something I said?"

"I'm not feeling good about things," Claire said impulsively. "You're acting like everything's back to normal, but it isn't."

"I'm not saying it is."

"I'm saying you're acting like it."

"Oh, jeez, here we go."

"Does it have to be 'here we go'? Can't I just say what I'm seeing?"

"What's this about? Should I be grieving harder? Am I not feeling as much as you?"

"Why is everyone so threatened when I pay attention to things? I don't get it. Are you competing with me?"

"Honestly, I don't know what you're talking about," he muttered.

"That's kind of my point."

They continued up Prospect, right past the spot on the sidewalk where she had kissed Mike, right up the steps where he had followed her, right into the foyer where she had climbed him.

Guilt pierced her body like an X-ray, but she couldn't look at the image it left behind. All she knew was that her marriage was a site of grief and conflict and lies, whereas her love for Mike was pure.

21.

Having finished repairs on the murder weapon with a day to spare, Mike cleaned the house for the first time since before Anne left, in preparation for Connor's arrival and, if they got that far, to show Claire she had revived his will to live. Much of the dust and dirt had been deposited during some very bad times, some of it by Anne. Sloughed skin cells, spilled wine, dried flecks of saliva sprayed during vicious arguments. This residue was also a type of evidence he was erasing forever.

When Connor stepped off the Amtrak in a plain T-shirt, shiny long basketball shorts, and a backwards ball cap, Mike embraced him as if he were a soldier returning from war. Connor seemed dazed and bemused by this reception.

He'd told Connor on the phone that he should sell the Honda for whatever he could get because he'd bought him a new car.

"A new used car," he'd corrected himself.

Though Mike had done a careful job of restoring the murder weapon to its pre-accident appearance, he worried that in passing Connor would notice a difference—the pristine windshield molding or the shininess of the new headlight or the sootless sound padding under the new hood—which when mystically aided by the amount of genetic material he and Connor shared, would facilitate Connor asking unanswerable questions and making amazing inferential leaps straight into the heart of Mike's guilt. Only a year apart, Connor and Emma had shared school buses and the occasional car pool over the years, and he'd no doubt heard of her unsolved death on social media. So Mike was picking him up in the replicar, hoping this would overload Connor's sense of Camry details, muddying any basis for comparison.

They walked to the train station's decomposing asphalt parking lot.

"There it is. That's your new car."

"So what'd you buy for yourself?" Connor asked, sounding a bit disappointed.

"Nothing. I still have my Camry. We've both got red Camrys now." Mike laughed nervously. "Except yours is an '06 and mine's an '05."

"I see," Connor said, keeping his eye on the car. It was plain he pitied his father for thinking father-son Camrys was meaningful. "Thanks, Dad."

Mike invited Connor to take the wheel for their short drive home, and Connor promptly steered for the McDonald's drive-thru across from the train station. Mike paid.

"This look-alike car is more than a joke," Mike said solemnly as they pulled into traffic with Connor's food. "If it stands for anything, maybe it's my degree from the School of Hard Knocks, which I transfer to you, *honoris causa*, so you don't have to go through the crap I went through in your relationships."

"Really," Connor said through a mouthful of Big Mac. He fished in the bag between his legs and pulled up a bouquet of fries. "Awesome, Dad." He bit all the fries in half.

A saucy, proto-rancid meat-and-potato smell filled the car, turning Mike's stomach, but he persevered. They had never had a frank discussion of the divorce.

"I know you're thinking I screwed up with your mom. But that's what I mean by hard knocks. I didn't treat her right."

"She did drink a lot—and still does." Connor shrugged.

"That's not a license to yell at her or get on her case about things. She needed help and I gave her criticism—a lot of bullshit criticism about tiny things besides the drinking."

Connor took a long draw on his Coke, considering.

Tandem

"Yeah, no one likes getting ragged on," Connor finally said. "But if you never complain, you're just a doormat."

"Not necessarily."

"Yeah, but likely."

"Don't sweat the small stuff," Mike insisted, "so when it's time to talk about the big stuff, the other person feels safe, and you can raise issues in a supportive manner."

"I guess, whatever."

"I'm thinking about your well-being, Son."

"Thanks, Father." Connor laughed like a burp, or maybe it was just a burp.

By this time, they were turning into the alley. Connor reached for the garage door opener.

"Let me out," Mike said. The garage was too narrow to exit on the passenger side once the car was in there. Mike stood in the driveway, bracing himself.

Connor got out of the replicar and said nothing about the twin vehicles. Mike had successfully inoculated him against the issue. He insisted on carrying Connor's backpack into the house. In thirty minutes, Connor left to meet up with friends, and they hardly spoke again for the rest of the visit.

22.

When her courage faltered, Claire told herself, "Don't go backwards."

Every night for a week, Nathan and Ryan had watched the baseball playoffs on the basement TV. From what she overheard, Nathan was not doing any play-by-play; they seemed to just be enjoying the games together. The number of dark beer bottles standing on the counter to be rinsed and recycled at the end of each night suggested Ryan was letting Nathan drink. They probably expected her to say something, but she did not. Let Ryan buy their son's allegiance with local micro-brews and televised sports. Let it appear she was the lone keeper of Emma's memory.

When she asked if the Tigers were winning, Nathan snorted, "They didn't make the playoffs." He grabbed a jar of peanuts and headed downstairs.

Left to her own devices, she was glad to text Mike. Was he watching the game? No, he was streaming old episodes of *30 Rock*—a show created by a woman, she noted to herself. She got a feel for how long the games lasted and made a point of going to sleep before they ended, to avoid Ryan pawing her on a vicarious testosterone high.

Ryan's beloved Cubs were in the playoffs, so she couldn't blame him when he begged off the neighborhood watch party for the second Clinton/Trump debate. In fact, it was a relief because she knew she would find Mike over at the Paulsons.

He looked fabulous, lean and crisp in jeans and a dress shirt. They briefly exchanged pleasantries by the snack table, as if they were only casual acquaintances. It was like being in a spy movie. She felt herself getting turned on, which was ridiculous and exhilarating.

Back home, she went down to the basement to check on the devoted fans. Nathan explained the game was tied in the bottom of the eighth inning.

"Who are they playing?"

Slouching deeply in a stuffed armchair, Ryan made an annoyed sound, implying this should be obvious from information on the screen.

"It's Texas at Toronto," Nathan said.

The pitcher threw the ball. The batter just stood there. The umpire gestured convulsively. Players suddenly abandoned the field, and a Toyota commercial came on.

Claire went upstairs to the kitchen, taking in the fact that the Cubs hadn't even been playing. Ryan wanted to watch baseball instead of accompanying her to what could have been the most consequential presidential debate in American history. The pussy-grabber vs. the first female major party presidential candidate, ever. Ryan had expressed appropriate levels of derision and outrage when the Access Hollywood tape broke, but after two days it had all proved to be lip service. Feeling sorry for herself, she continued up to the second floor without turning on any lights.

She had known she was going to do it at some point, she just hadn't known exactly when. Now she pushed open the door to Emma's room and climbed into her bed, slipping between the still-unchanged sheets. She lay sideways, hunched up, with her head on her daughter's pillow, which smelled faintly of her shampoo, Strawberry Herbal Essences Long-Term Relationship. Moonlight slanted through the window.

Serious-minded people like Joan Didion and Elaine Pagels wrote in their memoirs about hearing apt and comforting words from departed loved ones. She badly needed some reassurance, even guidance. She tried to quiet her mind and listen for Emma.

Emma would hate her for breaking up the family. Maybe Emma would also take perverse satisfaction in how horribly she was behaving. Could Emma imagine her mother might have needs of her own?

She tried to listen without trying to listen, like trying not to think of a pink elephant, but no good words from Emma were coming through the veil.

As soon as Emma had turned eighteen, she had gotten a word tattooed across the inside of her left biceps in simple purple script: *Patience.*

Claire had admired the sentiment, but she had let slip a caution about how tattoos were forever.

"Whose body is this?" Emma had demanded. "Whose body is this?"

Claire had no answer for that. Emma was just articulating a principle Claire herself would have leapt to in any other context.

She had to admire her daughter for standing up to her. If she wanted to give herself credit, she could have said, in that respect, she had raised her well.

She promised herself she would not let Ryan have sex with her. No more.

This resolution roused her from Emma's bed. She packed her suitcase and her garment bag and put them back in the hall closet, just in case. They looked the same packed as unpacked.

·

At the third debate watch party, Cheryl from book club patted Claire's knee and said in her ear: "I'm so nervous, tell me when it's over."

Claire's own stomach was twisting. The nation's verdict on Hillary had always felt personal.

When Chris Wallace turned the questioning to the latest accusations against Trump, Claire couldn't help but imagine herself standing at the lectern instead of Hillary, Trump pointing at her: "What we really need to talk about is *she* cheated on her husband. All these women, they lie, okay? They want their ten minutes of fame! It's very unfair, but she cheated on her husband, which is very bad—not good."

Tandem

Then as Hillary calmly explained how Trump denigrated all the women who had accused him—"Every woman knows how that feels," she said—Claire tried to formulate her imaginary rebuttal: "It's consensual. It's true love. You don't know what goes on in a marriage. You don't know what my grief is like!"

When the debate was over, everyone thought Hillary had won. She left before Mike, only catching his eye briefly on her way out. It was windy, and wild herds of brittle leaves brushed and swerved down the sidewalk. Mike was a good man who respected women.

Back home, celebratory whooping rose from the basement. She didn't want to be drawn into it, as if it would compromise her somehow, so she went upstairs and got ready for bed.

She lay awake for over an hour, replaying moments from the debate, imagining things Hillary could have said, which bled back into defending herself against Trump's, and the world's, likely accusations.

She was staring vaguely in front of her, mind racing, when the door opened and Ryan walked in. She was not in her sleep position. Her eyes were open and seemed to meet his in the darkness.

"Cubs win!" Ryan stage whispered. "Cubs win!"

"Wow," she said. "Congrats."

"Unbelievable. They blew them out *in L.A.* Evened the series."

"Maybe this is the year."

"Hey, how was the debate?"

"Awful in many ways."

"Did Hillary win?"

"Probably, but I don't think it matters."

"Aw, it's in the bag. All is good."

He stripped down to his boxers, crawled into bed, and turned to her. He touched her slowly and gently in the familiar ways.

"I've got to use the bathroom," she said.

She peed, put in a tampon, and washed her hands. She gave herself only a quick glance in the mirror.

Back in bed, she told Ryan, "Hey, I'm really sorry, I'm getting my period. Rain check?"

"If it means a double header..."

"I walked right into that one," she sighed.

Then she had to wait out his wordless handjob expectation, until with a theatrical sigh he turned over, apparently shifting his fantasy back to the Cubs winning the World Series.

She lay awake listening for the onset of his soft snores.

She couldn't go backwards. She had to choose what she would choose if she were strong.

When he seemed deep enough in sleep, she got out of bed, quietly got dressed, took her suitcase and garment bag from the hall closet, and walked over to Mike's house.

23.

The sound of someone knocking on wood finally penetrated Mike's exercise-deepened stupor. He found himself on the sectional. The TV wanted to know if he was still watching Netflix.

The knock again, more insistent. He moved and saw a shifting shape at the back door.

It was Claire. She had luggage.

"Wow, Claire, hello!"

"Can I stay here?"

"Oh. Of course! Come on in."

"I'm sorry to wake you."

"Oh, no, it's perfect," Mike said, taking the suitcase and garment bag out of her hands so she could come through the door.

He set her bags behind him, and when he turned back, her face burrowed in his chest. He gave her a bear hug, hoping it wasn't noticeable he had to think to do that. How to support her as she took this incredibly stupid action? He pitied her, he pitied Ryan, he pitied her son. He doubted he could live up to her choice.

"Thank you," she whispered. She squeezed him with what seemed like all of her strength.

"I've got you," he said.

"Thank you."

They unclenched.

"Can I get you something? Midnight snack? Glass of wine?"

"I'm ready for bed."

Mike mentally inventoried his house: the iPad mini had been destroyed and thrown out; all of his legal pads had been burned in his Weber grill; the car part boxes had been recycled; the disguises were disposed of; the replicar had been driven away. Yet the existence of some other incriminating evidence worried the fringe of his awareness—what was it? A part of him wanted to bar Claire from the house until he could remember, find, and destroy it. As he led Claire upstairs, toting her bags, he was sure her magnetism would draw the object (or objects?) to her.

"Surprisingly clean, eh?" he said. "That's all me."

"I'm impressed."

He pointed to the bathroom, offered her everything in the house.

In the master bedroom, Claire pulled Mike onto the unmade bed. This was another big scene in the movie of her life, he could tell. She seemed to be in a sort of trance, and eventually he got swept up as well. She got on top and rode him like a champ. At last, in their total privacy, she made sounds that would have had neighbors calling the police if the windows had been open.

Finally she collapsed on his chest.

"I'm so lucky," she said. "I've waited my whole life for you."

"I feel very lucky, too. Thank you for being here."

"I love you, Mike," she whispered.

In response, he hugged her to him. In his head, he was not bullshitting her, but in his heart there was more than a twinge.

He lay there, with her warm body nestled against his, wondering if she really did love him. He assumed she would come to her senses at some point. But what if she didn't?

"Can I ask you a favor?" Claire said.

His shoulders twitched with a realization: the Compact OED with the pages cut out to accommodate the mini—still on the shelf in the living room! What if she wanted to know the origins of "prevaricate"?

"Sorry, were you falling asleep?"

"No. What favor?"

"Can I take your car to work tomorrow? I left in a hurry. I didn't—"

"It's kind of a junky car..."

"Okay, well...I guess I can walk home first thing and get my car. It's not a—"

"No, of course you should take it. I walk to school. Please take it."

"I could walk, too..."

"Claire—" An abrupt, jagged laugh escaped his mouth. "Seriously. It's a total non-issue."

"Okay. Okay, thank you."

They were quiet for a bit. Mike hoped the sudden throbbing in his head might soon subside and all would be covered in sleep.

"This must be so out-of-the-blue for you," Claire said.

"No. Not at all. I've been visualizing this for weeks."

Maybe she would stop speaking and just let everything be. Any second, he was going to blurt some exasperation and expose something awful about himself.

"I can hardly believe things sometimes," she said.

She wound her hand into his. He could not sleep holding someone's hand. It was impossible. He squeezed her hand, though he wanted to shake it off and roll over. He could feel heat building under his shoulder blades. His butt was starting to sweat.

He could not tell her it was time for sleep. She must decide on her own.

It was like planking: he just had to hold still, minute after minute, endure the discomfort, say nothing, time would pass, and he would reach the end.

"You're super hot," Claire said mischievously.

"Am I?"

"Yes, you are."

Then she finally fell asleep and he almost fell asleep, too, trying to ignore his need to pee, but finally he got up and used the downstairs bathroom.

Afterwards, he stood naked in his dark living room in front of the OED. He could double-wrap it in two black trash bags and put it outside in the trusty rolling trash can through which he had disposed of so much evidence. But he was naked and the back door made too much noise.

Instead, he removed the box containing the two volumes of the compact OED from the shelf, rearranged other books to conceal the gap, and carried the box to the basement. He had just the bin for it: he nestled the near-perfectly opaque piece of evidence between layers of Connor's baby bath towels. It was extremely unlikely that Claire would go through the bins in his basement before she went to work tomorrow. Then, when she was out of the house, he would wrap the dictionary in two black trash bags and put it out in the rolling trash can.

His sweat was drying into a cold film. He went back upstairs and paused when he saw Claire lying asleep in his bed. She looked so small and helpless and trusting. In the dim light, with her eyes closed, he caught a resemblance to her daughter in the fog just before impact.

24.

She awoke next to Mike, luxuriating in his musky warmth, bracing herself for whatever would happen now. Reluctantly, she picked her phone off the nightstand and unlocked it.

A text from Ryan had come across at 6:52 AM—a half hour ago (she'd over-slept, but could still get to work at a respectable hour): *Whose house are you at? Are you OK?*

Her hairline tingled. She had forgotten they had each other on their "Find My" apps. He probably knew exactly where she was, but apparently not with whom—friend or lover?

Her first thought was to get dressed, slip out the back door, and speed walk toward the KIA, insist he had gotten a false signal. The app could be squirrelly, with obsolete readings and long bouts of buffering.

But she had to be ready for this. This is what a new life meant.

She checked Ryan's location. He was at their house on Prospect. Then the app buffered.

The circle with his first initial now pulsed at the intersection of Prairie and Grand—half a block away.

She sprang out of bed and threw on some work clothes with trembling hands. Mike stirred.

"Good morning," he said.

"Ryan's coming here. He knows I'm in this house." She flashed her phone at Mike and he squinted toward it.

She checked again. "Oh, shit! He's right outside!"

Mike didn't sit up. He didn't seem alarmed. "Are you going to talk to him?"

"I don't know."

"Do you want me there with you?"

"I don't know."

She didn't want to hurt Ryan. They had been through a lot together. What would she do if he apologized, begged her to come home?

She walked down the upstairs hallway and into a guest bedroom with a view of the street. In the small front yard was an enormous spreading maple tree that had already dropped its leaves. Ryan stood on the sidewalk beneath it, in his suit and raincoat. It was still dark out, and his face was lit by the post lamp in Mike's yard. Everything was wet, leaves plastered on pavement, and it was drizzling. He looked down at his phone and then up at the house, several times, back and forth. She saw fear on his face. His naturally mournful eyebrows were fully canted. She wanted to cry out to him; she wanted to comfort him; or maybe she just didn't want to see that look on his face.

His eyes seemed to search the first-floor windows. Then they flashed upwards.

She jerked back from the window. Mike came down the hall and stood in the doorway, in boxers and a T-shirt, watching her with a calm, benevolent expression.

Her phone buzzed. It was Ryan. The buzzing insisted and insisted and insisted, until, on its own, her fingertip slid the bar across.

"Whose house is this?"

"I'm sorry, Ryan. I can't sleep with you anymore."

"Who are you with? What the hell is happening?"

"I just can't. I need a break."

He sighed. She heard a car sizzle by on the wet street, in the world and, with a microscopic delay, in her phone.

"You don't have to sleep with me. Just come home. Can you please just come home?"

He didn't love her; he just wanted her back under his control.

Tandem

"Jesus Christ! It's me! What the fuck is happening? Who are you with?"

She edged to the side of the window, like a sniper, and saw him pacing back and forth on the sidewalk with a hand on top of his head.

"Whose house is this?" he repeated.

"Mike's. Mike Kovacs."

Ryan stopped and jabbed a finger into his phone, like poking out the eye of a small mammal, and the line went dead. He seemed about to throw his phone at the house—pitching a small electronic device was apparently his go-to expression of extreme displeasure—but he thought better of it. He yelled something. Through the closed window, it sounded like "Fuck me!" Then he stalked off.

Tears rushed to Claire's eyes, but she didn't want Mike to see them. She stood at the window, listening for what Mike was going to do. Radiators began hissing throughout the house.

After a bit, he entered the room and embraced her from behind. She gripped his arms folded across her chest.

•

Claire was a little taken aback by the condition of Mike's Camry. Unfortunately, it was similar in color to whatever vehicle had struck her daughter's bicycle, but she had gotten used to how many such cars were out there. The upholstery on the side of the console hump was streaked with brown stains she hoped were from coffee. The dashboard had probably never been dusted. It smelled bad in a complicated masculine way. The air freshener hanging from the rearview was a pale, pine-tree-shaped flag of surrender.

But for her first days living at Mike's house, these were her wheels.

Because after their dismal phone call across Mike's front yard, Ryan had gone home and thrown a stone the size of a cantaloupe at the windshield of her Prius. She found it embedded there when she went home over lunch the next day to pick up her car and get more clothes. The windshield cupped it like a curve in space-time.

At first, she had been shocked and frightened and sad, but it gave her back some of the moral high ground, which helped her talk to Nathan.

"Your father and I are upset," she told him. "It's not about you."

Ryan was out grocery shopping, and she sat with Nathan at the dining room table. She told him she would be "staying with a friend" for a while.

"I know who your *friend* is," Nathan said. "This really sucks."

"I know. I'm sorry. Your father and I love you very much."

"A certain amount."

"What?"

"I think you love me a certain amount. And you love other things more."

"You don't get to say that! Don't you ever say that!"

Nathan fixed his eyes on a random object on the shelf behind her and held them there in silence.

"I don't blame you for being mad about this. Ryan and I are going to be the best parents we can be for you, no matter what."

His stare did not lose focus, and finally she had to get up and walk back to Mike's house before Ryan got home.

•

Sex with Mike was escape, pleasure, and hope, all at once. She threw herself at him just about every night after they cooked dinner together, collaborating on her ambidextrous meat/vegetarian recipes. She couldn't believe she possessed his body. He was Mapplethorpe's Charles Bowman. He was Caravaggio's Victorious Cupid, with emblems of civilization broken at his feet. But he was also alive and in her arms, like something she had curated come to life. She worried she was wearing him out a bit. Tonight it took him some extra effort to get hard.

Tandem

They lay in bed. Tomorrow was Saturday, and they were going to pick up her repaired Prius from the dealer.

"Do you think Ryan is going to try to murder me?" she ventured.

Mike hadn't said much about the smashed windshield.

He sighed. "Nah, he's not the murdering type, I don't think. I bet he still loves you. Guys don't act out like that when they're done with the relationship. When Anne left me, I was devastated, even though I knew it needed to happen. Not like I was going to break anyone's windshield, but—" He laughed awkwardly.

"Did you do anything you regretted when you broke up?"

"For a while I regretted everything. I blamed myself for everything. But that wasn't making me a better person; it was just making me more twisted up. So I decided it had to be all about, you know, being a better guy going forward. And then I got to know you."

"Ryan and Nathan are hurting," she said. "And that's not good, but they'll deal with it."

Mike made no sound.

"They found little bits of windshield glass in Emma's face," she added, because she was hurting too. "They figured out who made the windshield—Guardian Glass, owned by the Koch brothers, if you can believe it—but they make windshields for everybody."

"Oh, that sounds really rough," Mike said. He clasped her hand under the sheet. "Oh, Claire, I'm so sorry."

He turned to her, pulled her hand up, and pressed her knuckles against his forehead.

25.

Mike found he was unable to forget the resemblance to Emma he'd glimpsed in Claire's face the night she'd slept in his bed for the first time. Seeing them both with their eyes closed, wearing a dreamy-but-expectant expression, had revealed a similarity he hadn't noticed before. But now it had gotten into his head to the point where he could hardly look at Claire during sex. He had to admit she wasn't exactly his type to begin with, and if he wanted to perform, he had to imagine Anne or get worked up on internet porn ahead of time.

He was not looking for trouble at Dave's 50th birthday party. Claire couldn't make it—there was a KIA reception, and in any case they weren't ready to go public. The gathering was lively and loud, unlike a typical colleague-heavy party. Dave and Sarah had a wide circle of non-College friends, from their synagogue to Sarah's job at Zoetis and beyond. And something about a 50th made everyone drink more than usual.

A woman with curly reddish-brown hair approached him, sweating Amstel Light in hand, and said, "Hi, stranger, what's your name?"

Her cheeks rounded beautifully when she smiled. The perfect pitch of jocularity in her greeting suggested the tonal sensitivity of a symphony conductor. She was tall and large-breasted. His relationship radar flashed a warning: batten down your life and seek shelter or this woman will blow you away.

"Good question." He pulled out his wallet, extracted his driver's license, and read from it: "'Michael Robert Kovacs.'"

"You don't know your own name?" she asked playfully.

"I wanted to get it right."

"Is this a new identity for you? Are you in the Witness Protection Program?"

"Yes, as of this morning. This is actually a going-away party for me, but no one can know."

She laughed. Evidently, she was charmed. The one woman in a million who would be. He had hoped she would think he was stupid and weird, and when he got home he could give to Claire the erection this woman was already starting to inspire.

Her name was Chloe. "I've got it memorized," she said, tapping a forefinger on her temple.

"Show-off."

She was a pediatrician. Her boys were eleven and fifteen: Ethan was into basketball and Luke was into soccer, both sports Connor had played.

"I miss my son at those ages," Mike said sincerely. "Old enough where we could shoot buckets, play one-on-one."

"I'm glad they're into sports," Chloe affirmed. "Gets them off the video games for a minute."

"Yeah," he said. "More risk of toxic masculinity, but less risk of shooting up the school."

"Trade-offs," Chloe deadpanned.

Mike laughed. He was being reckless, but Chloe seemed impossible to offend and he'd always been drawn to hard-to-offend women; it was one of the things he'd liked about Anne—until he finally succeeded at offending her and she left. A bell went off: this was the widowed doctor Sarah had wanted to fix him up with months ago. She had probably known his name all along.

"It would be fun to sit in the bleachers some time and yell at referees together," she said, smiling.

"I sometimes still go to games," he said. This wasn't true, only a lame attempt to deflect her invitation, as if his showing up might just mean he would have been there anyway.

"Maybe—" Her voice faltered. "I could get your number?"

He remembered something Dave had said about her just easing back into dating. If he hadn't hit the tandem, he would have had a moment like this himself, nervously asking a woman out for the first time in decades. He couldn't say no.

Of course he wouldn't call her.

When he got home, Claire was getting in the shower.

"How was the reception?" Mike called out.

"Come in here and I'll tell you all about it," she called back.

He stripped down, stepped in behind her, and thought of Chloe.

•

When Mike awoke Saturday morning, he regretted exchanging numbers with Chloe. Was he a two-timing douche as well as a drunk-driving killer? Besides, he needed all the emotional poise he could muster to drive Claire in the murder weapon to pick up her repaired Prius.

Claire asked if it was okay if they took care of some things on the way to Metro Toyota. Anne had always been an impulsive errand-runner, completing multiple discrete round trips a day like a hub-and-spoke airline. By contrast, Claire batched up her errands in the most efficient possible sequence.

The good thing about Anne was that she never expected Mike to accompany her, but Claire seemed to imagine they were best friends who wanted to spend all their time together. Mike surmised he might eventually have to draw some lines, but he resolved to give her everything she wanted for as long as he could.

They'd never been in the car together. Mike noticed she'd hung a new air freshener from the rearview, which made him self-conscious. He checked the windshield, to make sure it wasn't cracked; he eyed the perfectly sealed edges. He finally started the car. His head was getting swimmy, so he powered down his window a bit.

Tandem

The fresh air was good.

"Are you hot?" Claire asked a little peevishly.

The temp was in the low 40s after all.

"Whups," Mike said, and powered up his window.

The cabin instantly became stifling to Mike, but he didn't want to unzip his jacket and suggest he was in fact hot, which might read as a passive-aggressive criticism of Claire.

"Where are we going?" he asked, though she had told him.

"Can we stop at the mailbox in front of St. Augustine's?"

"Is that on the left?"

"Yeah."

He knew it was on the left side of the street. He was steeling himself.

Michigan Avenue was one-way into downtown, the counterpart to Kalamazoo Avenue coming one-way out of downtown. It was a busy street and, after putting Claire's letters in the box, Mike would have to merge into traffic to his right, which he hated. His whole driving life had trained him to be a left-handed merger. Merging to his right and making left turns against traffic at unregulated intersections or when leaving parking lots were the biggest threats to his accident-free driving record, and as he had gotten older, and in the wake of the accident that did not appear on his record, he had taken ever-greater pains to avoid such situations.

He was miffed at Claire. Why was she always putting pressure on his ability to function in a calm and loving manner? He knew it wasn't her fault and most normal people did not have the issues he had but, still, why?

He was used to taking the right lane as he traversed downtown, but instead he had to cross two lanes to his left to pull up to the stupidly squat blue mailbox in front of the church.

Claire handed him her letter. He exited the car and slid the letter down the chute. Then he assessed the traffic coming from his right. Many cars and trucks sped by across three lanes, some only inches away from his Camry. Some vehicles wove between lanes—one, he noted, without signaling. The parking lane was open in front of him, giving him some runway to get up to speed before trusting his eyes—could he trust his eyes?—and lurching into what he hoped was a clear lane. He remembered a car beeping at him when he'd pulled into traffic leaving the Arcadia Brew Pub on his way to the accident.

He got back into the car and looked across Claire to check his right mirror. A car went by in the center lane, the near lane was clear, but just as he turned to check his blind spot, a car whizzed by that would have killed them both. Jesus Christ! He took a moment to gather himself. Mirror, look back—a stray car at various distances in all three lanes. Maybe he could make it, but then he couldn't make it. Claire was going to say something any second. Mirror, look back, nothing. He eased the car forward, looked back, car in far lane, he sped up, looked back, car in center lane, double-checked not changing lanes, nothing in near lane, nothing. He accelerated quickly, trying to beat an unseen car he might have missed, merging right at last.

"Mike!" Claire screamed, reaching for the dashboard.

He looked forward just in time to see a speeding car from his left. He slammed on the brakes, knowing he wouldn't stop in time. A loud crunching sound, his lungs flattened by a medicine ball to the chest. Dust filled the air. His first aching dry breath set him coughing. His forearms burned; his nose felt punched in an ongoing way. The swirl of car horns died down. His foot was still jammed on the brake and he fumbled under the deflated airbag to shift into park. He touched blood where a mustache could have been; his nerves rang in a register only a dog could hear.

Through an uncracked windshield, they faced a pair of stopped cars pointing directly at their car, twenty-five feet in front of them. Another car approached from the right, horn stuck on crescendo, jerked to a near stop, then accelerated around the front of their car, between them and the onlooking cars. His view seemed all wrong until he intuited they had been knocked into a perfect 180 and were looking back at where they had come from.

26.

With Mike compulsively checking his blind spot,
Claire glanced to see what all the fuss was about—and by the
time she faced forward again, they were about to run the red
light at Westnedge. It was like one of those embarrassing
moments in bumper cars when you find yourself bearing
down on a stranger, not a friend. The bang of impact hurt her
ears. Her seatbelt violently cut her chest. A poof of talcum
powder. An unexpected Viewmaster slide clicked into view:
two cars facing them head on. A car blaring its horn rudely
cut across this vision, but then it went away. A deflated airbag
sat in her lap. Her left wrist felt snapped like a twig; pain
flamed up her arm into her neck.

"Oh, god, I'm so sorry," Mike moaned.

"I wish you'd been more careful," she mumbled,
trembling. She felt thrown from her body.

The EMTs insisted on a spinal board.

Claire told them they didn't need to go to any
trouble—she was dead, wasn't she?

"You're fine," a female EMT told her cheerfully, "and
your husband's fine, too."

"My daughter warned me about this," Claire replied.

The EMT seemed to lose interest in Claire's
statements and helped load her into the ambulance.

•

Reality clarified in waves, until things were more or less
stable again. A CT scan. An MRI. They put her sprained wrist in

a brace that left her fingers free. After they finally Ubered home from the hospital, Mike suggested they order a pizza.

"And make another person drive?" Claire asked.

Mike said he would cook omelets instead.

She lay down on the couch and tried to nap. She opened her eyes when Mike got a phone call in the kitchen.

"Hey, how are you?" Mike said in a low voice. "Yeah, that was fun...Good, good...Wow, that sounds great, but you're not going to believe this—I just got in a car accident... Totally my fault... Ran a red light... No, I'm totally serious... Not paying attention, I guess... Yeah, no, I'm fine, just a little freaked out. Just trying to lie low... Yeah, everything checked out... No, I'm glad you called... OK, I'll be in touch. Buh-bye."

"Who was that?" she called from the couch.

There was a beat, as if Mike had to swallow something before answering. "Dave."

"The birthday boy?"

"Dave's a friendly guy."

Mike sounded more polite with his friends than Ryan, who was likely to be profane or even mildly abusive.

When they sat down to their omelets, he said "I'm sorry" for the tenth time.

"No, I blame it on my karma."

"Oh, please don't go there."

"I try to talk to Emma sometimes," Claire admitted, "or I try to listen, in case she has anything to say to me. I thought maybe she would comfort me, but she hasn't. I know she would be upset about what we're doing, I mean, what I'm doing to Ryan and Nathan—and this happens."

"Magical thinking is not the best," Mike offered.

"It feels like that's exactly what's happening."

"That's how you know it's not what's happening. I mean, it's tempting, but there's no magic."

She sighed. She reminded herself she didn't believe in magic or third eyes. Did her new, adulterous self believe in stupid things? Maybe being in love changed everything.

"I know," she said. "I know."

Tandem

"And it's okay. And it means you had nothing to do with the accident. With either accident," he added. "Obviously."

They were both tired, and it was already dark, so they went to bed. They didn't have sex.

27.

For several days in a row, Mike woke in the dark, at an ungodly hour, feeling alert and doomed.

Claire usually slept turned toward him, wearing a foam collar for her whiplash, rhythmically blowing stale air at his face. She only wore the collar to sleep, but he didn't wear one at all; apparently she had pre-existing neck and shoulder issues, and the accident affected her more.

He had his own milder case of whiplash and would wake with a stiff neck and a dull headache radiating from his brainstem.

He would lie still and think of Emma's blue scrunchie on the crumbling pavement. He would contemplate some of the objects Anne had told him to go fuck over the years—a Christmas tree, a pepperoni pizza, his own self. He'd think of the grape pantsuit of the peppy insurance adjuster. The car had spun like a top because it had been struck up front, ahead of the wheel; somehow the frame had not been bent, the engine had not been damaged. He'd think of his father's rheumy, uncomprehending eyes watching boats on the Chippewa River. He'd think of cowering in a giant wooden maze, hearing the distant scratching of a huge rat many walls over making its way towards him. He'd fantasize about the murder weapon safely compacted into a cube—but he had not chosen that option because that's not what the dealer would do, they would resell it and it would be loose in the world, out of his control, and the adjuster was so friendly and the repairs were less than the book value and he must always act in front of Claire as if the original accident had never happened.

Eventually, lying there in the dark, he would imagine breaking up with Claire and hooking up with Chloe. He mentalized how in the course of normal relationships people got to know each other and parted or stayed, depending, and no one went to prison over such choices. Wasn't it perverse and terrible to sleep with the mother of his victim? Especially when he couldn't get their resemblance out of his head, especially when he knew he wasn't drawn to Claire to the degree to which he was drawn to Chloe? Wasn't that what his body was telling him whenever he had to work himself up to have sex with Claire? He would be happier with Chloe, and maybe Claire would be happier back with Ryan, and Nathan would be happier to have his parents together. And didn't Chloe need love and companionship? Wouldn't it be good for Luke and Ethan to have a sports-savvy stepfather during their critical teen years? Maybe there would be more net love and happiness in the world if he were with Chloe. And wasn't that the point of avoiding prison?

•

He ran into Dave, who was walking to his car on Academy.

"How are you feeling?" Mike asked. "Isn't fifty surprisingly great?"

"Hey, Mike," Dave said wearily. "What happened to your nose?"

"Car accident. But let's not dwell on it."

"Holy shit. What happened?"

"My fault. Honestly, it's not great. Dealing with some whiplash symptoms."

"Seriously? That sucks."

They stood next to Dave's white Honda. Stray students filtered by. The sun was going down, chilling the air. A murder of crows was going nuts in a grove of tall trees in front of one of the red-brick dorms.

"Hey, I saw you talking to Chloe," Dave added. "Are you two getting together?"

"She's great. She really is. But my love life has gotten super complicated all of a sudden."

"It's about time." Dave half-smiled.

"I know, right? Seriously, you're not going to believe this: I'm having an affair with a married woman, but I'm crushing big-time on Chloe."

"Whoa." Dave's high balding forehead rumpled.

"I shouldn't have given Chloe my number because now she's calling me, and I feel like I'm two-timing this other woman."

"Jeez. Well, sounds like you kind of are?"

The crows wouldn't let up, taking off from and re-alighting in the treetops fifty yards up the hill, cawing as if their long-planned attack on humanity was imminent.

"So you're saying one woman at a time?" Mike said.

"Chloe's already had her heart broken pretty bad."

"Same with this other woman."

"The adulteress?"

"Hey, you sexist bastard, it's not like that. Her heart's broken, too."

"Sounds like you're not in too deep with Chloe. Maybe if—"

"She's so perfect for me, it's frightening. Even Sarah knows it."

Dave looked off, then looked back. "How'd you get mixed up with the married woman?"

"If I have to get a job somewhere else, would you write me a letter of recommendation?"

Dave chuckled bitterly. "Mike is a wonderful colleague and a fine macroeconomist. But he's a flight risk." He eyed the crows himself as he went around the front of his car. "Lock up your daughters," he added with a sour smile, opening the driver's side door and getting in.

"I know it looks bad. I'll be kind to Chloe."

"Get thee to a counselor," Dave said, pointing at Mike. Then he slammed his door and drove off.

Tandem

Mike couldn't remember an important conversation in which someone told him what he wanted to hear. He wondered if there was a point in talking to people if this continued to be the case.

He got out his phone and scrolled his messages. A text had come from Chloe an hour ago, in the middle of Intermediate Macro:

How r u feeling? Luke plays Districts at KC 6:3o nxt Tues. Interested?

Mike remembered the yellow light in Otsego he had scooted through the night of the accident. If he had just stopped at that light, he would never have struck the tandem, Emma and Jeremy would still be alive, Sarah would have fixed him up with Chloe in due course, and he would be texting her now with clean thumbs. Could such randomness really be the line between unending misery and eternal bliss?

He had to walk past the crows. As they grew louder, high overhead, he ignored them as he did barking dogs. Dave was obviously missing the big picture. But could he leave a woman to whom he owed so much, and really did care about, for someone he barely knew? Couldn't he—shouldn't he?—get to know Chloe better before she slipped away or he did something rash to hurt Claire? There was also such a thing as friendship, in which people enjoyed spending time together without jeopardizing other relationships.

He typed: *Sounds great! Thanks!*

He pressed send.

The crows ebbed as he went along the familiar streets to his house, where he needed to cook dinner for Claire. The sidewalk curved over a swell in the earth. He envisioned a crow far down a branch, bobbing up and down in the breeze. This limb of sidewalk seemed long and sturdy. He kept walking until he lost track of when he stopped hearing the crows.

28.

A terribly thin woman with short, side-parted hair said she was very sorry but their car was not quite ready.

"Oh, well," Mike said.

They went into the elaborate waiting area, which had a snack bar, a TV pit, cubicles for doing office work, and original paintings on the walls. Metro Toyota's Service Department apparently valued art more than Emma. But why had she ever cared about the bareness of Emma's bedroom walls? She had mommed too much. It was depressing. They sat at a hi-top table, on chairs so tall her feet couldn't reach the floor. Mike sat with his elbows up on the table, tapping two fingers against his lips.

Ryan had called to apologize for smashing her windshield; he wanted to pay for the repairs, which made no sense because they hadn't yet untangled their money. He said he didn't understand what was happening to them. Claire said when he calmed down, they might be able to talk, a precondition which seemed to infuriate him, as she suspected it would. In the meantime, maybe he would better understand what was happening to them if he considered whether he really respected her. Ryan accused her of cruelty, said she was lucky he was even speaking to her, but he knew losing Emma was making things crazy, so he was—

She'd had to end the call. Maybe if she hadn't given in so often, the cruelty charge would have had more bite.

"Nervous about something?" she asked Mike. It was a way to keep her own composure.

Mike pressed both hands against the tabletop.

Tandem

"Hasn't this just taken forever?" he said. "I know it's my fault, but jeez. How are your symptoms?"

"A little better."

She was getting used to her wrist brace. At least she didn't have to wear it in the shower or to bed, and luckily it was on her left wrist, her off hand.

On the wall behind Mike, there was a huge painting of a street scene in downtown Chicago at dusk—the marquee for the Chicago Theater was prominent. It was impressionistic and thick with paint. A rushing cab in the foreground was just layered smears, more parfait than automobile. Mike hadn't seemed like the absent-minded professor type, but he had plowed right into that intersection like Mr. Magoo.

"Dr. Kovacs! I was hoping it was the one and only!"

A young man in khakis and a navy Metro Toyota polo approached them with an enormous grin and bright eyes. His center-parted hair framed his oily forehead in waves. He had a California dude accent.

Mike returned a broad smile. "Wow, great to see you," he said.

"Clay Witts." He spread his arms, presenting himself and the clipboard he was carrying.

"Yes, of course," Mike said hurriedly. "Great to see you, Clay."

"What's been going on, Dr. K?"

"Just picking up a car."

"Fantastic. How's things at the College?"

"The College is chugging along. I see you've entered the workforce. Congratulations!"

The moment when Mike might have introduced her had come and gone. She understood.

"Yeah, you sniffed me out, because, so, yeah, I'm actually on the job here." Clay brandished a business card, which Mike took. "Just wondering if it's time for a trade-in, Dr. K!"

Mike's smile puckered like a broken zipper. His eyes narrowed into a disbelieving squint.

"Wow, seriously? Is *this* why our car's not ready?"

There was a harsh edge in his voice she had never heard before. She was embarrassed for him, but Clay's puppy dog demeanor didn't flag.

"Professor Kovacs, I'm not gonna lie: our service team is pretty awesome. If I wasn't driving my dad's car, I'd definitely get service here. Now, I know you'd want me to do my research." He consulted his clipboard. "More than ten years old. More than 100,000 miles—a lot more. Sir, can I get you into a new hybrid RAV4?"

"Not interested, sorry."

"Um, yeah, so that seems pretty rash—just sayin'!"

"Clay, please...," Mike said quietly, briefly closing his eyes. His chest was rising and falling like someone preparing to lift a large weight.

"You were always hard on me, Dr. K, but you taught me resilience." Clay jabbed the air with his pointer finger; still the corners of his smile had lost a little starch. "Speaking of resilience, this '05 Camry's had some tough times—replacement windshield, headlight, looks like hood, too! Maybe not its first fender bender? Sometimes the structural stuff catches up to you at a bad time. Now I can—"

"Do you know why we're sitting here?" Mike stepped off his high chair and stood. "Because we've been in a serious car accident! Do you know how traumatizing a car accident is? No, evidently you don't, because you were a bullshit marketing major, not an economics major, which is a real goddamn social science!"

Clay's face fell. He took a step back. Mike was like a downed power line snapping and sparking on the street. She reached out and touched his arm, trying to ground him.

"Okay, okay, I'm sorry, but, I mean..." Veins bulged in Mike's neck. He simultaneously strained forward and held himself back until he seemed cantilevered. "You don't upsell traumatized people! You just don't! You don't upsell—period. It's offensive!" He raised his hands to the back of his head, trying to contain himself. "Now just please tell the porter to bring us that ever-fucking car!"

Mike strode past Clay toward the garage.

"I'm so sorry," she said to Clay.

Tandem

But he didn't seem to hear her. His eyes were glassy and stunned.

29.

As quickly as his temper had flared, his thoughts turned to damage control. By the time he had reached the desk of Dotty, their service captain, he didn't even care to mention the despicable act of upselling. When he tried to imagine what to say if Claire asked him about the Camry's previous repairs, he only spun his emotional tires deeper.

"What's the ETA?" he asked, unable to wring all the agitation out of his voice.

"He just brought it up," Dotty said, averting eyes already shielded by tinted prescription glasses.

Et tu, Dotty? Had Clay put her up to it, or had she put Clay up to it? It was a horrible world, full of lies and money grubbing. Capitalism didn't always bring out the best in people, it had to be noted.

Dotty busied herself at her computer, then went to get something off the printer. He was startled when he found Claire standing next to him.

"I'm sorry," he murmured.

He didn't hear her response, which didn't bode well.

They drove back to the house in separate cars, which gave him more time to think.

He waited for Claire as she pulled her red Prius into their—or maybe soon-to-be just his again—garage. He put his arm around her as they slowly walked to the backdoor. He remembered the horror of this walk the night of the accident. He found there were deep grooves in his emotions that felt continuous with that night, as if it had never ended, and there were moods and states of mind that had a tenuous, separate existence. Now he seemed to toggle between emotional states with each step he took with Claire. He wondered if he could hold it together. He understood how a lobotomy could seem like a viable next step, a way of cutting your losses.

Maybe she didn't want his arm on her just then. He removed it before they reached the back door.

Feeling light-headed, he prepared a plate of cheese and crackers.

She sat at the dining room table, sometimes fiddling with a saltshaker, sometimes looking out the window.

"You want something?" he asked her.

"No thanks."

Though he wanted to hide in the TV room and stream one of his sitcoms, he sat down with her.

"Are you okay?" she asked.

"I'm sorry."

"I know. I appreciate you saying that, but that's not what I'm asking. That was a little bit scary for me."

"I understand. So, you're wondering, what happened back there?"

She nodded.

"It was probably a couple things." He exhaled and, without willing it, his eyes went away from her, toward a random cupboard. It took some effort to bring his eyes back. "I'm still feeling super guilty for the accident, and it was hard for me to hear Clay putting it in my face like that. And the rest is kind of a long story."

She didn't nod; she just looked at him.

"Okay, my dad was a stockbroker, and he was always churning his accounts—always getting his clients in and out of investments, because he made money every time they traded. It's an insidious type of upselling. It was just more, more, more, all the time. He didn't exactly care about people. And eventually he bought a lot of stock for himself on margin, meaning with borrowed money, and he lost big. And my family went bankrupt and my parents split for a while because of that. And I just felt really…manipulated and hurt, you know, by that sales tactic. So I just kind of saw red."

"I'm sorry, that sounds hard to deal with." She turned the saltshaker around in her hand, then set it down. "What happened the other time?"

"What other time?"

"He said the car had been in another fender bender. Was that Connor?"

"Oh yeah, well, no, it was me. I hit a deer, two, three years ago. On 131." He was thinking of the dead deer in the breakdown lane the night of the accident. "I didn't see it until I was hitting it, basically. It was big, and the windshield cracked and the front end, the hood, whatever—and that little shit tried to use that to upsell me." He said this last thing very calmly, very mildly, to show Clay had been the real source of his upset, but he was over that now. But of course Metro Toyota didn't have a record of the other recent repairs; Clay must have gone so far as to talk to the technician, who must have noticed things while working with the car.

"It brought back that trauma for you," Claire stated.

"And I knew it was bringing back trauma for you, too! And I just couldn't stand that he went there, you know?"

"He was trying so hard to impress you."

"You're right. The poor stupid kid. I'll get back with him. I'll apologize."

She smiled faintly to herself.

"This is going to sound weird," Claire said, "but a part of me is relieved. I was beginning to think you weren't totally real. That maybe you weren't always yourself with me—you were so nice all the time."

"Hey, I am nice." He smiled his big smile. "That's one thing I definitely am."

"I know. You've always been so nice to me."

"Look, I want you to doubt me. I mean, I want to have to prove myself to you. I don't ever want to take you for granted."

"No, no, I don't want you to feel all that. I feel bad for questioning you. I fall pretty hard, and that's happened with you, and sometimes I feel vulnerable for no reason."

Tandem

"And I really surprised you. And that was bad. I get it. But you're special to me, and you don't have to feel vulnerable."

She looked back at Mike, openly staring into his face, looking for something, maybe, or just loving him, he didn't know, but he kind of wished she would stop, because he was hungry and irritable and feeling temporarily incapable of loving her well. He needed his cheese and crackers snack badly. But it didn't feel right to just eat something during this important moment, so he waited, and tried not to show anything on his face.

Finally she stood up from the table, and he thought it was okay to eat and was reaching for the plate, but then she came toward him, so he got up, and they hugged it out, and he held her lovingly, as if she herself were a square of sharp cheddar between two Wheat Thins, until she let go and went upstairs. Then he sat at the kitchen table and, at last, wolfed down his snack, telling himself it wasn't her fault their relationship was so stressful.

30.

A few days after Mike went ballistic at the car dealer's,
he abruptly announced after dinner that he had to head out. He
was going back to campus to watch a volleyball match.

"Conference tournament, so it's kind of big, and I've
got three students in my Intro to Macro class on the team,
which never happens."

"That sounds fun. Can I come with?"

"Yeah, I don't know if you'd really want to. I mean,
are you into volleyball?"

She had said some negative things about sports, but
she had meant big business professional sports, not students
getting exercise and making friends and learning teamwork,
all that good stuff. She tried not to be hurt. Maybe he just
needed some space. Insisting had hurt things with Ryan, and
she didn't want that with Mike.

After he brushed his teeth and left, a little abruptly—
the match started at 6:30—she found herself alone in her
lover's house.

Ryan had texted her yesterday. He said he was in
therapy and he was calm now and could they talk again, this
was really, really bad for Nathan. She had to figure out how
to respond to him. It was one thing to be convinced in her
mind and in her heart and another thing to take the formal
steps to dissolve a marriage of twenty-four years.

Was Mike already growing tired of her? Was he
having second thoughts? How well did she really know him?
"I mean, are you into volleyball?" A classic, Kevinesque line.

"How does volleyball speak to your own problems? Do you also feel batted back and forth over a net?"

She tried watching CNN, but it was all about the election, which made her even more nervous. She switched off the TV and found herself wandering Mike's house.

She went upstairs to the master bedroom, where she felt most at home. Overall, their sex life was very good, sometimes great. There were also a few times when Mike wasn't totally into it, or needed extra coaxing, but she attributed that to wanting sex more often than he did, of which she was secretly proud.

There was also a guest bedroom and Connor's old bedroom and Mike's small office, the most Mike part of the house.

The door to his office was wide open, making the space continuous with the end of the hallway; she entered the office thinking it was a sort of cul-de-sac, where she might turn around. She saw a folder splayed on his desk, labeled *Discover — October 2016*. It contained receipts, mostly trips to Meijer and Harding's. The desk was mildly cluttered with stacks of books and unopened mail and a laptop and class handouts. She was curious about him because she was in love with him.

An old metal file cabinet partially obscured a window. It was lockable, but the push-button mechanism protruded obscenely. He said he wanted her to doubt him. That seemed like a dare. What she was about to do was wrong, but so was the behavior of the tall, dark, and handsome men that had created her trust issues in the first place.

The bottom drawer was filled with folders labeled with the basics of life—*Appliances*, *Home Equity*, *Cars*, *Health*, etc. She found a report for an annual physical with a Dr. Zhang. 6'2", 189. His cholesterol and blood pressure were fantastic. No medications. The numbers stirred her ovaries, though she was well into the reproductive warning zone. The second drawer was brokerage statements from TIAA-CREF and Fidelity and taxes organized by year. Being suspicious about whether he was financially secure would hurt their relationship much more than sneaking a peek at his statements. His TIAA-CREF and Fidelity balances were very good. That was a huge relief, as she had recently read a *Times* article about profligate spouses duping their partners until the inevitable financial reckoning.

Mike was evidently a paper guy, which was quaint, if environmentally disastrous. Eventually they would have to talk about online statements, but that was for later.

Third drawer was academic stuff.

The top drawer had bank and credit card statements organized by months. She pulled out a folder labeled *Discover — January 2016*. Her pulse quickened.

Nothing really jumped out. He gave $10 to Michigan Radio. He had Netflix and *New York Times* subscriptions. He bought gas and groceries. There were no restaurants, airline tickets, hotels, clothing stores or liquor stores. No therapists or pharmacies. No dating sites. Each transaction had a small pencil checkmark next to it; each corresponding receipt had a small checkmark at the top. He paid his balance in full every month. His January bank statement was also sparse, with automated charges for Sprint, Consumers Energy, Republic Services (the trash guys). No large ATM withdrawals to purchase street drugs—no ATM withdrawals at all. He got his cash from grocery store top-offs.

She went on to February, curious if there would be a big restaurant tab around Valentine's Day. There was not. No florist or Bath and Body Works or Victoria's Secret. She feared he would be drawn to women who shopped at such places. He was making a monthly donation to Michigan Radio. He also gave good chunks to two universities.

Claire relaxed and started to enjoy the evidence Mike was what he appeared to be: a sensible and responsible man, even a somewhat austere and disciplined man. This made her snooping feel more benign, even positive, as if Mike would want her to know these good things about him without having to tell her himself.

March and April were more of the same.

She went on to May, when everything had changed for her. Mike's statement also changed, blooming with unusual charges. CarParts.com, a little over $400. But a day later, those charges were reversed. She wasn't surprised; frugality fit his hatred of upselling. A Greyhound bus ticket, a La Quinta in South Bend, and a $34 purchase from Omari Auto Sales, also in South Bend. Was Connor going to Notre Dame? She had thought U of M.

Late May, early June, she and Mike had started to run into each other. More new purchases—Etsy (of all places), Bell's, Goggin Rental, and The Prairies, a golf course by Harding's. She saw the MADD donation, in honor of Emma. Very thoughtful. There were two large donations—$500 and $1,000—to Ministry with Community, both the same day. She and Ryan only sent MWC $50 around Thanksgiving. Her man had a heart of gold! Also, in May and June, for some reason, there were no check marks. He had never gotten around to reconciling his receipts with his charges. In July and August, three CarParts.com charges reappeared, spread out over several days, and this time they were not reversed.

These were not Metro Toyota charges. They didn't bill parts separately. There were no new accessories on Mike's Camry; anything new would have flashed on that beater.

She looked for the corresponding paper receipts for the Carparts.com charges and couldn't find them. What she did find was a receipt from eBay. It was for a car windshield.

August 7th, 2016.
TOYOTA OEM 02-06 Camry-Windshield Glass 56101AA03083.
$692.92.

Didn't he say his broken windshield was two or three years ago? Or did he say two or three months? Mike was obviously a terrible driver. Or maybe a stray pebble had cracked the glass and he didn't think of it as an accident. He didn't suggest getting her a replacement windshield on eBay—they just went to the dealer—but men could be weird about cars. Her brother often did his own repairs to assert his rugged individualism. Maybe it was an insurance thing?

She was more curious about whether their relationship had changed anything. She saw a purchase from

This Is a Bookstore—probably *Tree of Smoke,* the day she emailed him about book club. It was gratifying to see him act so quickly on her invitation. Two weeks after they slept together for the first time, there was a run of Battle Creek restaurants, a significant charge at a Baymont in Battle Creek, and a big charge at Sunshine Toyota. Also Battle Creek.

He had never mentioned a trip to Battle Creek. She remembered that week, because they had almost gotten caught at Mike's office, which had freaked her out. The next day, she'd made a panicky call, and he had told her he was getting his car serviced and had a meeting with Dave to work on a report, so they couldn't get together. What was with this guy and cars? Why didn't he tell her he was going to Battle Creek? He'd sounded as if he had just woken up when she called. Why stay overnight when it was only a half hour away? Was he sneaking around with some *other* married woman?

She knew how stepping out involved half-truths and routine-adjacent activities. From the outside, the inexplicable bits only made sense when you added a clandestine lover to the picture. She remembered over-hearing his phone call when they got home from the hospital. Maybe she was being too gender normative, but it just didn't sound like a phone call with a longstanding male friend. Tonight's last-second outing where she wasn't welcome—just the sort of thing she had done to Ryan to spend time with Mike.

But he *had* gotten his car serviced. Maybe he stayed overnight because they kept the car to do the service. But why not just go to Metro Toyota and get a courtesy ride and sleep in his own bed and avoid $379 in hotel charges? Or whatever about the car service—why hadn't he just told her he'd be in Battle Creek? She looked for the itemized receipt from Sunshine Toyota, but she couldn't find it, just as she couldn't find the corresponding receipts for the Carparts.com charges. The Sunshine charge was $1936. That was a lot.

She went through September. The lack of new suspicious charges couldn't keep her stomach from clenching. She sat down in the desk chair, touched her forehead, which was damp. Who was Mike? What was he up to? Maybe there was a way to use what she now knew to test him.

Tandem

Fran from book club had retired to Battle Creek, where her mother was in assisted living. Maybe she could mention that Fran had spotted him at a place listed on his statement—say, Sojourner Brewing, or even the Baymont, picking up visiting relatives—and see how he reacted.

She remembered there was a folder labeled *Cars* in the bottom drawer. She found titles and paperwork for car purchases. She was a little confused at first, but as she sorted the documents, she realized Mike had acquired two different Camrys. A 2005 was purchased new in October of 2004. The second Camry, which was an '06, was bought used from Omari Auto Sales in South Bend, on May 21st, 2016—two days after Emma was killed.

But he only had one Camry. Was Mike cheap enough to trade in an '05 for an '06? But there was no trade in listed on the purchase agreement. Did he take a bus to South Bend to buy a car? Why would he do that? Both Camrys were red. Goosebumps rose on her forearms. Where was the other Camry?

Then she remembered: he had mentioned giving Connor a car when he'd come to town in August.

Her shoulders relaxed a bit.

Two red Camrys were weird and disturbing, but she'd been in the red-car haystack before. It was inconceivable the needle might come to prick her when she wasn't even looking for it.

It was inconceivable, too, that Mike would be out driving forty miles away, after dark, on a school night. The police said the car was going into the parking lot, not leaving it. To imagine he went to Saugatuck Dunes at that hour just to kill her daughter was the worst kind of magical thinking—the fault-finding kind. It was why Ryan and Emma hated her.

But it was all too conceivable he went to Battle Creek to cheat on her, with the car service as a cover story. He might be stepping out on her this very night.

She covered her eyes with her hands. She had to be careful—stress and grief and paranoia reinforced each other. She just needed to be with Mike, to feel the real Mike. The gem who donated $1,500 to Ministry with Community, the man who always seemed to understand her pain.

31.

Mike hadn't been back to Kalamazoo Central's lumpy soccer field since Connor's last game three years ago. Anne hadn't shown up, Connor hadn't been at his best, and the Maroon Giants lost. When they got home, Anne was three sheets to the wind in front of the TV.

He spotted Chloe about ten rows up, in the middle of the back row of clumped parents. There was no seat next to her, and he walked slowly up the bleacher steps, trying to figure out what to do. Chloe suddenly made eye contact, smiled, and stood up. She picked up her portable chair and climbed a few rows. She was wearing a sleeveless fleece and snug jeans. He sensed the woman Chloe had been sitting next to was giving him an extended look, so he took his eyes off Chloe's ass.

Mike's heart was fizzing more than beating—it was a high school type of excitement, a way he'd never thought he'd feel again. He was coming down her row, when the PA announcer introduced a choir student who would sing the national anthem.

"Hey" was all he had time to say.

It was odd standing next to her in ritualistic silence for the first three minutes of what felt exactly like a first date after all. Chloe's careful make-up suggested as much. He felt a pang of guilt for talking himself into this. The student sang with exasperating slowness about the rockets' red glare...the bombs...bursting in air...

Tandem

With their hands over their hearts, Mike and Chloe seemed to be swearing to something long and complicated as they began their relationship.

He remembered the look on Claire's face when he had said, "I mean, are you into volleyball?" He hoped some of his dick moves would be forgivable once he figured out whom to love.

"Sorry I'm late," he said when they finally sat down.

"You're exactly on time," she said in a plucky way, making him wish he could explain the difficulty of finessing dinner time with Claire.

Luke was only a sophomore but he started at right fullback. He had great defensive technique—never flat footed, always meeting the attacker at a good distance with staggered feet, and often ending up with the ball. Mike asked so many questions about Luke's history as a player and the fortunes of his current team that he got self-conscious and tired of himself. Luckily, Chloe asked questions, too. He enjoyed talking about Connor, and a version of his life in which he had not committed a hit-and-run and was not sleeping with a married woman. They both really wanted to learn about each other.

She was born on a commune in Virginia, but her parents had eventually re-entered the "regular world," as Chloe called it. Her mother had been a jewelry maker and still was, and her father had been a sociology professor at MSU but had passed away.

"I'm sorry," Mike said. "When did you lose him?"

"Oh, about fifteen years ago. He died from sepsis that started as a urinary tract infection."

"Gosh, that must have been devastating. I mean, how does that happen?"

"Untreated STD," Chloe said.

"Oh."

"Probably from one of his students. It was a simpler time, right?" She laughed.

"Wow," Mike said.

He didn't mind if she was signaling his student contacts would be a point of concern for her. Suspicions about things of which he was innocent gave Mike comfort.

Luke stole the ball again and cleared it up to a midfielder.

"Yes, good work, Luke!" Mike clapped vigorously.

Chloe didn't react, and he feared he'd gotten out of his lane. He'd become so used to making over-the-top gestures of love and support, his personal style was becoming warped and "extra," as his students said. Or maybe she was just signaling she wasn't planning on introducing him to Luke tonight, which made sense.

Neither team could keep possession long enough to mount a real offense. He couldn't help but think of Kalamazoo Central as Team Chloe and their opponent, Portage Northern, as Team Claire. Even the game clock seemed to be the time running down to make his decision. The longer he let himself exist in this emotional limbo between Claire and Chloe, the more damage he was likely to do to both of them.

"How about your parents?" Chloe asked.

"Stockbroker dad and librarian mom. They're retired but still kicking." Chloe's silence was probably an invitation to go on, but he changed the subject.

"How are you managing? What's everyday life like for you?"

He wasn't afraid of her grief or her dead husband. He sensed any relationship would have to be a threesome at some level and he wanted to give her that space.

"Good question!" She laughed again—ruefully. He had already counted about ten different laughs she had. "Well, Luke is my surrogate adult. I have to stop him from cleaning or trying to get into my business. Just do your homework! Our house is absolutely filthy—you're forewarned. But he *is* helpful. And Ethan? Honestly, he's our designated basket case. Night terrors, separation anxiety." She shook her head. "He acts out everything I can't—maybe that sounds dumb. I can adjust the number of patients I see— my practice partners have been very understanding. Honestly, that's what saved me."

"It doesn't necessarily get easier?" he gently asked.

Tandem

"A friend said to me, 'You give patients medical advice all the time, what advice would you give yourself?' I tell myself doing little things, even like drinking water, will help—little things, little placebos. It comes and goes. You just have to get through it when it comes."

Mike imagined Chloe unable to get out of bed. He would bring her a ham-and-cheese omelet. She would cry, set the plate on her nightstand, and pat the bed beside her. After they made love, he would make her a new omelet, so she could eat it hot.

"So what do you know about mice?" Chloe asked.

"Just what I've learned from cartoons."

She laughed. "About how to catch them?"

"Are you using have-a-hearts or snap traps?"

"Both."

"And they knock around your have-a-hearts and lick your traps clean?"

"Yup."

"Alright." Mike gathered his thoughts. "You've got to confuse them with more than one snap trap. I always set up three, in a T-shape along a wall. One trap perpendicular to the wall, baitside against the wall, then the other two parallel to the wall, with the baitside abutting the baitside of the perpendicular one. Are you following me?"

"Three traps, T-formation, bait cluster, along the wall."

"Usually one of the three gets them. There's a limit to how much a mouse can process."

"It takes Luke ten minutes just to set one up. He gets so frustrated."

"They *are* touchy," Mike said. "I could come over and do it some time." Maybe he wasn't ready to offer, but it would have looked bad if he hadn't.

"That would be a nice favor. It's so gross—I found one in the washing machine the other day. I was moving a load to the dryer and found the little guy drowned at the bottom of the tub!"

"Oh."

"I screamed so loud, Ethan came screaming, too."

Luke was growing up too soon, while Ethan wasn't growing up at all. If he ended up with Chloe, he'd take the boys fishing in the U.P., on the Fox, the model for Hemingway's salutary Two-Hearted River. He'd make Luke eat a s'more and Ethan drink some beers.

Chloe's friend on the bleachers below had her head turned far to the side, maybe trying to get a glimpse of them. Then she went into her purse.

The ball squirted out of a traffic jam at midfield. K Central's striker suddenly had a run toward the goal. A defender came flying at the striker, poked the ball away, and the striker went down. The goalie ran out of the box and kicked it clear. The striker was slow to get up. The whole K Central section was on its feet, calling for a penalty.

"Terrible no-call!" Chloe shouted.

The striker briefly lying helpless on the grass had sent a frisson of panic over Mike's skin. When he and Chloe sat back down, he said, "Yeah, they should have called that," with barely enough air to finish his sentence.

"Unbelievable," Chloe fumed. She suddenly stood back up. "Could've been injured, Ref!" she yelled through cupped hands.

Another mom—short, in a turtleneck sweater—stood up at the edge of the parent clump, giving the refs the what for. For a second, she looked like Claire in her whiplash collar.

"You tell 'em, Sheila!" Chloe shouted to the woman. Sheila turned back to Chloe and said, "Such bullshit!" There was real anger on her face. She caught Mike staring at her, and he had to look away. Of course it wasn't Claire.

"Well, that makes me want to use the restroom," Mike said, standing up. "Please excuse me." He was light-headed and his knees shook before he locked them. His intestines cramped; his need had become urgent all of a sudden.

"Good luck," Chloe called after him. She laughed lightly.

Mike emptied himself in a cold metal stall with a concrete floor. He balanced the greatest good for the greatest number (a comprehensive Pareto Optimal state) against his personal obligation to Claire. What was the morality of a

Tandem

consumer borrowing money from one bank but paying back another, even if the consumer gave the second bank a higher interest rate? Chloe's name and Claire's name began with the same sound, which reinforced his sense they could occupy similar positions in his love equations, represented by the same variable—c.

He finished, washed his hands, and pondered his worried face in the mirror.

"Have you lost your fucking mind?" he said out loud.

It occurred to him he could no longer distinguish between the care and attentiveness required to manipulate someone and the care and attentiveness required to love someone. He could no longer distinguish between what was self-serving and what was serving another. He felt he should know these differences. Was his heart in the right place—or any accessible place, for that matter? Or had he left it in Saugatuck after all?

A fit of weeping threatened to over-take him, but then a urinal flushed. He hadn't realized another guy, a teenage boy, was in there with him. He stepped back dramatically from the sink, and with a single ugly gasp, he sucked up his tears, finally discovering how the expression "suck it up" originated.

"All yours, buddy!" He gestured at the sinks.

The boy hurried out without washing his hands, slipping awkwardly behind Mike's back.

Mike got out his phone and composed a text to Chloe:

Yes, you are wonderful. Yes, I freaked out and left. Can I explain why? No. Except my divorce + your loss set off chain of thoughts I wasn't ready for. You're a real catch for a guy w his act together. I do not. Do not want to string you along. Sorry! Peace.

Before he could rationalize anything else, he pressed send.

32.

When Mike came in the back door, Claire was watching
Grey's Anatomy in the TV room. It was a wallowing-in-grief
thing to do, but she couldn't help herself. Some of her best
memories of Emma involved watching medical trauma
together. At first, she had found the emotional register at the
Seattle Grace Hospital to be too junior high. Luckily she had
managed to not make that critique in front of Emma, and it
had become their thing. She had some questions cued up for
Mike, but she wasn't sure she had the strength to ask them.

Mike was all smiles. "I got you something!" He
presented a clear plastic container of shelled pistachios and
a bottle of red wine. "It's the wine of the month at Tiffany's!"

She didn't get off the sectional, wary of his offering. He
brought his gifts over to her and set them on the end table at
her elbow. He leaned over for a kiss. She couldn't raise her lips
to him, but he kissed the top of her head anyway. Then he sat
at the other end of the sectional and looked up at the TV.

Bailey was arguing with Meredith about Meredith
having sex all over the hospital. Meredith couldn't believe
Bailey cared.

"Thanks," she finally said. "Who won?"

"I don't know. I left early. I missed you."

Claire paused the show. She looked over at Mike. He
was smiling benevolently at her. Kevin had been an excellent
liar. Her stomach hurt.

"How's your night been?" he asked brightly.

"Quiet. Except Fran called. Her mom's not doing well."

"Fran?"

"From book club. Don't you remember her?"

"Not really, but sorry to hear that."

"Yeah, well, she remembers you. She said she saw you at a brew pub, in Battle Creek."

Mike looked at her for a beat. He blinked.

"Well, she should've said hi," he said.

"She said you were occupied." Maybe that was going too far, but she had to test him.

"*Occupied*? By chewing?"

The shift in his tone warned her. She had to get back to what she knew for sure.

"I don't remember you taking a trip to Battle Creek."

"That was months ago. We weren't living together then."

"How long were you there for?"

"Oh, Claire," he said softly. "I know things have been stressful. And unsettling—super unsettling."

He looked at her with concerned eyes she wanted to punch. She looked right back at him.

"I don't remember—a day or two?" he said.

"I remember you telling me you were getting your car serviced and you couldn't see me because you had a meeting with Dave, not because you were in Battle Creek."

He sighed. "I just didn't think to tell you. Someone keyed my car and I needed to get the hood repainted. Metro Toyota doesn't have a body shop, so I took it to the dealer in Battle Creek and they kept it overnight. Dave's a beer snob and he wanted to try the beers at this place, so everything just worked."

"You have a lot of car things," she fumbled.

"Car things?"

"We got your car fixed at Metro," she continued as evenly as she could. "I thought they didn't have a body shop."

Mike put his hands over his face. She braced for an explosion. He lowered his hands.

"They sent it out. I asked the cop to tell the tow driver to take it there. Right before I went in the ambulance. I didn't want it to get impounded, which is a huge pain. It was all I could think of."

"Well, if they could just send it out, why did you take it to Battle Creek yourself?"

"I don't know. I mean, I *didn't* know they could just send it out until after the accident." He sounded tired.

She looked into his eyes and he looked right back, with the fixed calm of a staring contest champion. A stalk of pain rooted in her shoulder and pulsed in her neck. He had an answer for everything. Why did it matter where he had his car serviced? She should never have snooped. Whatever else she'd discovered in his file cabinet fled her brain. She couldn't hold back her tears anymore.

Mike didn't come over to comfort her. When she got her sobs under control, she said, "I'm sorry. Cars freak me out. Car accidents freak me out. I never told you the cops know the color of the car that did it—it's salsa red, the color of your car—and that really freaks me out! And I'm so sorry for doubting you!"

Mike came and sat by her. They hugged on the couch. Then he put his forehead to her forehead and whispered: "Remember, it's okay to doubt me. I just want to always treat you right."

He hugged her again and said, "You're okay."

Then he got up and took the bottle of wine into the kitchen. The pistachios sat on the end table. She couldn't take her eyes off of them, as if waiting for them to explain what was really going on.

33.

Mike found the corkscrew in the drawer. Anne's trusty friend. He cut the foil off the neck.

And Fran came back to him: dyed blonde hair, large smooth face, clear strong teacher voice. He tried to remember the patrons at Sojourner Brewing. He'd been by himself and had nothing to do but read Packers news on his phone and look around the dining room. There hadn't been that many people, and he probably would have recognized her or overheard her loud voice. Had she really surveilled him? How else could she have known he was there? What did "occupied" mean, for Christ sake? It *was* hard to keep track of all the possible traps.

He fought the sudden urge to confess, to get this over with, to in one gesture return to the self he was not unhappy with before he hit the tandem, no matter the cost, because his program of restorative love was making everything worse and Claire seemed on to him. He didn't love her. He couldn't love her. At least not the way normal people loved their romantic partners. He could only love her as penance. Or he could admit he'd been living a hopeless, cynical lie from the start—and confess. It might take years off the sentence he'd otherwise get when he was inevitably caught.

Or he could slip out the back door and drive to Chicago, long a magnet for outstanding macroeconomists, and make a new life there under an assumed name. But he knew leaving the house again was the exact wrong move. Claire could not be left alone with her thoughts.

Mozina

He poured out two glasses of wine. He prepared a cutting board of cheese and crackers. He was so angry he'd walked out on Chloe, he wanted to strangle himself. It was maddening to be trapped in the life he had made. But maybe the hardest and best way of loving people was being kind to them no matter what he was thinking and feeling, never taking his guilt and depression out on others. He would never lose it again, as he had with Clay and the La Quinta housekeeper and Anne and—

Never!

It would be a tremendous moral accomplishment, if he could sustain it.

He put the wine glasses on the cutting board. As he returned to the TV room, walking as carefully as he could, he watched the surface of the wine tremble in exactly the same way in both glasses.

34.

"Can I watch with you?" he asked, entering the room with a laden snack tray.

"Sure," she said.

The *Grey's Anatomy* episode was still paused. Mike put the tray down on a rolling ottoman and sat next to her, but she couldn't unpause the show.

He handed her a glass of wine.

She held it briefly, then set it back down on the wooden board. She had to be sure.

"I never asked you what kind of car you gave Connor."

He seemed not to have heard her, looking at the frozen image on the TV screen as if it were playing normally. Then he said, "I gave him the exact same car I have—another red Camry. Had to go all the way to South Bend to find one. It was an elaborate joke." He turned to her and smiled. "I just straight up told him: the divorce doesn't mean we're not father and son forever—these cars are a symbol of our bond!"

"And how did he take it?"

"He thought I was an idiot."

She gave a short laugh. "They do tend to think we're idiots, don't they?"

She picked up her wine glass and took a sip. Mike nodded and downed a gulp.

"Clay was right," she said. "I think you should trade in that car. It's a bad car. I kind of hate it."

If something bad *had* happened with that car, wouldn't he have taken the chance to get rid of it? But he hadn't, which meant he didn't feel bad about it, but she did.

"It's a very junky car," he affirmed. "Hell yes, we should trade it in. Connor won't care. I shouldn't have let my hatred of upselling get the best of me. I've got unresolved issues." He flexed his chin and shook his head, maybe ironically. It was hard to tell.

"Welcome to the club." She sighed.

Mike offered his glass. They clinked and drank.

"See, we belong together," he said. "Because we fit perfectly. We need each other."

"You think so?"

"At least, we deserve to pick out a new car together. One we can drive for the rest of our lives."

"Well, not one car the *whole* rest of our lives."

"Of course. When that car gets junky, we'll get a new one. Sometimes you be the driver and I be the passenger, and sometimes I be the driver and you be the passenger—if you still trust me to drive."

He had come back to her early, bearing pistachios and the wine of the month, like a sudden bright light waking her from anxious dreams. Her touch alone had been enough to temper his blow-up with Clay. He was here now—her tall, dark, and handsome man, telling her he needed her.

"I trust you to drive," she said.

He put his arm around her and she nestled against him. She unpaused the show.

Epilogue.

On the fifth anniversary of the death of Jeremy and Emma, after a morning spent laying fresh flowers on Emma's grave—as they did every year—Claire and Mike met the Vanden Bergs at their spacious mid-century modern house on Gull Lake. Suzanne Vanden Berg showed off her pair of Finn Juhl "Chieftain" chairs (impressing Claire in spite of herself, Mike could tell), and Mike took the design of chairs seriously for the first time in his life. Nathan and his girlfriend Amanda came along. Connor was living in Chicago, selling finance software to investment houses, and couldn't get away.

Everyone was vaccinated, but it was warm, so they spent most of the visit outside by the lake just to be on the safe side. Richard grilled enough steak and veggie kebobs for thirty people. Suzanne had made a quinoa and black bean salad for Claire. Nathan ate a bloody steak while looking haunted. He had just graduated from Grand Valley and seemed to be discovering the world was not especially kind to aspiring sports broadcasters.

Ryan had been invited, but he begged off. He had moved to Lansing to work in Governor Whitmer's Legislative Affairs Office on reform of the foster care system. Claire and Ryan were on reasonably good terms, and for a get-together like this, they could put aside any animosity, but Claire had been noticeably relieved when she learned Ryan wouldn't be coming.

She had also warned Mike that the Vanden Bergs would not necessarily be pleasant. She said they were very conservative, and religious differences may have inhibited the Vanden Bergs' embrace of Emma. But Mike found them to be hospitable and mostly warm, except when they caustically criticized the police for failing to solve the hit-and-run. He told them he was very sorry for their loss, which didn't seem to register, but he didn't dare attempt anything less rote.

The bereaved parents traded anecdotes about their dead children. The time Jeremy split a toboggan running into a basketball pole, the time Emma played Glinda in *The Wiz* with a head cold. If the family went to a movie together, Emma insisted on sitting apart from them, usually in the highest back row, so she could "get immersed." Jeremy had donated the proceeds from his childhood lemonade stands to a battered women's shelter in Grand Rapids. Mike found himself crying, which created an uncomfortable silence, and eventually they moved on to other topics.

Richard was serious and amiable, as well as a bottomless source on all things sand, gravel, and cement, and Mike quizzed him pitilessly. Suzanne and Claire took their wine glasses out onto the pier and stood in the early evening sun, one woman tall and surprisingly muscular, with prominent veins on her biceps, and the other petite and pretty, with soft hunched shoulders. He wondered what they were talking about. Were they parsing the old clues, comparing takes on the slowly receding details, like JFK truthers standing before the grassy knoll? It was all he could do to keep from calling them back to the table. Amanda and Nathan wandered the shoreline. The land around this inlet was unusually flat; it seemed the water need only rise a foot or two to flood everything.

While Richard explained the chemistry behind the hardening of cement, Mike remembered giving Claire a piggy-back ride right into the lake at South Haven, though she shrieked in his ear, "No, no, it's too cold!" They fell over in the waves and came up laughing. She was always jumping on him at odd times. It made him feel useful. Being dead inside was not as bad as it sounded, Mike longed to tell someone. Deserts brimmed with life, mostly unseen.

Cements are dry powders, Richard clarified, not to be confused with concretes or mortars.

"But I bet some people mix them up anyway," Mike said.

"Blockheads," Richard pronounced.

"No pun intended."

"How's that?"

Eventually Suzanne and Claire came back to the patio. Richard had grown expansive and said, without apparent irony, "One more for the road," as he topped off everyone's glass.

"You two seem happy together," Suzanne remarked, referring to Claire and Mike.

This was a borderline inappropriate (albeit positive) thing to say, but Mike sensed Suzanne's grief manifested in excessive frankness. Suzanne and Richard had lost their other son to crib death, years ago. Covid reaffirmed every breath was an accident waiting to happen. Mere survival felt like grace.

"Yes, arranged marriages work out more often than you think," Mike quipped.

"Arranged?" Suzanne asked.

"Yes, *arranged*?" Claire seconded. Her eyelashes fluttered with consternation, which pained Mike.

He had often thought about his marriage with Claire in those terms: he hadn't found her through romantic love but through a convoluted cultural obligation; and yet arranged marriages sometimes blossomed into something rich and affectionate, way beyond romantic crap—a practical partnership deepened by acute care for each other.

But he could never explain himself to her, just as he could never entirely escape the risk of giving himself away.

"By fate!" Mike said, pointing at the blue sky.

And everyone laughed.

Acknowledgments

Thank you to my draft readers who made wonderful suggestions: Lisa Lenzo, Deborah Gang, Bonnie Jo Campbell, Erica Ferencik, Heidi Bell, John Mauk, Cathy Bobbe, Mike Stefaniak, Glenn Deutsch, Lorraine Alberts, Susanna Campbell, John Fraser, Christopher Hermelin, and Ryan Harbage. Thank you to those who lent their expertise, even if what I learned from you did not survive all the revisions: MRAUTOGLASS, Alex Rubio of R Quality Glass, Katherine Ransbottom, Karla Niehus, Scott Wagenaar, Barry Johnson, Ken Barnard, Joe Mozina and Brian Stephenson, with special thanks to Tiffanie Stanfield, founder of Fighting H.A.R.D. (Fighting Hit and Run Driving), and the Mothers Against Drunk Driving Victim Impact Panel Program, Texas Township, MI. Thank you to my mother, Elaine Mozina, for a timely plot consultation. Special thanks to Jerry Brennan for fog-piercing editorial vision and several awesome, book-transforming suggestions. Thanks to Christopher Hermelin, Ryan Harbage, Caitlin Hamilton Summie, and Rick Summie for championing this book. Thanks to the Trustees of Kalamazoo College and the Kalamazoo College English Department for sabbatical support to complete the first draft. Thanks to the Kalamazoo College Center for International Programs, the Global Liberal Arts Alliance, and the Great Lakes Colleges Association for grant-supported travel research.

About the Author

Born and raised in Milwaukee, Andy Mozina majored in economics at Northwestern, then dropped out of Harvard Law School to study literature and write. He's published fiction in *Tin House*, *Ecotone*, *McSweeney's*, *The Southern Review*, and elsewhere. His first story collection, *The Women Were Leaving the Men*, won the Great Lakes Colleges Association New Writers Award. *Quality Snacks*, his second collection, was a finalist for the Flannery O'Connor Prize. His first novel, *Contrary Motion*, was published by Spiegel & Grau/Penguin Random House. His fiction has received special citations in Best American Short Stories, Pushcart Prize, and New Stories from the Midwest. He's a professor of English at Kalamazoo College.

About Tortoise Books

Slow and steady wins in the end, even in publishing. Tortoise Books is dedicated to finding and promoting quality authors who haven't yet found a niche in the marketplace—writers producing memorable and engaging works that will stand the test of time.

Learn more at www.tortoisebooks.com or follow us on Twitter: @TortoiseBooks.